FIND YOUR WAY BACK TO ME

a novel

William J. Donahue

Copyright © 2025 William J. Donahue

Find Your Way Back to Me
ISBN: 978-1-958370-30-8 (paperback)
ISBN: 978-1-958370-29-2 (eBook)

Published by Manta Press, Ltd.
Pickerington, OH 43147

Cover Design by John Errichetti (Tinhouse Design)
Author photo by Alison Dunlap

First Edition

W. S. Merwin, "Here Together" from *Garden Time*. Copyright © 2016 by W. S. Merwin. Reprinted with the permission of The Permissions Company LLC on behalf of Copper Canyon Press, coppercanyonpress.org.

Printed in the United States of America

"A dark and intense novel that has as much heart, soul, and depth as it does thrills and chills, *Find Your Way Back to Me* should bring some deserved attention to author William J. Donahue and help cement him as one of the voices on the rise in dark fiction. This was my first time reading him, but it certainly won't be my last."

—Greg F. Gifune, author of *Smoke, in Crimson*

"Tense and chill-inducing, *Find Your Way Back to Me* by William J. Donahue is simultaneously thought provoking and creepy. With an immersive atmosphere and relatable, multidimensional characters, Donahue has cleverly crafted a thriller that explores the dangers of burying our traumas a bit too deep. Riveting from the first page to the last, *Find Your Way Back to Me* mixes gory details you can almost smell with satisfying social commentary spanning back to the Vietnam War. A compelling and fresh supernatural thriller."

—Diana Rodriguez Wallach, author of *The Silenced, Hatchet Girls,* and *Small Town Monsters*

"Absolutely loved this book!!! It was so original and unlike anything I've ever read. Enjoyed the main characters and their backstory. Will definitely recommend this to everyone that I talk to."

—BookSirens Reviewer

"What a fun and unique story. I absolutely don't want to give any spoilers, but I loved the way the story seamlessly moved from the present to all throughout the past without ever feeling lost. I did not want to put the book down!"

—BookSirens Reviewer

For my father,
who probably would have liked this one.

HERE TOGETHER

These days I can see us clinging to each other
as we are swept along by the current
I am clinging to you to keep you from
being swept away and you are clinging to me
we see the shores blurring past as we hold
each other in the rushing current
the daylight rushes unheard far above us
how long will we be swept along in the daylight
how long will we cling together in the night
and where will it carry us together
— W. S. Merwin

CHAPTER 1

Crash

Jodi Avec-Georges stood at the kitchen window and studied the arid vastness of Crum, Arizona—nothing but red rock, desert scrub, and the sun-scorched bones of vertebrates whose time had come. Her hands rested on the edge of the farmhouse sink, the porcelain cool beneath her fingertips. The evening's warm breath seeped through the pores of the window screen.

"Best day of my life," she said. Her husband Martin had used the same phrase less than a year ago, just beyond the threshold of the Phoenix-area family home they had abandoned after an episode of shared trauma, torture, and abject terror. The phrase had spilled from her lips every day since, purely to remind herself of the things they had left behind, for better or for worse.

Martin tramped the yard, humping rounds of firewood from the pile behind the shed to the altar-like chopping block. Jodi had helped him fell a pair of dying cottonwoods nearly a month earlier, three days after they moved in, and he had been giving the splitting maul a workout ever since. They already had enough termite-ridden firewood to last them a dozen winters in the uppermost reaches of Maine, let alone the northeastern corner of Arizona.

Jodi ran the water until cool became hot and soaked the frying pan to wear down the film of bacon grease slicking the stainless-steel surface. She then tipped the tea kettle beneath the spigot until the vessel had its fill.

Thwack!

Martin split wood as reliably as a metronome. As the maul hit its target, each half of the log struck the hard ground, followed by the sound of Martin wrestling another chunk of cottonwood onto the chopping block. He repeated the sequence again and again until he had to return to the woodpile for more, always with the limp he had acquired eight months prior—the result of an injury suffered during the horror that drove them from their former home in the Phoenix suburb of Rio Vista.

Jodi placed the kettle on the front right burner, only to remember that the burner's coils heated too slowly. She was still learning the house's temperament, from the schizophrenic appliances to the problematic plumbing to the soft parts of the staircase in sore need of replacement. Homes were like people, she knew, rife with eccentricities and imperfections, in need of constant soothing and healing. She moved the kettle to the burner that had become her favorite, the reliable rear left, and fetched the tin of Darjeeling from the stone countertop, blue marble veined with white, gold, and gray.

"Tea, Martin," she yelled out the window. "Ten

minutes!"

"Or a goblet of gin," he hollered back.

She paused to admire the horizon and wondered where their thirty-two acres ended and Navajo territory began. The landscape seemed to stretch on forever, thousands of acres of featureless desert. Most people considered the space a waste of real estate because it went mostly unused and uninhabited, but Jodi saw beauty in the nothingness. Approximately two-hundred and fifty humans lived within Crum's twenty-seven square miles, per the most recent census data, and Jodi was proud to count the Avec-Georges clan among the hardy few.

The early evening sun had begun to dip behind a ridge of red mountains. Saguaro cactuses rose from the landscape, like fingers, like teeth, like horns, maybe a quarter mile away. She did not permit her attention to linger on the horizon, instead checking the sliver of darkness between the wall and the open cellar door. A feeling she likened to the unwanted gaze of a stranger weighed upon her. She cursed her imagination.

"Easy, old gal," she told herself.

Thwack!

She fed two tablespoons of loose Darjeeling to the steeping pot. The woodwork groaned from somewhere nearby—the floor, the walls, the ceiling, evidence of the house settling, even after so many years. She missed having a radio in the kitchen, for news, for classical music performed by the Phoenix Symphony, for the comfort of static, especially when Martin was out chopping wood or farting around in the yard, to remind her that she had company in the dusty, drafty house.

Funny how life worked out, she thought. While most of the friends her age were downsizing to cottages in retirement communities or single-story ranchers with no lawns to water or any property to care for, she and Martin had invested their retirement savings in this rickety old place. She guessed they would enjoy ten to twelve good years there, before the ravages of age staked their claim on the faculties they had not already lost. The home had two stories and a basement, surrounded by dead farmland riddled with holes made by black-tailed prairie dogs. Most landowners would be tempted to poison or shoot the adorable little pests and leave their inert bodies where they fell to fertilize the soil. Not Martin, who seemed to love everything about Crum. He had come all this way for good reason. She had, too, but she might have chosen a different end point.

Still, the place's charms outweighed the inconveniences and the less-than-perfects. The "new" house bore little resemblance to the last. Their prior address had been alive, first with the energy of children and family, and then, as the years wore on, with a dark heartbeat all its own. They had spent twenty-eight mostly happy years there, until that dreadful Tuesday evening eight months prior, when Martin's demons decided they wanted someone else to torment for a change. By comparison, the new house in Crum seemed lifeless. Jodi considered this an improvement, though she woke every morning with the same nagging thought: Sooner or later, the troubles they had left behind in Phoenix would hunt Jodi and Martin down to pacify an insatiable lust for cruelty and vengeance.

She turned away from the window and nearly tripped over Roy, the itinerant calico.

"Dammit, cat! You're going to break my neck!"

Roy took off like a shot bullet. A blur of black, white, and ginger, the cat's tricolored tail, disappeared behind the basement door. Jodi liked that Roy spent time in the basement, which was one of the few rooms in the house she did not care for—too cramped, too musty, and the dim lighting seemed made for a Hitchcock chiller. If any unwelcome visitors were beginning to exercise their hold down there or anywhere else in the house, Roy would be the first to sense it.

Thwack!

Memories from the final hours in Jodi's former home replayed in her mind.

When that *thing* pressed its ragged lips to hers …

When the shadows slithered in from all corners and bared their teeth …

When the creatures that found life in the darkness clasped their claws around her wrists and ankles, yanked the hair from her head, and sank their talons into the soft part of her throat as Martin screamed from the basement …

A knock at the front door jolted the coffee mug out of Jodi's hand. Ceramic splintered against the slate floor. She peeked around the kitchen table, into the foyer, to see a silhouette at the front door. The screen obscured the visitor's identity.

"Well," said a voice. "Sanctuary for a road-weary traveler?"

"Alison!" Jodi exhaled. "You scared me half to

death! Of course, come in."

Jodi hurried to the door and undid the latch.

"You're wound too tight, Mom," Alison said. "You'd think being way out here, on the edge of civilization, would calm your nerves."

Jodi welcomed her daughter into the foyer. The door creaked shut behind her. She draped an arm across her daughter's shoulder.

"Found the place all right then?"

"They say Siri knows all, but even she seemed unsure at some points in the journey. Took me longer to get here than I thought it would."

"Well, your timing is uncanny. Just put on some tea. You'll have a cup."

"You said this place was different, and you weren't kidding." Alison's eyes found the cracks in the ceiling and the shabbiest steps of the worn staircase. "Remote, like you wanted."

"Like *your father* wanted," Jodi said. "I would have been happy anywhere. If you passed the old cattle ranch a half-mile up the road, that's the neighborhood."

"All settled in?"

"Still finding our way, one room at a time." She motioned to a trio of brown boxes piled in the living room. Each box bore the word ADORNMENTS in black marker. "I don't know why we bothered packing up all those decorative teacups and saucers—useless knickknacks. Frankly, I can't remember why I started collecting the dumb things in the first place. Simple habit, I suppose. I might just haul those boxes over to the town dump, because who cares anymore?"

Thwack!

Jodi shuffled into the kitchen and leaned toward the window. Her cheek grazed the screen.

"Martin, your daughter's here!"

"Hey, Dad!" Alison yelled over her mother's shoulder.

"Give me a minute, Al," he replied, nearly out of breath. He carried another round of wood to the splitter.

"I swear to Christ, he's going to give himself a heart attack if he doesn't give me one first," Jodi said. "He's out there chopping wood every damned day, like we could possibly run out. He sits out at the firepit until two in the morning some nights. Quiets his mind, he says."

Her knee made a cracking noise as she bent to pick up pieces of the shattered mug. She would have to sweep up later to prevent any errant shards from nicking the cat's paw pads. She turned up the stove heat so the water would boil more quickly and then fetched another mug from the cupboard.

Alison stood at the window and watched her father heft an oblong piece of wood.

"I'm amazed at how well he still gets around, all things considered," she said. "I go to the gym two days in a row, and I walk like a corkscrew for a whole week."

Thwack!

"Oh, he has his slow days," Jodi said. "Age does that to you. A sixty-five-year-old body doesn't move nearly as well as a thirty-something- or forty-something-year-old one. He hasn't been the same since the bear, but he'll never let you see how his aches and pains affect him. Enough about that stubborn old man. Tell me how you've been, dear."

Alison took a seat at the kitchen table.

"No complaints, really," she said. "Work is killing my spirit, one shift at a time, but that's nothing new. I don't know how you did it for as long as you did—the nine-to-five grind. Retirement seems two lifetimes away."

"Work's not really work if you don't mind doing it. I never did."

"Well, you got to work with books and children all day. That's a far cry from red-faced adults screaming at you and accusing you of trying to rip them off."

"Every job has its kicks to the shins," Jodi said. "Even for an old librarian like me."

"You two have inspired me to follow your lead, got me thinking maybe it's time for a change. Maybe getting out of health care entirely. Maybe living somewhere else. Maybe moving to Thailand for a year, teaching English as a second language."

"You're serious?"

"You disapprove."

"I didn't say that. I asked if you were serious."

"I need some new scenery, too."

Alison's voice weakened mid-sentence, making Jodi think she meant it this time.

"Life's too short to feel stuck," Jodi said. "So go get unstuck. You know I'll support you if that's what you want to do. You have your dad's blessing, too. Just be safe wherever the little bouncing ball takes you."

"Things are good here?"

Jodi let a beat pass between them, as if waiting for

someone else—or something else—to answer for her. Her eyes turned to the shadows gathered in the corner, searching for the suggestion of movement.

"It's been quiet," Jodi said.

The teapot began to scream.

"So, nothing … weird?"

Jodi sighed.

"You know what I'm asking, Mom." Alison struggled to restrain a smile. "Nothing, you know, *followed* you?"

A dropped spoon clanged against porcelain. Jodi lifted a hand as if to silence her daughter.

"No reason to dig up old bones, dear. It's been quiet. Honest."

She pulled the tea pot off the stove and poured scalding water into the steeper.

"Honey for your tea? We get a full jar every week from an apiary five miles down the road, on native land. They say the local stuff is better for you than what you find in the supermarket. Good for tamping down allergies."

"Andrew and I just want to know you guys are all right out here. The way you two left home in Phoenix, and the few details you shared afterward, you can't blame us for asking questions."

"Tell your brother everything is just fine here in Crum, not that he'll come to see the place any time soon. You can sleep well knowing the same."

Jodi went to the window and yelled for Martin, but no response came. She peered around the window frame but saw no sign of him. Maybe he was taking a leak behind the shed—an ugly habit he had acquired since moving to the outermost rim of civilization, with no one around to witness the act. She dipped the honey wand into the jar and dribbled the sap-like fluid into the bottom of each mug.

"Martin!" she yelled. "Where in Hell's Bells did he run off to now?"

Then she saw the treads of his boots, his supine form hidden behind the pyramid of split wood. His right foot gave the slightest twitch.

CHAPTER 2

Tarantulas and Underthings

For a small hospital in a speck of a town, the ER in Tuba City bustled with more activity than Jodi would have expected at nearly ten p.m. on a Sunday. She paced between rows of chairs outfitted with olive-colored seat cushions, trying to keep the terror from showing on her face. Everyone around her looked like they could either cry, vomit, or curl into a fetal ball and sleep forever. She could understand, of course, because each of them likely had a loved one on the other side of the waiting-room wall fighting to stay connected to the mortal world.

She had accompanied Martin for the thirty-minute ambulance ride from Crum to the Greater Tuba City Hospital and Trauma Center, his body motionless on a gurney while a stone-faced EMT kept watch. Too much time had passed, she told herself during the ride, silently begging Martin to sit up, snap open his eyes, and declare, "False alarm, folks!" She almost wished Martin had died in the back of the ambulance rather than risk him withering away in a hospital bed. If his death was forgone, he would have wanted to die at home, or anywhere else for that matter. She would never forgive herself if he had to spend his final hours in an infirmary, surrounded by tired-eyed strangers in scrubs and white coats.

The automatic doors to the ER parted and swept in a warm wind. Alison followed. She found Jodi and wrapped her arms around her mother's neck, sobbing. Jodi disentangled herself from her daughter and said, "Don't cry until there's something to cry about. For all we know, he's sitting up in bed right now, flirting with the nurses and eating potato salad out of a Styrofoam cup."

Jodi said the words easily enough, but she found the sentiment much harder to believe. Even though they were surrounded by physicians, nurses, and other people whose paychecks depended on their efforts to get Martin back on his feet, her sense of optimism eroded with each passing moment. Martin had endured an abundance of suffering throughout their forty-six years as a couple, more than any single person should have to endure. She had never seen him so helpless as the moment she found him in the yard: limp, unresponsive, his face as blue as a day-old bruise.

"It certainly took you long enough to get here," Jodi teased. "You stop for a sandwich, or did you just take the scenic route?"

"Why didn't you answer your fucking phone? I must have called you, like, seventeen times." Alison wiped her nose with the back of her hand. "I lost the ambulance almost immediately, driving like a bat out of you know where. You also didn't tell me there were two hospitals in Tuba City."

"Don't worry yourself, dear." Jodi fished through her purse for spare change. "Find a place to park yourself and I'll fetch you a ginger ale."

"Missus Avec-Georges?"

Jodi lifted her head at the sound of her name. A man in a white coat stepped toward her. He was young, early thirties, and thin as a rail. The bell of a stethoscope dangled from the mouth of his coat pocket. His name badge read: JASON PAVLOVICH, M.D. He looked solemn.

"Fuck," she said.

The doctor led them to an unoccupied corner of the ER waiting room. He took a protracted breath, as if preparing himself to deliver news Jodi did not want to hear.

"Missus Avec-Georges—"

"It's pronounced *Avick-George*," she said. "Accent on the first syllable, silent S at the end."

Pavlovich looked at her as if her words did not matter. She supposed they did not, considering the circumstances, but she had been correcting people's mispronunciation of her husband's last name since she took it as her own more than four decades earlier.

"Your husband's condition has stabilized."

"Thank God!" Jodi said. She grabbed Alison's hand and squeezed. A laugh turned into a cry. "So, it wasn't a heart attack?"

"I wish I could tell you exactly what it was," Pavlovich said. "We're still running some tests and monitoring his brain activity."

"Can we see him?" Alison interjected.

"Wait a second," Jodi said. "Brain activity. You mean he's not verbal? He's not conscious?"

"No, ma'am," Pavlovich said. "We're running labs to rule out a heart attack, but I don't think that's the likely cause of his condition."

"So, what then?"

"A stroke, possibly. Like I said, we want to run more tests."

"So run them!" Alison yelled. "Wake him up!"

"We're going to move him up to the ICU and continue monitoring him there," the doctor continued. "Once he's settled, a nurse will find you and take you up so you can see him."

"What are we supposed to do until then?" Alison snapped.

Jodi shot her a look.

"Forgive my daughter, Doctor. She has better manners than that. She's just worried about her father. We'll wait."

"Your husband is in remarkable shape for a man in his sixties," Pavlovich said. "He's been through a lot, hasn't he? I understand he's a Vietnam vet. That would explain some of the scarring on his arms and chest."

"He's had a colorful past, yes."

"A modern-day warrior, by the looks of him, someone who knows how to fight," Pavlovich said. "Ma'am, did your husband say anything about an interaction with a snake or a spider? Maybe a scorpion? Tarantula hawk? Anything like that?"

"He was unconscious when I found him. Laid out by

the wood pile."

"So, he didn't mention anything?"

"You do know what *unconscious* means, right?" Alison added with snark.

Jodi pinched her daughter's arm.

"We live in the desert," she told Pavlovich. "Things that bite and sting outnumber us a million to one. I found a tarantula in my underwear drawer just this morning, for chrissakes. But no, nothing comes to mind. Why?"

"There's an irritation on the underside of his right forearm," the doctor said. "Could be a bite or a sting. It didn't look too serious when he first came in, just a little angry. The limb is now showing significant edema. Possible allergic response. A sting from a paper wasp might do it. Whatever it is, we'll keep an eye on it."

A heavyset woman shuffled toward the bank of chairs across from Jodi and Alison. She wore an oversized Arizona Coyotes T-shirt paired with lime-green Crocs and tight black capris, each leg streaked with a net-like mess of white cat fur. The woman eased into a chair, expelled a gust from her lungs, and fished a rosary from her oversized purse. A prayer tumbled from her lips in Spanish.

Jodi would have described the woman as "old," even though the two women were likely born within five years of one another. At sixty-three, Jodi guessed most people would consider her old, too, but most days she felt as though the year on her birth certificate meant nothing. Age had more to do with factors other than the passing of time. She cycled twelve miles a day at least three days a week, and she would still be running three to five miles a day if not for the nagging pain in her left knee the doctor back in Phoenix suggested would get no worse if she backed off the impact exercises.

She also did an hour of yoga at least once a day, at dawn or dusk, though she could admit yoga had become less enjoyable in recent months. Before the move to Crum, or before the night that led to the move, each yoga session was an hourlong meditation with closed eyes and a blank mind, and she always finished feeling invigorated. She no longer made herself vulnerable during yoga sessions. Her eyes stayed open from the initial calming breaths to the final corpse-like stillness of Shavasana, to ward off every possible incursion.

Another treasure stolen from her by the dark thing that had come to life in the old house.

Alison dozed on the chair beside Jodi.

Jodi checked her phone: one twenty-nine a.m. She wished she'd had the good sense to grab a book from the TBR shelf back home so she could take her mind off her real-world troubles. Even a weak-spined novel from her "favorites" pile—one of the classics, or a more recent darling from the contemporary shelves, such as Louise Erdrich's *Future Home of the Living God*, Ann Patchett's *The Dutch House*, or Elizabeth Strout's *Olive Kitteridge*—would have done the trick. Instead, she had to stare blankly into the glow of her smartphone, clicking unfamiliar icons and hoping to learn something new.

As she scrolled through her catalog of texts, Jodi

stopped on a weeks-old thread with Andrew and guessed at the time in Valencia, Spain. Her son had become the equivalent of a rock star in European culinary circles—an expat restaurateur with widespread critical acclaim, mentions in *Bon Appétit*, and enough "best of" awards to fill a trophy case. Alison had urged Jodi to let Andrew know about his father's "episode," but what exactly could she tell him at this point? Besides, Jodi knew how stressful running a restaurant could be. Suggesting the sky was falling half a world away would likely send a sensitive soul like Andrew tumbling into an emotional morass.

She saw no need to disrupt her son … yet.

The dimmed overheads made her drowsy, but who could sleep? She should be hungry, but who could eat? She would worry about her own needs once she knew Martin was all right.

The double doors parted. Two paramedics hurried a man on a gurney into the ER. Even from a passing glance, Jodi could tell the fellow was in bad shape. Some sort of head or neck wound, by the looks of things—a gauze-like bandage, soaked red, dangled from one of the gurney rails. A blanket of warm air drifted toward her.

"Who are you here for?"

The woman with the rosary eyed Jodi through thick, tinted lenses.

"My husband." Jodi pointed to Alison on the chair beside her and added, "Her father."

"I'm here for my daughter. Again. Second time this month. Every time I think she's clean, I find her junked up with another needle in her arm."

"That's just awful," Jodi said. "I can't imagine. My children weren't perfect—*aren't* perfect—but I'm thankful every day they avoided those kinds of problems."

"Every time my Luna has a relapse, I tell God in Heaven, 'Please let this be the last time.' He hasn't heard a word yet, hasn't listened. He may not forgive me for saying this, but I just want it to stop, no matter how. Three days from her eighteenth birthday, and this is where she chooses to start her adult life? I'll probably burn forever for saying what I'm about to say, but if they can't bring her back this time, I would be okay with it."

Jodi nodded politely, knowing she could add nothing to comfort the woman.

"A devil hooked Luna on that junk," the woman added. "Honest to God, a devil. I know how crazy that must sound, but it's true."

"My definition of *crazy* would surprise you."

"What's wrong with your husband?"

Jodi sighed and said, "We don't know yet. I found him unconscious in the backyard, unmoving, blue in the face—nothing good. Doctor says it's not a heart attack, so at least there's that. The ambulance got to us quicker than I expected. I just hope we got here quick enough."

She imagined the bony index finger of Martin's doctor pointing to a computer screen, an unbroken green line trailing off into infinity. The implication: brain death.

"How long have you been together, you and your husband?"

"More than forty years." Jodi smiled at the memory of the wedding, the honeymoon, a stitched-together collage of the tens of thousands of other moments they had shared since.

"My husband died the year Luna was born. She came in April. He left in June. Lung cancer. You should be grateful. You and your husband had a good, long run."

Jodi gasped at the woman's suggestion, that her relationship with Martin had reached some kind of terminus. Part of her wanted to say something sinister to afflict the woman and her rosary, as payback for suggesting Martin would lose his fight, but what good would it do? Stress made people do and say stupid things. Considering the daughter's addiction, the woman's life was difficult enough without Jodi piling on.

Jodi turned to Alison, tapped her on the arm, and told her she was going to the restroom. As she hurried past, she averted the gaze of Luna's mother.

CHAPTER 3

The Shift

Martin downs another cup of coffee as he stares at the wall clock, trying to will the early-morning minutes to pass more quickly.

The harsh white light from the overheads makes the painted-green walls look sickly, gross, like baby shit. His mind feeds him images of the few diapers he changed a month earlier, and their stomach-turning contents. He cannot fathom how Jodi does it, this childrearing business, especially with two of the little buggers at the same time. When someone loves another person so much, the way Jodi loves Andrew, the oldest by three minutes, and Alison, the baby, anything becomes tolerable, even if the task includes wiping liquid waste from the crack in someone's backside and the folds in their fatty legs. Martin adores the babies almost as much as Jodi does, but he has not found the same strength Jodi possesses. What does it say about him that he vomited both times he was assigned to diaper duty, to the point that she no longer asks and he no longer offers, leaving yet another undesirable task in Jodi's tired hands?

As with everything in life, Jodi exceeds him. She is the better human being.

He tops off his Styrofoam cup with a pour from the coffee pot. Nothing else will keep him awake. At least he has the aptitude for this, working the late shift at the all-night convenience store three blocks from the slums of Ceniza Park, selling half-sawdust hot dogs and cans of Tecate to gringos and wetbacks at three a.m. He eyes the clock, knowing his shift will end in another two and a half hours, just as the sun peeks over the horizon. Then he will head to his day job at the Ford dealership, sweeping up spent Marlboros and Salems from the lot and hand-washing newly sold sedans and pickups for yuppies in polo shirts. He reminds himself that he will catch up on his sleep when Andrew and Alison turn two.

He pages through a month-old *Playboy* his fifty-something-year-old co-worker, Arthur, left beneath the counter. His crotch stiffens. Anything does the trick these days, because nearly six months have passed since he and Jodi last made love. The wind blows the right way and his pants get tight.

"Quiet, you," he tells his genitals. "You're the one who got us into this mess in the first place."

The bell above the door jangles.

So, he thinks, *this is how it ends.*

The man in the canary-yellow ski mask levels a shotgun at Martin's face.

"Every fuckin' cent in the fuckin' drawer," the man yells. "Give it here."

Martin backs away from the register. A tobacco

display jabs him in the spine. Tins of Skoal tumble to the floor. The man leaps over the counter and slips on the dust-slicked tile. The gun blasts a hole through the Formica, deafening Martin's ears. The man gets to his feet and trains the shotgun back on Martin. Ribbons of smoke trickle from the barrel.

"Open the damned drawer, or you're next."

The man's eyes flit to the front door. Martin sees the distraction as his opportunity to pounce.

His fist connects with the man's chin, and the man drops to a knee. Martin rakes his hand across the man's face, so the mask occludes his vision. He rips the shotgun from his assailant's hands, and cracks the butt against the man's forehead. The man crumples to the floor. Martin kneels across the man's back and rains blows upon the skull, his ears, the side of the face.

Keep going, says the voice in his head. *Beat him until he breaks.*

An image flashes through his mind—that of a small, strange man in a gunmetal herringbone suit, a derby shielding his dark sores for eyes, his teeth like ivory needles.

He lifts the shotgun from the floor and slams the butt against the man's skull. The first three strikes sound the same, like the crack of a bat, but the fourth reminds him of a melon splitting. The off-white tile turns the color of a rose bloom.

Martin gets to his feet, heart pounding, and shambles around the counter, toward the back of the store. Each step seems to take an eternity. He plucks a neon-green Mountain Dew from the cooler, twists the cap, and drinks deeply. The ringing in his ears does not cease. It sounds like the whine of a mosquito. He moves to the front of the store, realizing he should call the cops. As he emerges from the aisle, he faces another man, also wearing a ski mask—orange to the other man's yellow.

The half-drunk Mountain Dew bottle falls to the linoleum.

The bullet pierces his chest and prangs off the collarbone.

The floor rises to meet him. The tile cools his back. His neck and chest feel wet. Warmth leaves his body breath by breath. He thinks of the dead man behind the counter, and wonders if he is about to join him in the afterlife. He thinks of Jodi, of Andrew, of Alison. They will be better off without him.

The minutes tick by as he fades in and out of consciousness. He wonders how much time has passed. The face of the wall clock blurs. He wants to crawl toward the front counter and die where someone can see him, but he cannot move.

The bell jangles faintly. A tall black man, dressed in dark blue from head to toe, stands on the floormat. The silver star pinned to his chest gleams in the blare of the overheads.

"*Shit*," the cop says. He reaches for his transceiver. "Nine-oh-one-S at the Gila Mart on Petaluma and Broad. Send ambulance."

The officer kneels beside Martin.

"Today's your lucky day, fella."

"Sure doesn't feel like it," Martin says, the words too soft.

The officer places a hand on Martin's shoulder. A spurt of blood warms Martin's cheek.

A hobbit of a man in a gray suit appears by the counter. The man's alien fists clutch an ivory cane. A black cloud shrouds his feet. The brim of a derby shades his eyes, but the pupils glow like white-hot embers.

Those eyes ...

"You're late," Martin says.

"Be thankful I didn't stop at the Circle K on the boulevard," the officer says.

"Not you," Martin tells the officer. He points a shaky finger toward the strange figure levitating by the counter. "Tell him I'm done with this shit."

The Little Gray Man taps the floor with the tip of his cane. Thick green fluid leaks from the tip of each tendril-like finger. He has come to feed, Martin knows.

The officer looks to the counter and then back at Martin, as if he has seen nothing.

"Take it easy, fella. Ambulance will be here soon. You're losing a lot of blood."

"How much more do I have to give?" Martin asks, before the world goes dark.

CHAPTER 4

Insatiable

A hand grasped Jodi's shoulder. As she heard her name spoken aloud, she opened her eyes to the shock of unfamiliar surroundings. Alison stood next to a nurse who seemed too young and fragile for such a serious place. Morning sunlight painted the eggshell walls copper. The clock on the wall came into focus, suggesting a few minutes before seven a.m. Still foggy from a night of restless sleep on an uncomfortable chair, Jodi struggled to decipher the nurse's words, let alone where she was. Then she remembered: *Martin!*

"Is he awake yet?" she asked.

The nurse—BRANDY BRAY, R.N., according to her badge—wagged her head no.

Jodi turned to Alison. Her daughter's eyes looked ready to burst.

"I'm afraid we can accommodate only one visitor at a time in the ICU," Nurse Bray said.

"Stay here and get some coffee or something," Jodi replied. "I'm sure I won't be long."

Alison protested weakly. "Are you sure?"

"No reason for both of us to see the horror show anyway," Jodi said, half joking.

She stood to follow the nurse to the elevator. Cramps seized her calves. Her eyes landed on the chair where the woman with the rosary had been sitting—Luna's mom. No sign of her, just an empty seat.

An awkward minute passed in the elevator, with Jodi studying the numbers on the control panel. When that became uninteresting, she found a paper sign taped to the wall reminding her to wash her hands. The doors opened with a ding, and Nurse Bray led Jodi out of the elevator and into the ICU.

Every detail of the experience seemed alien. Jodi's gaze wandered into darkened rooms, offering just enough light to show motionless bodies in hospital beds. Machines blinked and beeped, giving breath to those who could not take it for themselves. Nurse Bray stopped at the entrance to a corner room.

"The doctor should be by in a few minutes," she said. Her eyes did not meet Jodi's. "In the meantime, let your husband hear your voice."

Jodi stepped into the room and took a breath. Martin lay silent and unmoving in his bed. Someone had snaked a tube down his throat, with the showing portion taped to his cheek. An overhead sling elevated his right arm. The limb seemed twice as thick as it should have been, swaddled in white wrappings. Fluid dripped from a seam at the elbow and turned the dingy white bedsheet yellow.

"It's me, babe," she whispered. She wiped the corner

of each eye with a shirtsleeve and eased her weight onto the bed's corner. "What the hell happened to you, Martin? … Whatever it was that did this to you, it picked the wrong person. If you're anyone, you're a fighter, so fight like a son of a bitch. Don't you dare make me leave this hospital by myself."

Footsteps squeaked from the hallway. Jodi turned to see a doctor busily tapping the screen of a tablet. His red hair had begun to gray, far older than the sapling she had met in the ER waiting room hours earlier. The new doc had some seasoning at least, which she took as a good sign.

"You're the wife?" he said.

She rose from the edge of Martin's bed.

"Who the hell else would I be? I have a name, for chrissakes."

He said nothing, perhaps realizing he should let her vent.

"I'm scared, tired, hungry, and constipated," she added. "The least you can do is know my name. … It's Jodi."

The doctor bowed his head toward the tablet in his hands—Martin's chart, presumably.

"I understand, Missus Avec-Georges." He pointed to his badge and said, "Doctor Kristoff Stephens, critical care. I'm sorry your husband's condition has brought you here today."

"That's better. Now what's going on with my husband? Call him Martin. Please."

"For all intents and purposes, he's comatose. I know that can be a scary word, but coma is the body's way of protecting itself against injury. Most comas last a short while, a few days, sometimes a few weeks, but some can go for months. Rarely for years."

She turned her head. She would not let Stephens, or anyone else, see her cry.

"Does he even know I'm here?"

"His brain is functioning at its lowest stage of alertness. It's not like sleeping, so he's not dreaming, and he probably won't respond to your voice, though it can't hurt to let him know you're here. His brain is likely doing little more than recycling memories—running through old data, you might say."

"As long as he's not in pain."

"There's something else."

"Is it the bite?" Jodi interjected. "The ER doctor said his arm looked swollen. *Angry* was the word he used. He didn't seem overly concerned."

"Leave it to my colleague to be colorful when clarity is needed. Are you squeamish?"

"Not particularly."

Stephens moved to his patient's bedside and slid back the sleeve covering Martin's arm. Jodi's eyes grew wide. The underside of Martin's forearm had split. The edges of the wound had turned black and chalky, while a pudding-like substance filled the cavity once occupied by muscle and tendon. Milky fluid colored the white bedsheet butter yellow. The smell struck her, thick and pungent, and her hand instinctively moved to her nose. Her stomach turned. She had never seen or smelled anything like it.

"What we have here is a form of necrosis. In other words, the flesh is dead or dying. This could be as bad as it gets, but there's a possibility the condition worsens. If it does, we'll have to consider more aggressive means of intervention."

He hesitated.

"Amputation."

Jodi had guessed he would use that word, but the word was no less shocking when said aloud. She sat on the bed and rested an elbow on Martin's socked foot.

"How—? How can this be happening? He was fine. Just yesterday he was fine. Hell, *hours* ago he was fine."

"Did you see what bit him?"

She wagged her head, still wrestling with the implications of a one-armed husband.

"I'm assuming snakebite, based on the severity of the reaction," Stephens added. "Whatever it was that did it, you can see how the venom has eaten away at the dermis, and now it's attacking the subcutaneous tissue, tendon, muscle. Inflammation and symptoms consistent with necrosis extend from the fingertips to the biceps. Quite destructive."

He called in a nurse to re-drape the limb with a new cloth sleeve, the old one sopping with rancid fluid.

"His fingers swelled so much we had to cut off his wedding ring," Stephens continued. "I have treated my share of bites and stings: rattlesnakes, scorpions, black widows, tarantulas, Gila monsters, brown recluse spiders—name it, I've seen it. I can say I have never come across anything quite like this. Part of me wonders if it's a bite at all, maybe some sort of bacterial infection disguising itself as something else."

She imagined Martin, one-armed, struggling to split wood. He would rather be dead.

"If you do take the arm, then he'll be all right?"

"Like I said, we're in virgin territory. The most common snakebite we see around here is from the western diamondback. Its venom is mainly hemotoxic, meaning it attacks the circulatory system and the tissue surrounding the bite. It poisons the blood, to put it bluntly. I can't say I've seen a case quite as severe as this one. This venom also seems to have neurotoxic properties, meaning it's attacking his nervous system, too. His abdominal muscles have gone rigid. And he's showing other symptoms I can't quite pinpoint."

"Clearly we came to the right place."

The corners of Stephens's mouth curled into a slight smile.

"In residency, my attending physician once told me that medicine is a bit like an old-fashioned murder mystery," he replied. "Sometimes you find the culprit only by ruling out all other suspects. I have a colleague who works for the university in Flagstaff, and this is his field of study— venomology. I'd like to have him review your husband's bloodwork, examine the wound. Maybe he can help us understand what we're dealing with."

"Martin's been here all night. How can you not know *any*thing?"

"I can tell you exactly how to treat the body for a specific injury or disease, but first we have to identify the malady," Stephens said with a smugness that made Jodi want to smack him. "The gentleman I mentioned, he's an expert in this sort of thing—poisons and venoms. If we've learned anything, it's that nature rarely stands still. Snakes, spiders, and other venomous critters are constantly evolving, as are the weapons they use to immobilize their prey. Once we shed more light on the problem, we can figure out where to go from here."

Stephens patted Jodi's shoulder. The gesture felt forced.

"I want you to prepare yourself." He paused. "If I were a betting man, I'd say your husband's arm will need to go."

CHAPTER 5

Blood and Soil

Jodi stepped outside to escape the chill of the ICU. Goosebumps pimpled the flesh of her arms. The warmth of early evening felt like a blanket on her skin. Unmoored and adrift, she wished someone would step toward her, take her in their arms, and say, "Everything is going to be fine."

Naturally, she thought of her parents, Elliott and Helena Claybourne, both long dead. No one had ever said an unkind word about her parents, both sickeningly kind, inoffensive, and positive to the point of being saccharine. At fourteen years old, Jodi had stumbled upon a tattered cardboard box stuffed with mementos of her mother's first pregnancy, in which her mom had given birth to a stillborn infant that would have been her older brother. When Jodi confronted her parents about this shock, her father left the room while her mother said, simply, "It was a trial run for bringing you into the world."

Only later would Jodi learn that there was a monumental difference between positivity and blind ignorance.

To Jodi's mind, Elliott and Helena Claybourne had loved only three things in the world: their daughter, paperback crime novels, and hard candy. Her parents kept a bowl of butterscotch buttons, Jordan almonds, and chocolate straws perched on the end table between their matching armchairs until the day she left home to marry Martin. While she came of age beneath her parents' roof—studying, sneaking drags on cigarettes through her bedroom window, dreaming about the future—her parents sat in their armchairs, voraciously turning pages and dipping their hands into the candy bowl, smooth jazz on low in the background. When MLK was assassinated and RFK met his end, and with news programs reporting on increasingly worrisome developments in jungles on the other side of the world, Jodi sought explanations from her parents. Mom and Dad reliably offered one of two responses: "Don't worry yourself, dear," or "It's out of our hands," and then thrust their noses deeper into their paperbacks, their hands deeper into the candy dish. She still recalled, with no small degree of disgust, the sound of her father's lips smacking together as he sucked the sugar out of whatever sweet treat he had pressed into the pocket of his cheek.

The Claybournes had lived in a bubble of their own making, and they tried their damnedest to keep their daughter there with them. If some rival world power had dropped a world-ending bomb on Arizona's meaty middle, much like the U.S. had done to Japan to hasten the end of World War Two, she suspected her parents would have reacted by plopping down in their respective chairs, plucking a fresh book from the towering pile between them, and keep turning pages until the wave of nuclear fire tore through the wall and reduced them to columns of ash.

While her parents went about their lives untroubled by unsettling events at home and abroad, Jodi could not help but feel as though the world around her was coming apart at the seams. Protests roiled every American city. Politicians behaved badly. When Jodi started paying attention, catching wind of stories about the sons of neighbors coming home from Vietnam in body bags, or not at all, she began to realize how dangerous the world really was, and how tenable her place in it. She then began to appreciate her parents' penchant for looking the other way, for pretending the world was not eating itself.

When her father's heart and kidneys began to fail, Jodi wanted to intercede, to see how she could help. Her parents either downplayed the seriousness of her father's troubles or suggested he was making progress in his recovery. Dad's death had seemed sudden, but only later did she learn it occurred over the course of a season, much like a boxelder shedding its leaves. Mom had lasted less than a year after that, and she faded in much the same manner—slowly, quietly, and without ceremony.

Jodi wondered: If her parents had still been alive, what reassuring words might they have to share, as Martin lingered on the edge of some invisible plane between life and death? She missed their well-meaning lies.

An ambulance idled beneath the overhang of the ER entrance, *chug-chug-chug*. She breathed in a lungful of engine exhaust, the whiff of tobacco smoke riding shotgun.

A stocky man stood at the end of the walkway, puffing away on a cigarette. The sweat on his bald head glinted in the sunlight. She waved and he nodded in return.

She would give almost anything to have the past twenty-four hours erased, or to be far away from here, her feet tramping the soft earth of a shaded trail, where the world's many problems, and her own personal traumas, could not touch her. Instead, she had to settle for brick buildings, ambulance exhaust, and the likelihood that her family life would soon change for the worse. She brought her hands to her face and tried to wipe away her fatigue.

"You look like you could use a smoke."

The man at the edge of the curb held up a pack of Marlboros.

She stepped toward him, eyes on the open pack, and said, "I shouldn't."

"Misery loves company," he told her. "Have at it."

His hand trembled slightly as he held out the pack for her. She pried back the lid and pinched the tip of a marbled filter, withdrawing a fresh cigarette from the crumpled box.

"It's been an age," she said. "As good a time as any to fall off the wagon."

He handed her his cigarette, which she used to spark the tip of her own. She inhaled the smoke and fought the urge to cough.

"Much obliged," she said. "Who are you here for?"

She had learned the parlance of those in waiting from the unpleasant woman she had met in the ER only hours earlier, though it seemed a full week had passed. Time had stopped making sense the moment she found Martin laid out by the woodpile in Crum.

"Buddy of mine had an accident," he said. "More like a brother. You?"

"Husband's not feeling too good."

She felt no need to elaborate, to suggest her husband might lose his arm because of some freak accident no one seemed able or willing to explain. A lurid image jumped into her mind: Martin climbing out of the shower, the nub of scarred flesh at the ball of his right shoulder, and using his remaining arm to towel off.

The man gobbed a pearl of spit onto the asphalt. Pink, she noticed, as if tinged with blood. Jodi guessed his age as late twenties, no more than thirty. Up close, she saw he was not bald; rather, he had shaved his head down to the scalp. His bottom lip was torn down the middle, perhaps a lip ring that had been yanked free. Red-brown spatters discolored the fabric of a white T-shirt with the sleeves removed. Ink covered the entirety of his left arm. Some of the tattoos looked suspicious—the phrase *Blut und Boden* etched in a Gothic script, and intimidating red-and-black symbols she thought she recognized, if she recalled correctly, from a CNN report about homegrown extremism. His swollen knuckles bore fresh scabs.

"So," she said. "What's wrong your brother-buddy?"

"Busted orbital bone. Shattered elbow. Stabbed five or six times, once in the throat."

"Some accident. Did he fall down the stairs with a box of knives?"

"You're a funny one," he said without laughing. "Shit happens, right?"

"It certainly does. To some more than others."

"He going to make it? Your fella, I mean."

"That's what we're here to find out. Your buddy?"

"No telling. He got cracked up pretty good."

Caution urged her to hold her tongue, but compulsion made her dig deeper.

"Couldn't help but notice your tattoos," she said. "I'm making some wild assumptions here, but was the trouble you two got into worth the fuss? Was it worth your busted-up face and a knife to your buddy's throat?"

He squinted as he sucked in smoke. "You've got to fight for what you believe in," he said.

"Which is what, exactly?"

He pointed to his inked-up forearm, almost as thick as her thigh. "Blood and soil," he said. "Blood and soil."

"The three-dollar bags of dirt down at Ace Hardware hardly seem worth shedding a tear over."

"You know what it means. Anyone who gives a shit about homeland and heritage knows what it means. You see how things have changed around here, around everywhere. What we've lost. Who's taking our place. A lot of good people in pain because of how far this country has fallen."

"That's what I don't understand. You look around and see enemies. All I see are people struggling to get by, make a life, get from one day to the next without falling apart. It's a beautiful world, if people stopped to notice. You should open your eyes and have a look around, too."

"It's got potential," he said. "Maybe one day we'll get back what we lost. Reclaim it. I hope I live to see the day. If I don't, you can bet your ass I died trying to pull it back from the brink. This ain't no small thing. It's a goddamn revolution. If I fall, a hundred thousand others like me will rise up to take my place."

"Can't we have peace and quiet for a change?"

"The world's all wrong and upside down. You'll have your peace and quiet when the world gets right again."

"I find that hard to believe," Jodi replied. "To some people's way of thinking, there's always going to be another enemy who needs a boot on his throat."

She took a drag, long and deep, and stubbed out the cigarette on the side of the building. Ash marred the buff brick. She held up the cigarette's remainder for him to take.

"When I was your age, snipes were a form of currency," she said. "I'd hate to see this one go to waste. But you should quit, you know. You might live longer."

He took the half-spent cigarette and re-lit the tip. Puffs of gray-blue smoke leaked from the side of his mouth. He then dropped his spent butt to the curb and snuffed the cinder beneath the toe of his oxblood boot.

"Good luck to you, funny lady," he told her. "Your husband, too."

"Same," she replied. She wanted to say more, but she had her own children to mother. Hard as it was, she tried not to judge the man, because on some level they were the same person, both nursing their respective wounds, both hoping someone they loved would make it out of the hospital alive, preferably with all their limbs intact.

CHAPTER 6

Nowhere to Hide

Martin arranges his dull-green army men on the windowsill, Allies versus Nazis and Japs. Raindrops speckle the windows of his bedroom. A curtain of water obscures his view of the outside world as the gutter overflows and drowns the flowerbeds below.

Martin inches an Allied sapper along the sill and twists his fingers so the figure sweeps its landmine detector from side to side. He hurries to a shelf on the far wall, where a German sniper peeks out from behind a stack of baseball cards. His cheeks bulge as he makes the sound of an explosion, and he draws a line from the tip of the sniper's rifle to the curve of the sapper's helmet. He flicks the sapper with his middle finger. The figure topples to the wooden floor and skitters beneath the bed—another one of the good guys lost.

"What are you up to now, boy?"

Martin's father fills the doorway.

"Nothin', Dad. Just playin'."

He silently prays for his mother to appear, but she does not. Still shopping for groceries, he supposes. She will not save him this time.

"Instead of wasting time in here, you should be outside, learning how to make an honest buck," his father says. "The lawn needs cutting. The fence needs painting. Did you take care of those rabbits like I told you?"

A mother rabbit built a nest for her two babies beneath the northwest corner of the shed. Martin hoped his father had forgotten, but he has not. His father dislikes animals and believes they deserve eradication. He sees the matter as "us" versus "them," though Martin cannot quite understand why.

"It's raining," Martin says. "Mom says it's supposed to rain all day. She'll be home soon, right?"

"Look at you, pretending to make war with a baby's toys. You know nothing about shooting and getting shot at, boy. Maybe you should."

Martin's father grabs his son by the shirt collar and drags him into the hallway. The fabric groans and tears. A steely hand squeezes Martin's shoulder, pushing him forward. Martin cannot see his father's face. He prefers to be dragged rather than pushed, because then at least he can see what his father is doing with his hands.

Martin faces the back door.

"Out," his father says.

Martin looks up at his father, pleading. He wears corduroys and a T-shirt, no shoes or socks. Mid-April in the Pacific Northwest means heavy rain, and he knows the temperature can be no higher than the low fifties.

When Martin hesitates, his father opens the door and roughly pushes Martin outside. Rain soaks his hair, his shirt, his pants.

"The lawn, boy. The mower needs exercising."

"Can I get my raincoat and boots?"

"I'm not going to tell you more'n once. When your superior tells you to do something, you do it, no questions asked. You think I wanted to walk a thousand miles across Europe, hunting town to town for those kraut sons of bitches? Hell, no. But I did it anyway, because that's what men do. Are you a man or a whiny little tit sucker?"

"I'm eight," Martin whispers.

He trudges across the sopped lawn and opens the shed. Rain pours over the eaves in a sheet. Every part of him is wet and cold. He yanks the push-reel lawnmower from its cobwebbed corner and starts cutting.

"Incoming!"

A small stone strikes the side of Martin's face.

"Bull's-eye!" Martin's father laughs from a dry spot beneath the awning. He holds a handful of stones in his palm. "When you're in a war, you have to be aware of your surroundings. Keep your eyes peeled, boy."

His father throws another stone, and Martin ducks. Then another, and again Martin evades the assault. A tossed stone ricochets off the mower's handle. As Martin turns the mower to start a new row, he sees his father whip his arm, and another stone veers straight toward him. He sidesteps just in time, and the stone pings off the top of the chain-link fence.

Martin smiles at his cleverness, though he immediately recognizes his mistake.

His father empties the rest of his cache. A dozen stones pelt Martin's head and torso. One hits his cheek, and the skin breaks. The side of his face warms.

"Don't forget to take care of those damned rabbits!"

His father goes inside and slams the door behind him.

Martin's forehead, jaw, and left cheek throb from where the stones hit, but he is glad to be alone. At least he can finish his chores in peace.

An hour later Martin goes back inside, soaked to the bone. He disrobes and stands in the middle of his room. He cannot stop thinking about the baby rabbits, how he hesitated over the first one, the sound it made as he brought the shovel blade down, and how the second one was easier. As much as he wants to cry, he cannot. Excitement builds in his gut as he dreams of taking the shovel to his father, but he shakes the thought away. He wishes he could stand up to his dad. Maybe when he is older, bigger, stronger.

Martin hates his age, his powerlessness. No longer can he afford to indulge in childish things. He goes to the window and sweeps an arm violently across the sill. His army men sprawl to the floor. As he lifts his gaze, something odd catches his eye. A small man in a gray suit stands on the front lawn. A derby the color of smoke shades the man's eyes. The rain seems to bounce off his hat and shoulders. A dark handlebar mustache contrasts his alabaster skin. His purple lips form a grin, as if struggling to hide teeth too big for his mouth. He holds an ivory walking stick with a sharp hook at the end. Gray fog shrouds the man's feet. His fingers look unlike any Martin has ever seen—long, green, and wet, like tendrils or tentacles. The man wags an eel-like finger, as if beckoning Martin closer.

A memory, or perhaps a dream, burns in Martin's brain. A year ago, when he was home sick with the flu. He stayed in bed for days, plagued by dark, vibrant dreams in which this strange little man stayed by his side and wiped the sweat from his fevered brow.

Martin turns away from the window and howls as he steps on one of his army men.

Something hard taps the window.

Martins turns to see the Little Gray Man at eye level, somehow hovering, on the other side of the rain-streaked glass. Martin may be only eight years old, but he knows the man is not all right.

"What do you want?" Martin asks.

"To be friends, of course," the man says, the glass muffling his response. "You will find I am a most sympathetic and generous friend. And you will repay me with your generosity, won't you, dear boy? We will share everything, like best buds."

"Who are you?"

"Call me Pappaduffus. Mister Pappaduffus, if you prefer."

"Why do you want to be my friend?" A fair question, because few others have.

"Perhaps no one else has told you, but you're a very special boy. You possess something I consider most precious. Surely I'm not the only one who thinks so."

"I'll have to ask my mom," Martin says.

"Oh, there's no need, dear boy," Pappaduffus says. "Why, I can't imagine what others might say, might think, if you go blabbing on and on about me. We'll keep us between us."

"No one else can see you?"

"Only if I permit them. Just the most special among you, the best of your kind. … Well, I see no point in being nasty."

"What if I don't want to be friends with you?"

The emotion seems to drain from Pappaduffus's face. The skin around his eyes and jowls begins to sag. Bits of flesh slide from his face, like drops of rain.

Martin pulls the lace-like curtains across the window. He sees Pappaduffus's silhouette through the lacy veil, and he wonders how well the man can see him in return. If Martin's mother were home, he would run and tell her so she can chase the strange man away. He does not dare voice his concerns to his father. No telling how he might react, other than pinning the blame on Martin and making him beg for contrition one lash at a time. Martin creeps across the floor, staying quiet, so Pappaduffus cannot track his movements. The carpet burns his knees and the point of each elbow. He crawls into his closet and creaks the door closed until only the faintest light filters through. He decides to stay there until Pappaduffus finds someone else to hector.

The tapping on the window grows more insistent. It sounds as though the glass might crack. Then, abruptly, the tapping stops.

Martin buries his face into something soft—a pillow, clothes fallen from their hangers, maybe his unfurled sleeping bag. Just as he reaches the edge of sleep, the pillow shifts as if it is alive. The smell overpowers him, like something gone rotten paired with the smoke of his father's Winstons. He retreats into the corner, hugging his knees to his chest. Two white pinpricks cut through the darkness. Eel-like fingers caress his arm. He hears the unmistakable sound of someone drawing a breath.

"Tell me, dear boy," Pappaduffus says. "Who are we hiding from?"

A scream forms at the back of Martin's throat, but it catches there, frozen.

Pappaduffus smiles. His fangs glow like burnished silver.

CHAPTER 7

Angels and Devils

A noise jostled Jodi out of a dark dream. A puddle of drool dampened the bedsheet. She lifted her head off the corner of Martin's bed, half-expecting to see Alison, only to remember the ICU's policy of one guest at a time. Instead, she saw Doctor Stephens accompanied by a younger man she did not recognize.

"Sorry to wake you, Missus Avec-Georges," Stephens said. "I'd like you to meet someone."

Jodi struggled to make out the newcomer's face. Stephens turned to the man behind him and said softly, "Now remember where you are this time."

The man stepped into the center of the room. Jodi's assessment: handsome, thin, and well dressed, his face bisected by eyeglasses with teal frames. Only a silly ponytail that jutted from the back of his head diminished his stylish appearance. She put him at no more than forty years old.

"This is the gentleman I was telling you about," Stephens told her. "Douglas Exelby, a biology professor at the University of Northeastern Arizona in Flagstaff. Venom toxicity is his primary area of research."

"*Doctor* Douglas Exelby," the man corrected. "I have a Ph.D., and I did go to medical school. About a year away from getting my M.B.A., too. Pleasure to meet you, ma'am. Mind if I have a look at your husband's arm?"

Jodi backed away from the bed and took a seat in the corner. Still lost in the fog of sleep, she struggled to process Exelby's words. The biologist reached into his back pocket and retrieved a pair of blue nitrile gloves. He then went to the bedside and removed the sleeve covering Martin's disintegrating arm. A substance resembling liquefied chicken fat dribbled onto the bedsheet. Exelby promptly brought a hand to his nose and made a noise that suggested surprise, or perhaps disgust. The smell hit Jodi a moment later, worse than she remembered. Exelby gave a thorough examination and then carefully re-sleeved the arm. He took a seat in the chair beside Jodi, wiped his glasses on the tail of his fitted shirt, and cleared his throat.

"Jodi, right?" he said. "First, some questions. Has your husband been to South Asia recently? India, Pakistan, Bangladesh, anywhere like that?"

"Of course not."

"Your husband fell ill at your home, correct? Not far from here?"

"Small place called Crum. Maybe thirty miles east."

"And I'm guessing he doesn't collect exotic animals, correct?"

"*What?* No."

"Then this is truly fascinating."

"I'm sure Martin would agree if he were conscious."

"He means no disrespect, Missus Avec-Georges," Stephens added.

"As Doctor Stephens told you, I lead the university's biology department, specializing in venoms and poisons," Exelby said. "Now, believe me when I tell you I have traveled the world to study the venoms of snakes, spiders, scorpions, fish, platypuses—you name it. In fact, I would have been here sooner, but I needed a day to recover from my latest trip to Costa Rica. Don't know if you've ever had the pleasure of visiting, but I spent most of my time there at a sanctuary to study *Lachesis stenophrys,* the Central American bushmaster. Absolutely stunning reptile, world's largest pit viper, and also owner of one of the most potent ven—"

"Douglas," Stephens interjected, "perhaps it would be best if we kept the discussion focused on the patient."

"Right, right. Curious case, your husband. I'll do my best not to bore you with the biology of it all, but some background seems necessary." He wrinkled his brow as if straining to recall some arcane detail. "All venoms are masterfully complex, though some are more sophisticated than others. Some attack the nervous system, the respiratory system. Others assault the circulatory system. Others break down the body from a cellular level. In only the rarest of cases, they do all the above."

He paused as if to make sure Jodi understood.

"From a venomologist's perspective," he added, "the culprit in your husband's case is the grandest of all jackpots. There's almost no end to the symptoms he's battling right now: necrosis of a spreading swath of tissue, sky-high blood pressure, coagulation defects, partial paralysis, the beginnings of organ failure. It's almost like a bomb went off inside your husband's body."

Jodi pinched the bridge of her nose.

"Every venom is alive in some way, with its own signature of enzymes and non-enzymatic proteins," Exelby continued. "The venom of the creature that stung your husband—and it was a sting—matches nothing native to this area. Nothing native to the New World, in fact. Based on the blood workup and the ferocity of the disease progression, what we have here is likely the handiwork of a scorpion in the Hottentotta genus, specifically, *H. cavestanii*."

"Get to the point, Douglas," Stephens added.

"Just want to make sure we all understand where our story begins," Exelby said. "*H. cavestanii* is native only to some of the remotest parts of India, Pakistan, and surrounding areas—caves and crags a world away from here—so there is no easy explanation for why its venom should be coursing through your husband's body."

"Martin's dream was to become a medical mystery," Jodi said. "So, if this damn thing lives so far from here, how the hell did it end up in my backyard?"

"How does an Egyptian cobra slither onto a grandmother's patio in suburban Philadelphia? How does a school of piranha wind up skeletonizing a poodle in a public swimming hole in Austin, Texas? How does an Asian bearcat terrorize toddlers in a daycare center in downtown Sacramento? It hitched a ride somehow."

"Or something put it there on purpose," Jodi offered. "Some*one*, I should say."

"Like, attempted murder? That seems unlikely."

"You don't know what I know. You haven't seen the things I've seen."

"Be that as it may, I'd like to have some of my graduate students poke around your home, scour the property to see if we can find the culprit. It's your typical needle-in-a-haystack situation, but you have to start somewhere. It's highly unlikely we'll find anything at all, but we want to make sure an invasive population hasn't somehow taken root. For your own safety."

"Fine, whatever you want," Jodi said. "What about Martin?"

"Now, if this is what I think it is, your husband is in for a rough ride. When we think about venom lethality, we consider toxicity and dosage. Some venoms are incredibly potent, and others kill by the sheer volume injected. *H. cavestanii*, I'm afraid, checks both boxes, which is rare for a scorpion. It's one of the most virulent venoms on the planet, comparable to the omega box jellyfish and the Bengal sea krait, and each sting tends to produce an absurd quantity of venom. Whereas most venoms weaken as they become more diffuse, the venom of *H. cavestanii* actually gathers strength, seeming to multiply when it has room to roam—the 'spreading factor,' as it's known, courtesy of the hyaluronidase enzyme. There's no good reason a creature whose diet consists of cave crickets and desert mice should have such a powerful weapon. It's one of nature's bizarre miracles."

Exelby became wildly animated, spitting out more words Jodi had never heard before—bradykinin-potentiating peptides, procoagulants, myotoxins, rhabdomyolysis. Each sentence came faster than the preceding one. Jodi suspected cocaine.

"Now, I may be the *closest thing* to an expert in this hemisphere, but that hardly qualifies me as an honest-to-goodness expert on the matter," he said. "I counted twelve *H. cavestanii* interactions with humans in the Global Venom Index. Only twelve. In South Asia, you can find reams and reams of data on bites from the deadliest snakes—cobras and kraits, Russell's vipers, saw-scaled vipers—as well as stings from the red scorpion and other highly venomous arachnids from that part of the world. To have only a dozen confirmed cases of envenomation by *H. cavestanii*, all from halfway around the world ... Well, it makes your husband's case all the more astonishing."

He paused, as if his brain struggled to retrieve a memory, like fingers trying to pluck a piece of thread from the end of a spool.

"I am vexed by a case in Arles that no one seems able to explain," he added. "It's a city in southern France, right on the Rhône. A woman brought her husband of some years to the hospital with a mysterious mark on his hand—a bite or sting of some sort. His health deteriorated so rapidly, no one had any clue how to handle it. Poor fella's organs shut down one by one. His lungs filled with fluid in under an hour, the hospital staff couldn't do anything about it, meaning the guy pretty much drowned in his hospital bed. Everything about the case screams *H. cavestanii*. If I'm right, I'll chalk that one up to an exotics collector who got sloppy."

"I understand why you're over the moon about this little bugger, but forgive me if I don't share your excitement,"

Jodi said. "Those twelve prior cases—unlucky thirteen, we'll call it, considering the guy in France—what do they suggest about my husband's chances of getting through this mess? Doctor Stephens suggested Martin might lose his arm."

"Consider that the best-case scenario," Exelby said flatly. "None of the cases I mentioned had a happy ending. All concluded in death, in some cases because the envenomation occurred so far from capable medical help. Even so, I'm afraid there is no known antivenom. HC-Ab camelid antivenom has shown some promise in treating the neurotoxic effects of envenomation by other scorpions in the Hottentotta genus, but *H. cavestanii* is unlike any of its peers. Perhaps I should mention *H. cavestanii*'s common name: the death angel scorpion."

"So," Jodi started. She exhaled and added, "You're saying Martin's days are numbered."

Exelby and Stephens eyed each other, and neither gave an answer.

CHAPTER 8

A Field of Fire and Ruin

Martin holds his M16 above his head as he steps into the river, maybe sixty feet separating one bank from the other. He follows a few paces behind Samuels, the soldier just ahead of him, though every part of him wants to turn around and head in the opposite direction.

Samuels sinks up to his waist. He hums as he always does while out on patrol, or when things make him nervous, presumably to keep his mind off the killers lurking beneath the river's surface—crocodiles, pythons, leeches, and, if the rumors are true, tiny fish that pry their way into unguarded urethras and make themselves comfortable—or hidden in the jungle beyond the shore.

"Shut your trap, Samuels!" Blatty, the lieutenant, hisses over Martin's shoulder. The words mingle with the din of moving water.

"Like that's ever going to happen," adds Horowitz, the soldier at Martin's elbow.

Each member of the patrol crosses the river without

incident and sloshes onto the opposite bank. Wet feet have been the worst thing about Martin's time in Vietnam so far, the mosquitoes a close second. Two months in the bush have yielded nothing worse than one of his fellow soldiers, Lobel, needing a Medevac to treat a centipede bite on the cheek. No sign of "Charlie" so far, though they can hear him all around almost every night. With any luck, by the end of his tour, Martin will have completed a hundred-mile walk through the rain-sopped jungle and come away with nothing worse than blistered feet and a pint less blood in his veins, courtesy of the "nighthawks," Samuels' nickname for the ravenous mosquitoes; Martin considers this a misnomer, because the needle-beaked pests feast on their flesh morning, noon, and night.

Only trouble, Martin realizes, is that he has never been particularly lucky. Blatty already warned them that the nighttime operations farther north would increase the likelihood of an encounter. Martin's dreams in the periods of restless sleep the past two nights, his ass planted in moist soil back to back with either Samuels or Horowitz, seemed to foretell something horrible—warnings, omens. The prior night, when Blatty roused them from their brief rest, some internal force beckoned Martin to shoot himself in the foot or stab himself in the leg, purely to stop the advance into the jungle, closer toward a firefight that seemed all but inevitable.

Sweat dangles from the point of his chin as he studies the heavens. Stars dot the blue-black sky. Samuels, nearly seven feet tall, takes his place beside Martin and props an elbow on his shoulder.

"It'd be pretty if we was anywhere but here," Samuels says. He sticks his hand down his pants to make sure nothing unwanted has made a home of his genitals. He excised a leech from his inner thigh a week earlier, and he keeps insisting that sooner or later one of the slippery little suckers will take a bite out of his "coin purse," as he calls it. Rather than getting shot in the ass or getting locked in a bamboo cage as a POW, Samuels is more worried about something altering his manhood in a way that might prevent him and his wife, Tilda, from adding to their brood back home in Cincinnati.

Samuels and Horowitz have been a boon to Martin. He met both of them the first day on the ground in South Vietnam, and the trio has been inseparable since.

Demetrius "Monk" Samuels—the son of a jazz musician—is Martin's closest friend in Vietnam, and a friend he intends to keep once they escape this hellhole and return to normal life back home in the States. At twenty-four years old to Martin's not quite twenty, Samuels is the older brother Martin never had. He does everything a good friend or brother should do, including making Martin laugh when he needs it most. Samuels reminds Martin of Bob Sweems and Frank McGoldrick, his childhood friends from the neighborhood in Phoenix, but somehow better. Samuels' towering stature makes him seem superhuman, impervious, immune to tragedy.

Eli Horowitz, on the other hand, reminds Martin of a baby bird. How he passed basic training and made it this far into the jungle, no one can quite explain. Horowitz jokes endlessly about having come to Vietnam to die, saying, "Just bury me where I fall, fellas." Martin has done everything in his power to protect Horowitz, however and whenever needed. Extra rations. Ribald jokes. Stepping in when other members of the patrol try to take liberties.

Martin once asked Horowitz why he talked so freely, so morbidly, about his supposed fate, and Horowitz responded, in one of his few moments of seriousness, "Because if I say the bad things out loud enough times, maybe they won't come true." Horowitz is as scared as the rest of them, or maybe a little more.

Just as Martin looks after Horowitz, Samuels looks after Martin.

"I don't know what we're supposed to find out here," Martin says, "because none of us can tell shit from Shinola."

"Just do what I do," Samuels says. "Sleepwalk through it."

"Man, I'd kill for a full night's sleep."

"Shit," Horowitz chimes, "I'd kill for a half-decent *nap*."

"Get used to it, my man," Samuels says. "Charlie's a busy beaver when the sun goes down, restocking the shelves while the rest of us are getting our shuteye."

The rest of the patrol must be as miserable and exhausted as Martin is. The distant echoes of small-arms fire grow less distant each night. Rocket and mortar explosions resound in the moist night air, making sleep impossible. This, he thinks, is no way to win a war.

The patrol's task: to proceed northwest, toward the Laotian border, and intercept any VC on a branch of the so-called Ho Chi Minh Trail. Disrupt the supply lines that have kept Charlie in the fight for longer than anyone could have anticipated. In their three nights out on this campaign, no run-ins with Charlie so far, but Blatty keeps telling them to "keep your trigger fingers horny," whatever that means, "'cause Charlie's itching to engage." Martin hopes Blatty is wrong, because he does not want the deaths of impoverished rice farmers—or anyone else, for that matter—weighing on his conscience. Likewise, the last thing he wants is a bullet to the brain or a bayonet to the gut. Jodi waits for him back home, and he intends to hold her to the promise she made the night before he shipped out for basic.

He finds it difficult to believe he is here, on a battlefield, charged with confronting the enemy and, when needed, gunning him down. Basic had required him to spend countless hours at the firing range, which he enjoyed, riddling the heads and torsos of human-shaped targets with too many holes to count. He had driven his bayonet into dozens of sandbags, each simulating another man's middle. But he cannot help but feel he lacks an essential skill, some vital nugget of wisdom or fortitude someone higher up the chain of command should have imparted. His superiors may have taught him the mechanics required to kill another man, but none of his training prepared him for the moment when he would have to put those skills to use. Not in basic training, not even in AIT, where he was supposed to have become an expert in his role as an infantryman. Coaxing a jammed M16 into working again, coping with hot- and cold-weather injuries, surviving behind enemy lines—AIT had shaped him into a more lethal and resilient soldier, at least in theory.

Martin supposes he learned everything he needed to

know from his father. Killing was a requirement while living under his father's roof in Oregon—rabbits, mice, baby birds in their nests—not that Martin took any pleasure from ending the life of another creature. No matter how small, ugly, or insignificant the organism, a life was a life.

None of it seems to help him now, on the ground in Vietnam, a situation unlike anything he has experienced in his two decades on the earth. Two more nights of this trek through the jungle and the patrol would return to base camp. Channeling his mother, who projected optimism even in dire circumstances, he tells himself he can do anything for two more nights.

"Samuels and A-G," Blatty says, using Martin's nickname. "See this?" He motions to a break in the foliage, or what appears to be a game trail. "You two dickweeds clear the path. Take it for a few hundred yards, have a look around, and double back. And Samuels, shut the fuck up for once in your life."

"I'll go, too, sir," Horowitz says.

"Keep your ass where I can see it," Blatty tells him.

Blatty whispers for Krebs, the forward air controller who joined the company less than a month earlier. Krebs has the important job, Blatty reminds everyone, because he is the one who will radio to the plane on standby and tell the crew exactly where to deliver two tons of ordnance. With Krebs's say so, Uncle Sam drops the bomb on Charlie's front porch and incinerates anything worth the trouble.

"Well, A-G," Samuels says, "let's take a stroll through the woods."

"Right behind you," Martin says. He claps Horowitz

on the shoulder and says, "Hold down the fort until we get back, pal."

They leave the shore and step into the jungle. The path is slight, but unmistakable. Other men—VC, no doubt—have preceded them on this trail. Martin can almost smell them, and they, in turn, can surely smell him. To them, he is an invader, a barbarian intent on vanquishment, while they see themselves as patriots defending their way of life. Both are the heroes of their respective stories, and Martin supposes neither perspective is incorrect.

Martin hears the blood pulsing through his veins. Why he signed up for this bullshit, he cannot recall. He would pay almost any price to be back home, stateside, in Jodi's arms.

A sensation prickles the back of his neck as some internal mechanism alerts him to an unseen threat. His boots freeze in place. Samuels presses forward, consumed by the jungle. A voice whispers Martin's name.

"*Run*," the voice tells him.

He looks to his right, beyond the fernlike fronds, and peers into a patch of darkness. Two pinpricks of bluish light stare back.

Those eyes ...

The first crack of gunfire comes from the left, then another, and another still. Martin drops to his belly and aims his M16. He fires wildly into the jungle. Bursts of gunfire turn the darkness red. The air smells of sulfur and hot metal.

Again comes the voice: "Run for the river."

"Samuels!" Martin screams. "Fall back!"

Martin fires off three more rounds before turning

back. His helmet slips from his head and bounces into the undergrowth. A bullet slices the stalk of a broad-leaf plant and lodges in the trunk of a banyan, so close he can hear the hiss of hot slag biting into the woody pulp. He runs blindly until the trail drops off. He falls face first into the shallows.

Enemy fire strafes the river's surface. Martin scans his surroundings for familiar faces, familiar bodies, the members of his platoon: Blatty, Donovan, Doyle, Hirsch, Krebs, Lapahie, MacDonald, Maniscalco, Paz, Santucci, Schoenebeck, Walker. Krebs, who has made his way back across the river, barks into his radio—numbers, orders, coordinates, curse words. Two bodies float with the current, facedown.

A ball of fire engulfs the opposite bank. Mortar or rocket. A hail of dirt falls from the sky.

"Samuels!" Martin screams. He fires off another three rounds and hugs the shore, his shoulder pressed into the soft mud.

The firing stops as abruptly as it started. In its place Martin hears the sound of the river and the rustling of leaves lifted by the warm breeze. A moan disrupts the stillness. Doyle, a nineteen-year-old kid from somewhere in western Pennsylvania, inspects his mangled left hand. The pinky finger dangles by strands of sinew.

Blatty stands knee deep in the river, Horowitz right behind him, as if Blatty might somehow deflect incoming rounds.

"Fall back and regroup," Blatty says. "A-G, help Doyle."

"Samuels!" Martin screams. He hears a faint

response that sounds like Samuels, but he cannot make out words.

"Fall back, A-G," Blatty says.

"I'm going after him," Martin says.

"Get the fuck across the river, Avec-Georges. I'm not going to say it again."

Blatty freezes in place, moonlight revealing the look of horror on his face. Then Martin hears what Blatty hears: the roar of an engine overhead.

The incoming plane, eager to deliver its payload.

"Call it off, Krebs!"

No response from Krebs.

Martin looks toward the opposite shore, smoldering and torn from the VC's rocket assault. Krebs lies on his side, unmoving, also smoldering. KIA.

"Fuck!" Blatty screams.

The roar grows louder. Martin feels the jet pass, and he knows he has only a second, no more than two. He leaps into the river and claws toward its center. He dips his head beneath the water. He waits for a moment, and nothing happens. Just as he readies to rise and take a breath, the world turns orange. Flames boil the surface. The pulse of the explosion batters his core, even from beneath the water.

His lungs about to burst, he surfaces to find a field of fire and ruin. The towering trunks of banyans, bishopwoods, and gums splinter and fall to the earth. Every leaf on every downed branch glows red until pieces of it drift away as ash. Martin overhands toward the far bank, where the remnants of his patrol huddle together. Blatty looks too stunned to notice the tongues of fire licking his leg. A motionless mass lies at the edge of river, face buried in the mud, legs submerged up to the knee. Horowitz.

Martin lumbers onto the shore and turns his friend onto his back. He wipes away the mud, tries to shake Horowitz awake. Then he notices the hole in Horowitz's throat and the stream of blood pouring from the back of his neck. The bullet went right through. A brother lost. Martin stands and screams for Samuels. Again and again, he repeats his friend's name, though he knows better than to expect a response. Hirsch, Santucci, and Donovan struggle to drag him into the jungle, away from the ruined bank.

Two months later, Martin stands on a tarmac in Saigon. He boards the Lockheed C-141 StarLifter, bound for Germany for seven months of desk duty and then, his obligation complete, back home to Phoenix. The burns to his face and hands have healed, but he knows his wounds will linger. He turns for one last look at a part of the world he hopes to never see again. A hot wind abrades the polished flesh of his burn-scarred cheek. He thinks of Samuels' fate, either a charred corpse coming apart on a decimated jungle floor or, worse, a military prisoner forced to rot in a bamboo cage. No mistaking Horowitz's end. A bullet to the back of the neck severed his spinal cord and shredded his jugular.

Martin tells himself to put his friends out of his mind, if not forever then at least for now. If he lingers on the horrors Vietnam showed him, he knows the memories of his friends' words and faces will drive him to the brink of madness.

CHAPTER 9

On the Topic of Horror

Jodi dragged her fork through the half-empty bowl of pasta salad. Oil-slicked noodles gleamed in the hard yellow light spilling from the cafeteria's overheads. She speared two spiral noodles and a ring of black olive, right down to the Styrofoam, and forked them into her mouth. Alison, seated across from her, munched on a rippled potato chip.

Jodi looked around the hospital cafeteria, thankful for the change of scenery. Change of smell, too, considering Martin's decomposing arm. Martin's ICU room had sapped the energy from her, not that she had much to spare. She pushed the bowl toward the center of the table and thumbed through her book.

"Have you had a good life, Mom? With Dad, I mean."

Alison's voice seemed small in the openness of the cafeteria.

Jodi looked up from the pages of Elizabeth Gilbert's *Eat, Pray, Love*—slim pickings in the hospital gift shop—

and closed the book on page eighteen, with the receipt as her bookmark. The cafeteria emptied in the span of a minute, as if everyone but them had been warned of some scheduled cataclysm. A dark-haired woman in a hairnet emerged from a set of double doors with a tray of paper-wrapped sandwiches. She shuffled out from behind the counter and set the tray on a table beside a warmer. Jodi watched the woman place each sandwich in its designated spot, one in back of the other, each lovingly arranged with its front-facing label. A gentle humming escaped the woman's lips. Her music followed her until she exited the cafeteria through the same double doors through which she had entered.

Jodi returned her attention to her daughter and said, "Why would you ask just a thing?"

"Because, after all these years, I've never known the answer."

"That's a whole lot of honesty," Jodi said. "I was a happy girl who became a happy woman. Your father gave me a lot of reasons to smile. You kids did, too, of course. Some days weren't easy or fun, but I'm thankful for every one of them. Even the shit we had to trudge through taught me something. In fact, the shit taught me the most. Forty years is a long time to spend with someone. Ninety-seven percent of it, I wouldn't change a thing."

"And the other three percent?"

"Chalk it up to bad decisions, bad luck, and the calamities life drops in your lap. The things you can't control."

She used a spork to tousle the pasta noodles languishing in the flimsy Styrofoam bowl. She craved something other than food. Her desire for a glass of gin, or any other kind of alcohol fit for drinking, had reached the point of obsession.

"How did you know Dad was *the one*?"

"I didn't. Not always, anyway. Our courtship ended when he left for the war. I was still in high school, still a know-nothing baby, and it got lonely with him not here. All the boys in my class were biting their fingernails, praying the war would end—or the draft, at least—before their numbers got called. I became close with one boy in my class. His name was Leonard."

Leonard Strohm. Jodi had not thought of him in years, not since Alison and Andrew were in high school, and Jodi saw his name on the school's masthead, as a history teacher and fencing coach. Neither of the kids had ended up in one of Leonard's classes—*Mister Strohm*'s classes, rather—nor had they any interest in fencing, so Jodi had no good reason to reach out to him. Even so, she had considered manufacturing a reason to "just say hello." More than once, in fact. Last Jodi had heard from one of the few girls she still spoke with from their high school days—all women in their sixties at this point—Leonard had retired from teaching to focus on his ailing prostate.

Jodi had quietly kept tabs on him over the years. The incipient guilt she felt in doing so was easy enough to tamp down. Leonard had reached the end of his teaching career without taking any arrows in the back, his tenure untarnished by scandal or the slightest trace of controversy. No whispers of inappropriate conduct with students. No extramarital goings-on. Not even a single complaint from a colleague about an off-color joke or a petty remark offered on a bad day. It was not that everyone had loved him; rather, it was more like no one had bothered enough to dislike him. Leonard Strohm had blended in, like wallpaper, like eggshell-colored paint. The passionate beast of a boy she had known so long ago had gone missing, either left behind somewhere, or overcome by a tamer, lamer version of himself.

"Leonard was a smart boy, handsome," Jodi added. "He was almost the exact opposite of your father—book smart, ambitious, built on the smaller side, but trim."

"Did you love him?"

Jodi dissected a curlicue of pasta with her fork. She watched as Alison bit into her sandwich, egg salad on rye.

Memories of the hours spent in Leonard's arms, her slick body against his, warmed her core. Their relationship had begun innocently enough, with brief flirtations in the halls between classes, and prying talks as he walked her home at each school day's end. Their first kiss was tentative and shy, but it unlocked an animalistic hunger in both of them. In the weeks and months that followed, they satisfied their ravenousness for each other in the backseat of his father's red Chrysler New Yorker, on blankets in the shade of boxelder trees, and in the privacy of other out-of-the-way places where they could be unbothered by the inconvenience of modesty. They kissed so deeply their teeth clinked and, on one occasion, she drew blood. The metallic taste did not dissuade her.

Meanwhile, Martin's letters from Vietnam piled up, unopened, on her parents' kitchen table.

Leonard was the first boy—or *man*, as he had just turned eighteen—to whom she had shown herself, naked, and she prickled at the feeling of his smooth body against hers. She gave herself to him fully in the New Yorker, wincing as the sticky vinyl squeaked and squealed beneath her. Shame overwhelmed her at first—because of Martin, mostly—but the feeling faded after a few days. Soon enough she and Leonard were getting their fill of each other almost daily. After each time she felt both drained and exuberant. If Leonard would have asked her to marry him, she likely would have accepted his proposal. Better, she would have preferred they get an apartment together, just big enough to do little more than eat, sleep, and fuck.

Their coupling slowed to a trickle in the weeks after they graduated from high school. Leonard pulled away as he prepared to leave for college in New Mexico, while she began taking classes at the community college in Glendale. From then on, she swore off the idea of falling in love with any other boy. The pain of getting left behind—yet again—would not be worth the pleasure she might take from the experience.

Then came another letter from Martin, this one promptly opened. After having been injured in a firefight with the VC, his missive suggested, he would leave Southeast Asia to finish up his military commitment on a quiet base in Europe. He ended the note with "I'll find you." The sentence elicited no feeling in her, but that changed when he returned home to Phoenix and shared a secret that cracked her open. Her parting words to him on a blanket by the Gila River the night before he left for basic training gave him the strength to endure his perdition in the green hell of Vietnam.

Jodi had since become an old woman. At least her eighteen-year-old self would have considered her old. Reminiscences of her time with Leonard Strohm had sustained her during the years in which she reared the twins, marred by prolonged stretches of inactivity, without romance or sex or a meaningful social life, as Martin fought to make his way in the world. Though brief, her dalliance with Leonard made her feel whole, as though she had lived, loved, been broken, and then healed from the trauma. Sex with Martin, though occasionally inspired, paled in comparison to what she and Leonard had accomplished. Yet, while Leonard had been her equal in this one crucial respect, Martin completed her in almost every other way.

"Your father is the only man I've ever truly loved," she told Alison.

Jodi sensed a shift in her daughter's mood.

"Are *you* happy, dear?" she asked. "I told your father not long ago that I was starting to worry about you. Do I have reason to be?"

"Not like before. Just the usual self-pity and regret I'm sure all single people my age wrestle with. Sometimes I feel like I'll never have a plus-one, at least not any plus-one I would want. It's almost like the good ones can smell me coming—my disorder—and run like hell in the opposite direction. You can't imagine what it's like to be alone for as long as I have."

"Don't be too sure. Besides, I'd wager that being alone is far better than being stuck with the wrong person."

"Says the woman who has been with the same man for forty-something years. I have no one."

"That's not true, dear."

"You're right. I have Mister Sticky."

"The lizard?"

"Yes, the lizard. Tokay geckos are hardly good company, and sometimes it terrifies me to think there's some other creature whose survival depends on me. I guess it's a good thing I never bothered to procreate."

"Well, marriage is no walk in the woods either."

"I'm at the point where I doubt I even *want* to share my life with anyone, but I just feel sort of *less than* because I'm not joined at the hip with someone else. Honestly, how would I tolerate sharing my personal space with another person? Even if the man of my dreams walks into my life tomorrow, we move in together and I'm going to want to choke the life from his body after three days. Humans are noisy, smelly, repulsive creatures."

Jodi cracked a smile at her daughter's dead-on observation.

"So, stay single."

"You just have *all* the answers—don't you, Mom? I wish you could see inside my head and tell me how to fix what's broken."

"Blame your father. I don't have the chemical issues you two do."

"That's what I'm getting at. You always seemed so hard and tough and put together. An unbreakable woman if there ever was one."

"I *used* to be soft," Jodi said. "Life gives you calluses. A tough exterior makes for a good shield, but you can't let the toughness penetrate you fully. My advice to you: Keep sight of the things that bring you joy. I fully expect your dad to make it through this, but both he and I will pass on one day. Maybe Andrew will precede you, too, making you the last of us. Those kinds of tortures are bound to happen in a long life, but don't focus on the horrible things that spill in your lap. I know that's difficult to do when you're in the middle of the horror, like we are now."

Alison seemed to sense an opening, a weakness Jodi had not intended to expose.

"Interesting choice of words," Alison said. "While we're on the topic of horror ..."

Jodi forked two noodles and a C-shaped slice of celery into her mouth. She took her time chewing.

"No more stalling, Mom. What happened back home?"

"Best to leave settled things settled," Jodi said. "Best to let the unpleasant memories fade."

"Do you know what it was like for me to find out from Melinda, the bitchy class-president type from high school? She IM'd me with a link to some ridiculous news story, asking me, 'Isn't this your house?' I just about wanted to die. Imagine what it's like to see your childhood home on the Channel Nine News for a story about a local haunted house for sale. A 'portal to the underworld,' the reporter called it. I was, like, 'Is this a fucking joke?'"

"We were surprised, too," Jodi admitted. "No one asks for that kind of publicity. We didn't ask for a lot of things, but we thought it was our responsibility to be upfront with the future owners. If it makes you feel any better, the house found the right buyer—some Goth spinster who claimed to be a witch or something."

"It *doesn't* make me feel better. I spent my whole childhood in that house, and it was quiet and wonderful. 'Haunted,' my ass."

"It changed after you left. You wouldn't believe how much it changed. When your dad and I escaped that Tuesday night, we took nothing with us, not even Roy. The next morning I had to call Tracey, our Realtor friend, and beg her to go collect Roy and the litter box, and a few other things we needed. I sure as hell wasn't going back in there. Never did again."

Even then, Jodi felt she could never adequately repay the debt she owed Tracey Shea-McEllish. Tracey said she had seen and heard a lot of strange things in her years of helping clients buy and sell their homes, so when Jodi told her what happened, Tracey responded, simply, "How can I help?" In addition to rescuing Roy, Tracey took a smudge stick to every corner of the house to drive off any traces of cosmic weirdness that might have lingered. When Jodi told Tracey her efforts were not enough to make her stay, and that they *needed* to move, Tracey suggested playing up the haunted angle, "just to be fair," she had said, "in case anything strange happens to whoever lives there next." Jodi had neither seen nor spoken with Tracey since the day of settlement, figuring no news was good news.

"No trouble in the new place, honest to goodness—at least not until this crap with your dad," Jodi said. "It's not even worth talking about at this point, like waking up from a bad dream."

"Details, Mom. If you don't tell me what happened,

I swear I'm going to scream until I pass out."

Jodi folded her hands on the table.

"You're not going to believe it," she said.

Alison stared her mother down.

Jodi saw no point in keeping quiet any longer. She lifted her chin to scan the cafeteria, to make sure no one was within earshot.

"When your father came home from Vietnam, he was different from the boy who went off to do his duty for God and country."

"Like, PTSD?"

"Not quite." Jodi sipped cautiously at her coffee, once boiling hot but since gone tepid. "We got married two months after your dad returned from the war. Every young marriage takes some getting used to, ours included. Your dad didn't sleep much early on, and he had night terrors when he did sleep. I kept pressing him to tell me what was bothering him. Finally he broke down and told me. He said he'd see things late at night, and things kept finding him, almost like metal shavings being drawn to a magnet. I knew your father had troubles, because of the war, because of his upbringing, but I always thought his problems were purely in his head. Then, last year, the air in the house went sour, stale, diseased. Slowly, whatever was there revealed itself."

A shadow that did not belong. A dish skittering from the counter and shattering on the floor. The downstairs furniture rearranged, the couch cushions on the floor or a chair several feet distant from where she had left it. When her toothbrush ended up in the toilet, she knew something was seriously wrong—either with Martin, with herself, or with the house. Roy had been the canary in the coalmine, the first one to make her realize the house had gone bad. The cat had begun to spend most of its time either hiding in the basement or pawing at the front door and begging to be let out.

"It was like some unnatural force was gathering power and learning how to use it."

A yearning built in Jodi's gut. She would trade a pinkie finger for half a glass of gin—Martin's drink of choice, and hers.

"When did it begin, Mom? The weird stuff."

Jodi considered the question and said, "Why, the day you were born, dear."

Alison swatted her mother's arm. "Not funny."

"Your father used to say he saw death over there, in the war, which I always thought was obvious, because awful things happen when countries fight. Every day you saw some terrible news about the things Americans were doing to the Vietnamese, or vice versa. I don't think he'll ever tell me about the bad things he saw and did over there. Well, *would* have told me."

"I guess it's my turn to remind you that it's not over yet. Dad's still with us."

"What I came to realize is that your dad meant to say he met Death over there, as in capital D. He wasn't referring to the state of unbeing, of life coming to an end, but he meant some sort of supernatural or otherworldly entity that ushers people from one plane of existence to the next. Not some big skeleton in a black robe, but a dark creature."

Alison sucked on the edge of a potato chip. Her tired face wore a look Jodi found difficult to discern.

"'Death was everywhere,' your dad used to say about his time over there," Jodi continued. "He said he could almost touch it, that he could feel the possibility of his own life being snuffed out, as if it were meaningless, as if *he* were meaningless. He wanted to be anywhere else in the world, but he also said he didn't want to leave once he got there, because of the friends he made on the ground. Or maybe he just wanted to die there."

"Jeez, Mom."

"I told him how twisted it was to think like that, and his response was, 'I guess you had to be there.' You know he had a strange sense of humor."

"*Has*, Mom. Has."

"It makes sense to me now, the things he talked about. If Death exists, it just sort of rides the edge of reality, between this world and another, maybe more. It's bound to linger in a place with so much suffering—all that killing and rape and destruction. And I'm sure all sorts of nasty things ride along with it."

Jodi drained her coffee cup.

"I'm going to tell you something," she added. "Something your father made me swear never to tell you kids."

"That sounds ominous."

"Something followed him back," she said. "You recall the imaginary friend you had growing up?"

"Miss Ellie Egret," Alison said. "Sure, I do. She was a stuffed animal."

"Your dad had an imaginary friend, too, only it wasn't imaginary, and it wasn't much of a friend. He saw it for the first time when he was eight years old. An ugly little goblin of a thing. He called it the Little Gray Man."

Alison repeated the name, almost laughing as she finished the third word.

"It went by another name, a name your father didn't like to use, but the Little Gray Man is how he first described it to his parents," Jodi added. "It was just as it sounds: a creepy little character in a gray herringbone suit, with a gray bowler and an ivory cane to go with it. Your dad didn't talk about it to anyone, barely even to me. It told him to do things, told him it could protect him from the pain in the world, for a price. He thought it was all in his mind, something he dreamed up. Then he went to Vietnam and learned about evil. He came back knowing the Little Gray Man was not some figment of his imagination, or at least hoping it was real."

"Why?"

"Because it would mean mankind is not as bad as it seems. If some evil entity was whispering in people's ears, pulling the strings, it meant maybe humankind wasn't so terrible after all. In his mind, being weak and malleable in service to some demonic force was far more palatable than being cruel and malicious for the sake of cruelty and malice."

"Dad told you all this? About the Little Gray Man?"

"He didn't have to. I've seen it."

CHAPTER 10

Parting of Ways

*M*artin winces as fork tines pierce the skin of his left hand. One of the prongs sinks deep enough to bruise a metacarpal bone.

"Stop playing with your damned food," Martin's father says. As he withdraws the fork, four red pinpricks mar the skin an inch from Martin's knuckle.

Martin squints the pain away as he shovels a forkful of over-gravied mashed potatoes into his mouth. The meal is too salty, but he knows better to complain. Martin's father prefers salty food, so he figures his son should like it, too, and demands that he does, which is why the father seasons the son's food for him. Martin would kill for a bland meal every now and then.

Martin's eyes move to the crucifix tacked to the kitchen wall. Every room in the house bears a crucifix or some other symbol of the family's Catholic underpinnings. A statue of the Virgin Mary stands on his mother's dresser, the same one she drapes with a red cloth just before his father closes the door on weekend afternoons so his parents can do the noisy things adults do in private.

The air goes foul and thick, like a hardboiled egg gone rotten. Martin feels the presence behind him, but he has no desire to look.

Martin's father slaps the table.

"You know better than to break wind at the table, boy."

"I didn't," Martin whispers.

"Don't sass me, boy."

"He said he didn't, Arlo," his mother says quietly. She keeps her eyes on the table.

"Don't defend him," his father snaps back. He turns to Martin. "If you act like a pig, you eat like one, too. Keep it up and I'll scrape your dinner onto the floor so you can eat like a fat-assed porker at its trough."

"Yes, sir."

The stench gains strength. Martin turns his head in a circle, his nose scouting for air that has not gone rancid. He cannot escape it.

His father's fist hits the table. The saltshaker topples.

"Come here, little pig," he says. "I'm going to whip the bacon off your back."

"It wasn't me," Martin insists.

"I said come here."

"It wasn't me!"

The presence looms closer, drawing a breath behind Martin's ear.

"You'll be sorry if you make me get up from this table, boy."

"Arlo," his mother says. She stands.

"Shut up and sit down!"

"It's not me!" Martin insists. "Blame Pappaduffus!"

Martin's father laughs. "What the hell's that?"

"The Little Gray Man who lives in my room."

"Hear that, Luanne? We have an uninvited houseguest." Martin's father stands. "Boy, you want to behave like a brain-damaged chimpanzee at the dinner table, you're going to take your lumps. Now get your ass over here."

Martin feels the air change. The crown of Pappaduffus's gray derby rises above the table's edge. The light dims as shadows crawl in from the corners.

His father takes a step backward. He sees Pappaduffus, too. Pappaduffus lifts his left arm and slams his alabaster cane flatly on the kitchen table. The clatter sounds like a gunshot in such a confined space. His tendril-like hands wriggle across the table. The tendrils of his other arm snake across Martin's back and around his arm, drawing him closer, as if to proclaim: *Mine!*

"Get the hell out of my kitchen, boy," Martin's father says. "I always knew you were a damned devil."

The priest arrives the next morning. Martin stays in his room, as ordered, which is fine for him, so he can try to get some sleep. He lies face down on the bed, the welts on his back still tender. The priest spends more time in Martin's room than Martin would like, speaking his blessings in Latin and making the sign of the cross with every step.

Hours later, as the sun goes down, Martin's mother calls her son down for dinner. He limps down the stairs and takes a seat at the kitchen table, careful to keep his bruises from touching the backrest. His father tells him to get up and stand in the corner. The smell of pot roast hangs in the air. Martin's stomach grumbles as he listens to his father's utensils clank against the ceramic plate. His mother, always kind, cuts her meat so quietly she barely makes a sound.

"The priest came today," she says.

"Fine," his father says. "Not another word about it."

A tear rolls down Martin's cheek. He is glad to face the wall so his father cannot see.

The door to an upstairs room creaks open and slams closed. Heavy footsteps echo throughout the house. Dust falls from the kitchen ceiling. The bulb in the overhead fixture flickers. The staircase groans under purposeful stomps. A moment later the front door hisses open and shuts as loudly as the blast from a cannon.

In that moment, Martin feels something in him change, as if a switch has been flicked, or a spigot turned off. The ache behind his temples dissipates.

Martin's father rises from the table and goes to the front door. He tries to open it, but it seems stuck. Finally, on the third try, he wrenches the door free. Cracks split the paint around the door's casing. Martin's parents then venture upstairs, and he follows. His mother and father exchange looks at the entrance to the master bedroom. His father struggles to open this door, too. When he succeeds, he enters the room for a look around. His foot clips an object on the floor and sends it windmilling into the corner.

Martin's father bends to retrieve the object he kicked. It looks familiar to Martin, though he cannot quite place its origin. As his father turns over the object in his meaty hands, the light reveals the severed head of a ceramic figurine, her hair covered by a white veil. Martin looks to the dresser and sees the statue of the Virgin Mary, her head absent—a clean cut, as if sliced off with a hot blade.

Both parents turn to Martin, who trembles in the doorway.

Martin stares out the window of the slate-blue Volkswagen Beetle. The landscape blurs past.

"Another three hours maybe," says Luanne, Martin's mother. "You can do anything for three hours. We both can."

"You can't hold your breath for three hours," he responds.

"No harm ever came from trying."

Mom has not been the same since Dad left, less than a week after the incident with the Blessed Mother statue. On second thought, Martin is confused about the sequence of events. Had his father left, or had he just told Mom and Martin to get out and find somewhere else to live? All he knows is that they—Martin and his mom—have been cast off to fend for themselves.

"It's a lot warmer in Arizona, and a lot less rain," Mom says, plucking the same threads she plucked at least a dozen times already in the three days since they left home in Eugene, Oregon, for a new life in the Southwest.

"I need to pee again."

"Next gas station, okay?" She pats the top of the steering wheel with both palms. "We'll give the old girl another chance to rest her old bones."

They took breaks every couple of hours to let the Beetle cool down, and to give his mother's eyes a break. She is not used to driving such long distances, she reminds him—not really used to driving at all, in fact, as his father does most of the driving. *Did* most of the driving, he corrects. Mom will have to get used to not being "taken care of," as Dad used to say, though Martin never saw it that way. Mom was the one who tended to the family's every need, including waiting on Dad every minute he was not at work or, as Mom said, "wasting time and money we don't have" at the corner bar two blocks away.

"I'll miss the trees," Mom says.

Again, with the trees. Martin does not see the big deal.

"We'll have new trees," she continues. "Yuccas and cactuses—big ones, as tall as a house!"

Martin has said little since they started their road trip. He cannot help but replay the events in his mind, trying to determine if he is the reason—he and the Little Gray Man, better put—Dad decided the family would be best served by being broken apart.

"Pappaduffus," he whispers.

"Martin," Mom says sternly. "No."

Mom instituted a prohibition on speaking the Little Gray Man's name aloud. Martin is not even supposed to *think* about the Little Gray Man anymore, and he certainly is not supposed to mention anything about the Little Gray Man to his Aunt Ruth and Uncle Stu or their two kids—cousins he has not yet met, and whose names he does not yet know—who will be putting up Martin and his mother for the foreseeable future, until Mom can "get my feet under me," whatever that means. He dislikes the idea of living in someone else's home, of sharing a bedroom, but he is smart enough to know he has no say in the matter.

"I want you to tell me the truth, Martin. Have you seen the … the *little man* since we left?"

He pauses to scroll through his memories of the days that have passed between then and now. "Nah," he says.

"You tell me if that changes, okay? We can have you talk to someone who can help. Anyway, you're going to love Arizona. Your aunt tells me there are two boys your age who live on the same street. You'll make new friends. We both will."

He knows better than to say it out loud, but he feels fine with no longer having a dad—at least not *that* dad, with his cruelty and coarseness, his temper with Mom and the hardships he piled at Martin's feet. If Mom ever decides to find a new man to love, he hopes she picks a better one, a good one, not another monster.

"I have to pee," he reminds her. He jams the heel of his palm into his crotch.

"Just a little longer. I don't want to pull over and risk breaking down in the middle of nowhere."

"Okay," he whispers. His knees close more tightly together.

"You're going to love Arizona," she repeats.

Martin wonders who she expects to convince.

CHAPTER 11

X Marks the Spot

"We need to take the arm."

Doctor Stephens had left Martin's room an hour earlier, but his words echoed in Jodi's brain, like alarm bells, like gunshots, as she balanced on the edge of Martin's bed. The venom had rendered Martin's right arm unsalvageable, Stephens said, and leaving the limb intact could give the bad bacteria a staging ground in which to gather strength and poison other parts of Martin's body. Stephens insisted the surgery was "relatively straightforward," and it might even shock his body awake once the anesthesia wore off. She imagined the whine of a surgical saw, a spray of red spattering the stark-white tile walls, and Martin's disembodied arm lying on a stainless-steel Mayo stand in a puddle of black blood, pus, and other rank fluids.

Martin had undergone something Stephens called "ultrafiltration," a treatment to address fluid overload intended to improve Martin's cardiac and renal function. Assuming his body continued to respond positively, early the following morning Jodi would have to accompany Martin to pre-op, where she would have to consent to the surgery on Martin's behalf. An orthopedic surgeon named Rhonda Till, M.D., would then explain the surgery in detail, how she would likely sever Martin's arm above the elbow, and prepare the distal end of the remaining limb to accommodate a prosthesis in the event of Martin's recovery. Yet another *if*.

To limit the possibility of a surgical screwup, Stephens said Jodi would either have to watch the surgeon scrawl an X on the arm in need of removal or, to her horror, put the X there herself. As if there was any question which arm needed to go. The last time she had seen the exposed limb, when the venomologist had come in to share his brilliance in his particular area of esoterica, the gangrenous limb reminded her of the picked-over carcass of a Thanksgiving turkey. Oh, and the smell. The head ICU nurse, Olivia Leary, had visited at least once an hour to spray the room with Lysol or some other chemical disinfectant, probably because the stench had begun to waft toward the nurses' station and make everyone sick to their stomachs. Jodi would never forget the ghastly stink, as if it had been burned into the lining of her nose.

An unhelpful thought crept into Jodi's tired mind: *What if the surgeon somehow lopped off the wrong arm?* If such a disaster occurred, Martin would then have to go under again and have his remaining limb taken away, leaving him armless. No worse fate could befall him. She imagined her armless husband sitting silently by the bay window overlooking the farmhouse's front acreage, gut gathered in his lap, drool dangling from his lower lip, realizing he neither had anything to live for nor a good method for ending it all.

Jodi tried to lose herself in *Eat, Pray, Love*, but she kept reading and re-reading the same paragraph, the words just not sticking. Her brain would not allow itself to be distracted. Although she could appreciate the writer's style, she had little interest in the story of a young, healthy, educated woman with no measurable problems, droning on about her struggles to find and accept love during a globetrotting trip likely funded by someone else's dime. Everyone should be so lucky, Jodi thought. She probably would have loved the story at a different time in her life, before age and catastrophe had upended everything.

At the chapter's end, she tossed the book onto the sill and leaned toward her husband unmoving in his bed. She brushed the hand of Martin's left arm—the one that would stay—and told him, calmly, "I won't lie to you. You won't be the same after tomorrow. None of us will."

Tears obscured her vision. She was grateful for the hospital's policy of one visitor per ICU patient, so she could weep without an audience. Then she remembered she had sent Alison away, to check on the cat at the farmhouse in Crum. Worry knotted Jodi's stomach as she envisioned the conversation in which she would share the bad news with her daughter. Alison would likely fall apart, Jodi figured. What a scene she would make. Jodi felt cheated, in a way, because ICU doctors got paid good money to perform the dirty work of wrecking someone's day.

Martin had been unbreakable before some mystery scorpion from South Asia had cut him down. The surgery would alter him forever. He would struggle with his newfound weakness, which is how he would see it. Stephens suggested medical manufacturers had made astonishing steps forward in prosthetics technology, advising her to focus not on what Martin would lose but on the possibilities ahead for the man the surgery would leave behind. Easy for Stephens to say, though Jodi knew he was right. She remembered staring at the TV screen, open mouthed and teary eyed, at a news report from years earlier about veterans who had lost limbs while fighting the wars in Afghanistan and Iraq. Despite their trauma, those amputees had mastered their prosthetic limbs to accomplish some truly inspirational feats: scaling Everest and Kilimanjaro, competing in Ironman triathlons, reinventing themselves as fine artists with exhibitions in the toniest art galleries of New York, Chicago, and L.A. People far weaker than Martin overcame worse odds every day. One guy, despite having been *born without arms*, somehow went on to become a world-champion archer, for chrissakes.

Martin could get there, too. He *had* to, but he would have to become someone else in order to accomplish such a feat. She almost wished he could stay comatose until his "stump"—Stephens' seemingly vulgar term for the remainder of Martin's arm—healed and was ready to accept the prosthesis. In truth, she wished she could sleep through it, too, fast-forwarding to the good parts, because the recovery would test both of their wills.

"I can't be there with you for the surgery," she told his motionless form, "but I'll be right outside the room. The doctors think this might be the best thing for you. You'd agree if you were awake to see what's happening, *smell* what's happening. Your arm is dead, Martin, all rancid and rotten. So, the doctors are going to do what they have to do, you're going to wake up, and then we're going to do whatever the hell we have to do from that point forward so you can come back to the farm"—her voice faltered—"and keep on living."

A memory from long ago revealed itself to her, from a moment they had shared early into their courtship. Something she had told him, something that stuck. She squeezed his thumb as tightly as she could.

"*Find me*, Martin," she said. "Get through what's to come. Of everything you've had to endure in your life, don't let something as simple as this beat you. A hiccup is all it is, you hear me? Now you wake up and find me, dammit. We'll get past this speedbump like we've gotten through every other damned hole you've fallen into since we met."

CHAPTER 12

Shaking the Pillars of Heaven

Martin squints into the late-day sun. His thigh touches Jodi's. Her head tilts onto his shoulder, her arm looped through his. She smells amazing, like lavender and sex and eternity. He closes his eyes and inhales her, holding his breath so she can linger inside him.

He expected a different sendoff, figuring they would find someplace remote and quiet where they could park and maul each other like animals. The sendoff she has given him, sitting quietly on a blanket a few yards from the Gila River, with a pristine view of the Laguna Mountains at sunset, is somehow better. Infinitely better.

"I'll never tire of this," he says.

"That's why I wanted to come here," Jodi says. "The landscape will be a thousand times different than where you're going. Maybe the memory of this view will sustain you when things get tough over there, or wherever you go. You know, if you get homesick."

"I didn't mean the mountains and stuff. I meant *this*—us."

"I'm so glad we met," she says. "The past year wouldn't have been the same without you. I still can't believe you're not going to be around for my senior year. Homecoming. Formal. Graduation. All of it. I'll miss you terribly, but you'll be safe."

"Watch, I probably won't even wind up going anyplace interesting. Something boring like desk duty at a base in Colorado Springs or guarding a munitions warehouse in Reno."

Two months ago, with the next draft looming, Martin decided he would rather control his fate than sit at home, waiting for Uncle Sam to pick his number and send him halfway across the world to tamp down Communism in Southeast Asia. He marched into the recruitment office across from the automotive warehouse where he worked and told a guy in a mint-green shirt with bars on the sleeve, "Send me anywhere you need me to go."

Now, here with Jodi, he regrets his impulsiveness.

His orders say he will depart tomorrow morning for Fort Huachuca in Sierra Vista, a stone's throw from the Mexican border. From there, who knows? The war might end by the time he finishes basic training. Based on the bloodshed and bombs in the headlines, though, not likely.

"You'll go to college, and God knows where I'll end up," he says. "You'll come out of it with a degree, and hopefully I'll come out of it with my hide intact and a few good stories to tell."

"If only we'd been born at a different time, in a different place. We wouldn't have to deal with any of this. It doesn't seem fair."

"*Fair*. My dad used to say that word should be struck from the dictionary. What's fair?"

"Are you afraid?"

"Nah," he says.

He is terrified. Two boys from his neighborhood got taken in the draft the year earlier, and both talked big and tough about how many "zipperheads" they would kill, about how they could not wait to get over there and stick their boots up the Viet Cong's collective ass. No sign of those boys since they left, making Martin wonder if they survived, or if they are still over there, taking the ears and scalps of mowed-down zipperheads. He sees no need for tough talk, no room for it. Ever since his growth spurt in the summer before sophomore year, he let his size and strength speak for him. He was the biggest ox in the crowd during the graduation ceremony from just a few months earlier, but now he feels small, as vulnerable as a newborn fawn. War will change him, but only God knows how much.

She begins, "No matter what happens—"

"Don't finish that sentence," he says. "I'll write. You'll do the same. We'll stay connected. Please say we will, even if it's not true."

Her eyes glisten in the sun's dying rays. She kisses him. Her lips feel soft and dry at first, and then the kiss turns wet and deep. She rises off the ground and straddles him. Her hands rest on the back of his head, caressing his neck. She pulls away and holds him tight. Her warm breath soothes the delicate hairs on the ridge of his ear.

Jodi is unlike any other school-age girl he ever met—practically a woman, but not quite. They have been dating for no more than four months, but the tightness of their bond suggests a much older relationship. She is thoughtful, funny, and kind, more so than any other seventeen-year-old girl in his circle. She reads important books and seems to retain their lessons, often reciting the authors' choicest words back to him. He cares nothing for classic tomes the likes of *Persuasion*, *Moby-Dick*, and *Slaughterhouse Five*, but he loves that she cares. She intends to go to college and study subjects that matter. She will make something of herself one day, of this he is certain.

Of course, he is drawn to more than just her mind—her body thick and firm in every place a man his age could want. He salivates at the contour of each chiseled calf, the silkiness of her movements, the firmness of her belly and breasts beneath his eager fingertips.

Both Martin and Jodi are fully clothed, yet the moment feels more intimate than the steamiest and stickiest of heavy-petting sessions he enjoyed with any other girl. They have not yet had sex, he and Jodi, for no reason other than they have not yet gotten around to it, because four months is not a long time. Besides, she insists she is still a virgin. He is, too, not that he would admit such a thing. He hoped to remedy their failing on the blanket overlooking the river, on their last night together before he ships out for unseen shores. It feels perfect, this moment, so perfect he could die happily if the world ended at sunset. He wonders if he should go home, dig his uncle's shotgun out of the closet, and put the barrel to his forehead so he can avoid the trauma military service would inevitably bring. Only the possibility that he would survive the tribulations to come, and that the experience might somehow make him a better person, stronger and more complete for Jodi, nudges the thought from his mind.

"Promise me one thing," she says.

"I'll be careful," he whispers into her ear. "I promise."

"No, something else. Find me. Come home in one piece and find me, no matter where I am. Do that and we'll set the world on fire. We'll start a life together. Get married, if you want, maybe start a family. I know we haven't gone all the way or anything, but if you make it through—*when* you make it through—find me. Find me and take me. We'll shake the pillars of heaven every day thereafter. By screwing, I mean."

He laughs out loud. She has cussed only twice before in front of him, and never in such a crude context, however welcome.

"You have a deal." Regret builds in his chest. He does not want to leave—not this place, right now, and certainly not tomorrow, after which he will no longer be a civilian. "One more thing," he tells her. "I love you."

She does not respond, but she does not have to. He can sense the depth of her affection in the might of her embrace and the moistness of her cheek against his.

Now, he thinks, he has something to live for. Now he has everything.

CHAPTER 13

Waiting for the Hammer to Fall

Jodi and Alison started their second lap around the hospital grounds. Mountains rose in the distance. The far-off view seemed cruel considering the blandness of their immediate surroundings: mostly empty parking lots, an ambulance bay, flashing traffic lights, and a monument sign for the Del Taco, Dollar Tree, and 7-Eleven in the retail strip across the way.

"Thanks for the company," Jodi told her daughter. "If I had to stay in that room for another minute, I'd take the elevator up to the roof and leap off."

Alison grunted in assent. She had been quiet since Jodi told her a surgeon would have to take Martin's arm. Her silence aside, she seemed to take the news better than Jodi anticipated—"I see," she said calmly—almost as if she had been expecting an even worse prognosis.

"Why in Hell's Bells don't hospitals have bars, taverns, even a vending machine that dispenses flights of Patrón?" Jodi asked. "If there's one place in the world where someone could use a shot of tequila or a tumbler of whisky, it's right frickin' here."

"How's the book?" Alison asked.

Jodi held aloft her ragged copy of *Eat, Pray, Love* and shrugged.

"About as good as I expected," she said. "You reading anything good?"

"I don't have time for reading."

"You don't *make* time for reading. Big difference. Your loss."

Jodi took it as a personal affront that neither of her children had inherited her fondness for the written word. Based on the look on her daughter's face, Alison seemed surprised by Jodi's irascibleness.

"Sorry," Jodi said. "I have a lot on my mind, as you can imagine."

"Try not to think about it, Mom."

"If you can tell me how I'm supposed to do that, I'm all ears."

"Just wishful thinking. What time is the surgery?"

"Five or six a.m., they think, depending on the surgeon's schedule. I don't know what they expect us to do with ourselves until then. They should give out free morphine drips or something."

Alison seemed a step or two behind, likely the result of a good night's sleep after too many days in a fog, stealing naps on an uncomfortable chair or laid out on the thinly carpeted floor in a quiet corner of the ICU waiting room. Jodi was glad Alison had overnighted at the farm in Crum, primarily to feed Roy, the dispassionate calico, but also to give Alison a break from the heaviness of her father's collapsing health.

"Everything okay back at the ranch?" Jodi asked. "Roy all right?"

Jodi missed seeing Roy, petting Roy, having Roy wake her at four in the morning by standing on her chest for a scratch behind the ears. She treated Roy as reverently as one of her children. Martin did, too, even if Roy rarely returned the favor. The cat had more nicknames than any animal should, courtesy of Martin. First came Roy Boy, naturally, even though Roy was female, and then Roy Polloi, which evolved into Roy Rogers and Rodgers 'n' Hammerstein. Then came Hammerhead and, her favorite, The Hammer, reserved for occasions when Roy brought them a slaughtered house mouse or kangaroo rat in tribute. Jodi smiled at the memory of shuffling into the kitchen to the whiff of fresh coffee, the morning sky still gray, and finding Martin reading the latest issue of *Smithsonian* at the kitchen table. He would look up from his spot on the page and say, "The Hammer brought us another sacrifice last night." Later she would go upstairs and scour the bedroom for evidence of Roy's dirty work—and, sure enough, she would find tiny red spots speckling the floral comforter.

A decade had passed since Martin had begrudgingly agreed to adopt Roy. Before then, he would offer slightly different iterations of the same complaint as a reason not to take on a house pet: "The last thing this place needs is a nocturnal allergy machine that shits in a box and has straight razors for hands." Alison had been living with them at the time, just about ready to venture out on her own, and Jodi had convinced him that the house would be too quiet without her. Of course, the damn cat had taken immediately to Martin and treated Jodi mostly with indifference. At night, as Martin watched Ken Burns documentaries or Diamondbacks games, Roy would curl up in his lap. Jodi would sit on the loveseat with her headphones clamped to her ears, turning the pages of the latest Margaret Atwood or Kazuo Ishiguro novel, and smirk at her cold, empty lap.

She had not seen Roy in almost a week, so the cat would have appreciated Alison's company, with the additional benefit of Alison getting to take a shower and sleep in a comfortable bed for a change. What Jodi wouldn't give for a warm bath, a soft pillow, and a night of unbroken rest. Her body's interworking systems seemed on the verge of shutdown, but the line from the Frost poem reminded her that she had promises to keep and miles to go before she could sleep.

"The cat's fine, Mom. As ornery as always. Did you get any rest last night? Any at all? Eat anything more substantive than cheese puffs from the vending machine?"

"I'll eat and sleep when all this is behind us," Jodi said. She smiled and added, "I certainly was glad to see *you* eating yesterday, dear. Glad to see you engaged with the world."

"That was twenty years ago, Mom. Almost, anyway."

"A mother never forgets her children's wounds. There were days when your father and I thought you wouldn't live to see thirty."

God, how difficult those years had been. Depression, anxiety, and bouts of mania had dogged Alison's teens and early twenties, not eating, not sleeping, not showering, acting out, fits of rage. Then, one Saturday, Martin had discovered the empty pill bottle on the counter in the hall bathroom. They found their daughter on her bedroom floor, unconscious, in a mummy-like pose. They got her to the ER in time to undo the damage, but a long, hard road followed. Alison spent the next three years in and out of behavioral health facilities in Arizona, Nevada, and California, testing Martin and Jodi's resolve and also burning through their modest nest egg.

Whereas Jodi thought Alison had been going through "a phase," Martin had the sense to realize Alison needed professional help. He stayed by his daughter's side while she sobbed beneath the covers. He held her while she raged and spat and butted her head against his, leaving a gash above his left eyebrow that required seven stitches to close. When it became clear Alison needed inpatient care, Martin was the one who dropped her off at her first facility—and the second, and the third—and then picked her up when she was ready to come home. Jodi had wished she had it in her to help, but she could not stand the idea of seeing another person suffer, especially when the person was her daughter. She always wondered if Alison held it against her for not being there for the goodbye at the facility's front door, or the hello to follow two months later. No wonder Alison seemed to have a closer bond with her father.

"Sorry if I made life difficult for you," Alison said. "At least you had golden-boy Andrew to balance the equation."

"Your brother was no cakewalk either."

Andrew had left home in the middle of his sister's troubles—at Martin's suggestion, as Jodi would learn later. Months passed before she forgave either of them. In hindsight, leaving home at twenty turned out to be the best thing for their son, who would go on to hone his culinary skills in the kitchens of some of the finest restaurants in Boston, Philadelphia, and New York. He then headed overseas to open his own restaurant, *Turista*. He also found Mateo, a business attorney who became the love of his life. Jodi just wished she saw Andrew more than once a year. Given the precariousness of Martin's condition, she supposed her son would be coming home soon enough.

"Andrew tells me you two have been texting," Alison says. "He knows about the surgery, right?"

"He'll just worry."

"Mom, he *should* be worried. Call him. If you don't call him and tell him what's happening—like, now—I will. It makes me wonder if you would have bothered to let me know if I hadn't been there to see what happened."

"Of course, dear. Your brother just lives so far away. You know how busy he gets—too busy to let his family know he's getting married, for chrissakes, too busy to invite his family to the damned wedding."

"You have to let that go, Mom. Andrew had his reasons. And he'll be back at Christmas. I think it's nice that he and Mateo want to have a ceremony here, just for us."

"We'll see about that, given the circumstances."

"I don't know why I'm surprised you've told him next to nothing. It wouldn't be the first time you kept us in the dark. Dad's run-in with the bear is the best example. We didn't even know it happened until you were driving him back from the hospital in Kamloops."

"Well, maybe you should check in on your parents more often. I'll call your brother as soon as we finish our walk. Promise."

Alison's shoulders seemed to relax. Whereas Andrew had always been the independent child, the dramatic one, the wanderer, Alison had been the worrier, the brooder, the wannabe peacemaker.

"Andrew and I still talk about what it must have been like for you and Dad, parenting a couple of weirdos like us. We couldn't have been easy on you."

"We signed up for it, dear. We knew what we were getting into."

A lie, though Jodi saw the invention as a kindness.

When Jodi was preparing to graduate from college, and waiting for Martin to return home from the service, her parents, aunts, and every other adult woman she knew began to pester her about starting a family. "The best decision you'll ever make," they promised. "You won't know the meaning of love until you hold your baby in your arms for the first time," they said. Those things turned out to be true, but no one could have prepared her for the difficulties of motherhood—not so much the toil of pregnancy or the trauma of childbirth or the sleeplessness of colic, but more so the hardships that grew out of nothing as children learned to cope with the likes of disappointment, grief, and ostracism.

"You kids gave me no trouble too great that I wanted to send you back to the stork," she added. "Your father, he was the one with the heavy load."

"You don't give yourself enough credit, Mom. Dad could have pounded a nail through a two-by-four with his fist, but you were the tough one. The strong one. You're the one who kept the walls from coming down."

The walls. Jodi thought of the old house in Phoenix the night they left, every darkened corner alive with unnatural things, glad she would never see the place again. She pulled herself back from the brink, not wanting to think about the impossible things she had seen, the whispers in the darkness, the putrid stink of something long dead. Such thoughts, she imagined, might somehow draw those things back to her.

"Well," she said, "even I have my breaking point."

"After everything Dad's been through," Alison replied, "it's almost funny that a freakin' bug might be the thing that does him in."

"Arachnid."

"What?"

"Arachnid, dear. A scorpion is an arachnid, not an insect. Show some respect to the critter that brought your dad to his knees. And you keep reminding me that we have no reason to give up hope. Your father's as strong as an ox, and sometimes as dumb as one. Let's talk about something else for a change."

Alison pounced on the opening. Jodi supposed she should have expected an ambush.

"Yesterday you told me about the supernatural thing—the Little Gray Man," Alison said. "You said you saw it. When, where, and how?"

"In our house," Jodi said. "Our *old* house. Its—"

She could still recall in vibrant detail the memory of her first encounter with the Little Gray Man: its foul odor, its taste, its oppressive nature, its ability to spoil the tranquility of her yoga studio at the family home.

A chill snaked up her spine.

"Go on, Mom."

"I smelled it first, like a mix of old fish and charred wood. I figured maybe something went bad in the refrigerator or your father left out a sandwich he forgot to eat. Then I felt it, something in the room with me. I opened my eyes and scanned every corner. Nothing but empty space, so I went about my routine. It happened when I moved into upward dog, lifting my head toward the ceiling. Contact. Its lips touched mine."

Her eyes had snapped open to see it, close enough to touch. A dwarf-like man, wholly unnatural, hovering in the space before her.

"His face was white as soap," she added. "Ugly little fu manchu and these horrid little eyes. Inhuman arms, like greased snakes, its feet shrouded in black mist. In a blink, it was gone. I thought I was losing my mind."

The delusional fantasies of Parkinson's, she began to suspect, but deep down she knew otherwise. She would never forget the sight of it, the smell, the violation.

"Everything came undone the next night, the night we had to escape," she said. "That's when the damned thing revealed its true form."

"I'm starting to agree with you, Mom. A stiff drink or two would hit the spot right about now."

"Dear, if you think what I've told you so far sounds strange, just wait."

CHAPTER 14

Dark Rider

Martin hears the music of his name, distant, as if he is underwater. Clawed hands wander his body, rake his throat, pull his hair. He opens his eyes to see Jodi's panicked face, surrounded by the hellscape that has consumed the basement of the family home.

"For chrissakes, Martin!" Jodi screams. "Get up!"

She props him against the basement wall. Eyes wild, hair mussed, shirt torn at the collar, she looks no better than he feels. Claw marks blight the skin beneath her left eye.

Pappaduffus has delivered on his promise to punish Jodi.

The urge to vomit doubles him over. His chest aches. His legs feel weak, especially the left one; he remembers the damage done to his knee by the hammer's clawed end. Somehow, Jodi gets him to his feet. Her hundred-twenty-pound frame propels his nearly two-hundred and fifty pounds of muscle, fat, and dense bone. Shadows rise from every corner. Tongues of fire surround them, but the fire gives off no heat. Devilish laughter fills his ears.

Martin begins to doubt he performed the rite effectively. The only thing he knows for certain is that he and Jodi must escape if they want to live. Pappaduffus has claimed this house as his own.

Jodi leads him up the stairs, one creaking step at a time. She moves calmly, deliberately, even though the danger multiplies with each passing second. Talons slash his back. Teeth sink into his calves, his sides, the lobes of his ears. Each assault draws blood, but nothing compares to the agony Pappaduffus put him through earlier. He cannot determine how many hours have passed since then, the pain so searing and intense he must have forgotten how to tell time. An hour or a full day gone—either option seems plausible.

"Come on, Martin," Jodi implores. "Hurry."

Shadowy figures slither down the walls, rise from the seams between floorboards. Jodi tries to swat the smaller ones away, though Martin knows they take bites of her, too. A hyena-like beast barrels down the staircase and drives a shoulder into Jodi's gut. The blow drives the wind from her lungs. She stumbles onto a lower step, but maintains her grip on the railing—giving no quarter. Compelled by her determination, he finds the strength to climb. He collapses at the top of the stairs.

A whirl of flame fills the hall, and inky darkness consumes the space beyond. The far end of the hall morphs into a portal, a doorway, and across its threshold lies an alien landscape blooming with darkened planets and the pinpricks of distant stars. Shafts of blue lightning spill from the portal's mouth, crackling, showing a glimpse of a hidden world.

An aberration billows from the portal's mouth. Jodi

screams at the sight of it.

The humanoid figure rides an enormous reptilian beast, similar to a crocodile, though the beast's body glows yellow. Five sets of eyes adorn each side of the beast's gnarled black head. Lines of sinew stretch from the crocodile's jaws to the clutches of the rider, its identity somehow familiar. The rider's chiseled face sports a full beard. Although it has the human-like torso of Adonis, its lower half resembles a python's sleek body. Its coils encircle the crocodile's middle. A crown sits atop the rider's head, each point lit with a small red flame. Sinewy green tentacles flow from the rider's shoulders in lieu of arms. Each tentacle's tip bifurcates like a snake's tongue.

The rider's eyes give him away. Martin knows those eyes. He points and whispers, "Pappaduffus," the Little Gray Man.

Pappaduffus lashes the walls with his steely tentacles. Framed photos tumble from their hooks and nails. Glass shatters against the hardwood. He whips the sinewy reins, urging his reptilian steed forward. In response, the crocodile-like beast snaps at the air and clamors toward Martin and Jodi. Floorboards crack beneath its weight.

Jodi drags Martin away, toward an exit he cannot see. The weight of icy darkness presses on him, forcing the air from his lungs and pinching the thoughts from his mind. A pulse similar to a heartbeat batters his eardrums—the room, the entire house, alive with a dark energy that tries to gnaw its way inside him. The room seems to spin, the walls and ceiling threatening to come down around him.

The crocodile comes to within a foot of Martin. He

cocks a fist as if a right cross will pose any sort of threat. Pappaduffus yanks the reins, and the crocodile rears back, marches backward. Pappaduffus's throat unleashes a bellicose roar. A patch of drywall falls from the ceiling and crumbles across the crocodile's dragon-like back.

A moment later, warm air caresses Martin's skin, and he feels the cushion of scutch grass beneath him. As he lifts his head, the house's front windows buckle, bow outward, and then explode. Glass shards shower the lawn and driveway. He shields Jodi with his shoulder. Bits of glass strafe his back. A deep, throaty hum oozes from the empty window frames. He turns over to see a kaleidoscope of color—blues, reds, oranges, purples, and, somehow, shades of black, shadows—bleeding from the home's front. The humming ceases. Then, one by one, the colors fade, until the house goes still and dark, lifeless and colorless.

Martin lies back and stares into the heavens. Jodi flops beside him, her blood-streaked cheek against his. Where he has failed, Jodi has succeeded. She got them out. As if he needed any more proof that she exceeds him in every possible way, she saved him from the full extent of Pappaduffus's wrath.

Neighbors trickle out of their front doors and garages to inquire about the disturbance.

The lightness in Martin's gut tells him the ritual worked. His tormentor has gone elsewhere. Finally, he will have peace. His family will have peace. They are safe.

"Martin," Jodi says. "What the *fuck*?"

"It's a long story."

"You're all right?"

"More than all right," he says weakly. He kisses the top of her head. "Best day of my life."

Martin pulls up to the La Quinta Inn on the edge of Glendale. Jodi, seated beside him, jolts forward as the front tires smack the concrete parking block.

"What's the plan, Martin?"

"Simple. Go inside. Get a room and a have good night's sleep for a change. See how the world looks in the light of a new day. I'm starved. For a hotel restaurant, the Mexican's actually not too bad here."

"I won't ask how you know that," she says. "I have no interest in sitting down to a meal. I feel like hell, and I must look like hell."

"Well, you've *been* through hell. Quite literally, I would say. Come on, the lighting's dim inside. No one will know any different. If anyone asks, we'll just tell them we conquered an emissary from the shadow world and, by the way, 'How's the guacamole?'"

Martin limps inside and checks in at the front desk, and then returns to collect Jodi. She looks noticeably shaken, drained, but he feels invigorated despite the hole in his knee and the toothmarks perforating his body. He leads her into the restaurant and they wait by the reception stand. A moment later, a squat woman with bleached-blond hair and too much eye makeup greets them. The woman looks them both up and down, shakes her head, and guides them toward a table in the corner.

"Something to drink?" she asks.

"Gin and tonic for me, just a splash of citrus," Martin says. "A margarita on the rocks for her. Please and thank you."

"Make that two G and T's," Jodi corrects.

The hostess-slash-waitress passes through a terracotta archway, presumably to fetch their alcohol.

"I could eat a whole suckling pig if they had one ready," Martin says. He drums his torn knuckles on the tabletop, its borders edged with blue mosaic tiles. The drumming stops abruptly. "Oh, shit. What about the cat? What about Roy?"

"Roy can take care of herself until we collect her tomorrow. Or, someone can. I'm not stepping foot in that house again. Ever."

"It should be fine now. Everything's fine. It's over."

"*Fine?* Martin, what the fuck did I see tonight?"

Her fingers find the scabbed-over scratch marks on her left cheek.

"His name is Pappaduffus," he begins. He tells her as much about the Little Gray Man as he can stomach: the origin of their pairing, the painful things his tormentor said and did, the ritual Martin performed to evict the diabolical son of a bitch from their lives.

"Martin, that's crazy," she says. "Although …"

Jodi tells him she had seen a character much like the one he described, just the day before, in her yoga studio. She tells him she thought she was losing her mind, adding, "I'm beginning to think the battle's already lost."

The waitress returns with a basket of tortilla chips, a

salsa dish, and two gin and tonics, each glass garnished with a pale lime wedge. Martin immediately brings the glass to his lips and drains half of it.

"Any food tonight," the waitress asks, "or are we just imbibing?"

"Mole poblano for me," Martin says. He turns to Jodi. "Dear?"

"Surprise me," Jodi says.

"Bring her a bowl of the pork pozole," Martin tells the waitress.

The only other occupied table in the restaurant clears.

Martin leans back in his chair and gulps down the rest of his G and T.

"So," Jodi says, "you're telling me some sort of interdimensional demon has been plaguing you for your entire life, and that's the hideous thing I just stared down in our living room?"

"And his many underlings, yes. How else would you explain what you just saw?"

"Gas leak? Mass hypnosis? LSD in the drinking water?"

"This is real," he insists. "I'm sorry I didn't tell you the whole story sooner, but I need you to believe me now. I need you to believe your own eyes."

"You've never said a damned word about it! We raised our kids in that house!"

"I told you pieces of the whole. I shared stories."

She pauses, as if measuring his words against her reality.

"I guess ... I guess I didn't realize your demons were

so literal."

"I sort of promised him I would keep him a secret. Pappaduffus, I mean. I had my reasons. He always promised he would leave you alone, leave the kids alone. Once he started to suggest otherwise, I had to do something about it. I wanted to tell you a thousand times, but how the hell could I? You'd think I was losing my mind. I couldn't risk you turning the kids against me, taking the cat, having me committed to an asylum."

"How can you think that, Martin? I would have let you keep the cat."

Her lips form the slightest smile.

"Don't hate me for saying this," he says, "but I'm almost glad you were there tonight to see what I saw, to experience the things I've been dealing with all these years. If one of us has cracked up, then I guess both of us have. Even if we're both nuts, at least we're on the same page now."

Jodi reaches across the table and places her battle-scarred hand atop his.

"So," she says, "what now?"

"We start over. We start anew."

"I can't go back to that house, not after what happened tonight."

"I'm glad to hear you say that." He extends his leg beneath the table and winces from the pain in his ruined kneecap. "Ever hear of a town called Crum?"

CHAPTER 15

Lies and Omissions

Jodi followed the familiar route, down the stairs, through the ER lobby, and toward the squeaky side door adjacent to the ambulance bay. The heat of the day comforted her, and made her glad to know at least the mechanics of the universe still held true: sunrise, sunset, and hot as a boiling pot in between. She scanned the sidewalk, keeping an eye out for Mister *Blut und Boden*, the misguided skinhead, so she could talk some sense into him. More so, she really wanted a cigarette.

She checked the World Clock app on her smartphone and then dialed Andrew's number. It was almost one o'clock in the afternoon in Arizona, nearing ten p.m. in Valencia. Likely, her son was still manning the kitchen of his restaurant, cooking or cleaning or doing whatever chef-restaurateurs did toward the end of a shift. The call went to voicemail after two rings. She nearly cried when she heard her son's voice instructing her, first in English, again in Spanish, to not leave a message and send a text instead. Rather than try to explain every detail of Martin's predicament, she told Andrew to call when he had a spare moment. She finished with two words: "It's important."

A few minutes passed as she waited for a return call. None came, nor did any kindhearted smokers who might permit her a drag or two. After coming to the realization that she would not get her tobacco fix, Jodi made a beeline for the cafeteria and found her seat at their "regular" table. Alison returned from the restroom a moment later, her hands slick with sanitizer, and Jodi let her know she had reached out to Andrew. Alison seemed pleased, or simply unburdened.

"I hope he comes home," Alison said. "For good, this time."

"I'd be surprised. He found his way over there, living the expat life. The entire world would have to go mad for him to come back to a place he left for a good reason."

Alison faced her mother and settled in.

"I've been thinking," she said. "If I saw what you said you saw—I mean the little guy in the gray bowler hat—I'd think I was going out of my mind."

Jodi understood why Alison wanted to hear more about the Little Gray Man, but the backstory felt too heavy for the moment. She needed a break from all of it—mentally, physically, and every other way.

"Most days I still don't know what to believe," she said. "In a normal world, no lucid person would believe the things that revealed themselves to me. Sometimes I wonder if I went temporarily insane or maybe ingested some sort of hallucinogenic. That's how I think they would want you to feel, if *they* exist: doubtful, vulnerable, alone. Only the fact that your father was there with me, seeing the same things I saw, assures me that I don't belong in the nuthouse."

Jodi's palms rubbed her face clean.

"What do you think it is, Mom? What *is* the Little Gray Man?"

"Just ask Google," she said. "Type in his name and you'll find a dozen websites devoted to him and others like him. Hat Men, Shadow People—diabolical creatures of vaguely human form that come to life in the shadows, who trade in cruelty and feed off the darkest parts of human life: pain, grief, suffering. Some of these websites are devotional, worshipping these figures as if they're deities, gods.

"You don't have to dig too deep to find stories from other people who claim to have had experiences, all of which sound remarkably similar to ours," she continued. "These beings are almost always male in appearance, and they usually have on some sort of formalwear—a nice jacket, a top hat, a walking stick. It's almost like they're trying to blend in, to assimilate, offering a facsimile of what they think humans are supposed to look and act like. Their true form is infinitely more disturbing."

The discussion rendered Alison speechless.

"Somewhere on the spectrum between a ghost and a demon—that description stuck with me, though who knows what the hell that means. Some people describe these things are interdimensional travelers, like extraterrestrials, while others refer to them as fallen angels. The one that's been terrorizing your father, I found its name on a Reddit discussion board. The writer characterized the little bugger as a Grand Duke of Hell, a powerful demon with knowledge of alchemy and metallurgy, and more than a hundred underlings to do its bidding."

"Why Dad? Why did it choose Dad?"

"Your guess is as good as mine. If you read what people have to say, you find that every person who has had an encounter with one of these creatures says the entity extends an offer to the human it targets. Whether or not the offer is accepted, the human wears a bull's-eye from that point forward."

"Like, forever?"

"At least until it's had its fill. Maybe until it gets bored and finds someone else to torment." Jodi's eyes roved the pockmarked ceiling. "Personally, I don't think it's through with your dad, or with us. It could be listening to us, right here, right now, taking notes, dreaming up inventive ways to break our necks."

"If it's all true, if some demonic force *is* trying to disrupt or ruin Dad's life, putting a lethal scorpion from halfway around the world in your backyard is a pretty good way of doing that."

Jodi paused to consider Alison's suggestion.

"The same thought occurred to me, but that seems needlessly complex," she said. "Sometimes you have to give coincidence its due."

"How have I lived forty years of my life not knowing any of this?" Alison asked. "I swear, I never noticed anything strange about Dad—no more than any other dad."

"Your father had a deal with this thing, the Little Gray Man—a deal your father intended to break. It didn't appreciate what it considered a betrayal, so it started getting more insistent, more aggressive. That's around the time I noticed a big difference in your father. He's always been moody, your dad, always talked about how drained and tired he felt, which I just attributed to the passing of time, let alone everything he's been through. Turns out, this thing had been taking pieces of him, like draining a battery. After your dad started cutting this thing out of his life, he was happier, lighter, more energetic. It was almost as if he was trying to keep the Little Gray Man at bay, depriving him so he could send the little bugger on his way. He wanted to starve the damned thing, if he could."

A memory from a year earlier returned to her. A smile spread across her face.

"I woke up one morning to find your dad watching *Sesame Street*, singing along with Elmo and Big Bird," she said. "Can you imagine?"

"*My* father? Watching *Sesame Street*? That's the most preposterous thing you've said since we sat down. … What did it want? The Little Gray Man, I mean."

"To see your father suffer, so it could feed. So it could be nourished."

Alison's mouth hung open. Jodi could imagine what her daughter must be thinking, because Jodi once had the same thoughts.

"I was mad at your father for not telling me sooner, but I understand why he didn't. He knew how crazy it all sounded. I felt like such a fool. *Still* feel like a fool. Imagine spending most of your life with someone, but they had this ugly little part of themselves that they never showed you. It makes everything else seem like a lie."

Men and women in white coats and green scrubs

filled seats at surrounding tables. Jodi piled her mostly uneaten lunch onto a plastic tray and nudged the tray off the table, nearly dropping it. She hated the idea of Martin being alone in the hours leading up to his surgery. Every minute that passed was a minute she could be spending in his room, telling him everything would be all right and reminding him of how much she loved him.

"It wasn't like a gambling problem or a porn addiction, Mom. Whether or not all this is real or in Dad's head—"

"You think I'm blowing smoke? I'm telling you the truth, dear."

"That's not the point, Mom. It makes me sad to think that Dad struggled with this problem for so long and didn't get help from someone. It makes me even sadder to think that neither of us noticed, that *I* didn't notice, because he was always there for me."

"Well, your father had a gift for hiding things."

CHAPTER 16

Pleasure and Pain at the World's Edge

*M*artin *stares out over the ocean and wipes a tear from the corner of each eye.*

He did not expect the Great Head trail to humble him. The scents of salt and pine, the crashing waves and whistling wind, the black speck of a lobster boat chugging across the horizon. He did not expect any of it to steal his breath the way it has. He now understands why so many people make the pilgrimage to Mount Desert Island in coastal Maine.

Like moths to a flame, like Muslims to Mecca, like the miserable to misery.

"Can we please go now?" whines a far-off voice, all rasp and irritation.

Martin turns to see his companion balanced on a lichen-bleached boulder, squinting into the sun. The wind tugs at the ends of her hair, dyed red to the point of looking purple. She has been uncharacteristically nervous since he picked her up at the airport in Bangor. He wonders if she has been having second thoughts, too.

She walks uneasily toward him in her clog-like shoes, nearly tripping over a loose rock, and whispers in his ear. No second thoughts from her, turns out. She wants to proceed to the hotel room now and do the things they came here to do.

"A few more minutes and we'll get a move on," he promises. "Are you taking all this in?"

"Mm-hm, sure. The scenery—very nice."

He retrieves the flip phone from his jacket pocket. He snaps a photo of the small boat working its way across the greenish-blue expanse. The sun-streaked Atlantic glimmers like a million jewels. He wishes Jodi were here to see it with him. She, more than anyone, would appreciate the simple beauty of this place. If only she would have agreed to come east …

He curses himself for blaming her. If anyone deserves the blame, it is him. He should have fought harder to persuade her. What's done is done, he figures, and now he must find out where his choices will lead him. He tries to send the photo to Jodi's phone, but the message does not go through. He holds his phone as high as his arm will let him, not as high as it used to reach, given his injuries. Still, the message does not send.

"Martin!" the woman yells. "Can we *please* get the hell out of here already?"

Rarely does regret find a person before he or she has had the chance to do the regrettable. He hopes the terrible acts he will soon commit will not tarnish his memories of this sacred place. As long as he stays put and keeps looking forward, staring out over the Atlantic, his problems do not belong to him. His sins have gone uncommitted. His curse does not exist.

He checks his phone again. Still so signal. The message refuses to send.

His gaze returns to the ocean. Not a single cloud blights the sky.

Except—

A small black smudge, like a puff of smoke, hovers maybe a quarter mile out over the Atlantic. The cloud bears the weight of a small, dark rider, topped by the rounded nub of a crown and a wide brim beneath—the unmistakable shape of a bowler. Nausea stirs in Martin. Unease builds in his gut, his throat, his head.

"Martin!"

The woman's insistence breaks Martin out of his trance. He stands for one last look before turning to find the rocky path that will lead them back to the worn gravel trail, toward the rental car, and, later, toward an unremarkable hotel room where he will endure an experience with his companion sure to bring immense pleasure, as well as nagging pains that will outlast him.

CHAPTER 17

Visitors

The smartphone buzzed in Jodi's hand. An unread text from Bob Sweems, as in one of Martin's oldest friends, sat in her inbox. The two men had not seen each other since Martin and Jodi abandoned Phoenix for Crum. They had not even spoken since, as far as she knew.

WE R HERE, Bob's text read.

She rose from Martin's bedside and went to meet Alison in the waiting area just beyond the ICU doors.

"I'll be right back," she told her daughter.

"Where are you going?"

"Visitors," she responded. "I won't be long."

"Who is it?"

"Just a friend of your father's. No one important. Why don't you go in and see him for a bit? Keep your dad company."

"But ... what if something happens?"

"Nothing bad will happen, dear." She patted her daughter's shoulder. "Just let your father hear your voice. Tell him something good. Tell him a dirty joke or two. He'll like that."

Jodi backed away from her daughter and stepped into the stairwell. She expelled a breath, slowly, and descended the stairs to the ground floor. She knew the route well by now, the quickest and least populated path to fresh air. An empty cigarette pack—Natural American Spirit—sat crumpled in the corner of the landing before the ground floor. Her feet skipped down the final flight and led her into the waiting room for the Emergency Department. Bob Sweems stood just inside the front door. Bonnie, his wife, positioned herself just behind him.

As he saw Jodi, Bob raced toward her and took her in his arms. He always gave the best hugs.

"I'm so sorry, Jo," he said, crushing her. His lips nearly touched her earlobe.

She saw past him and locked eyes with Bonnie, who looked shellshocked.

"I've been a shitty friend," Bob added. "I haven't called him since the move, purely to spite him for leaving, and for taking you with him."

"He loved you like a brother, Bob—you *and* Frank. The three of you were brothers. More than brothers. Something else. When Frank died, you and Martin became that much closer. You know better than anyone how tough he had it after that botched hunting trip, and you helped him through the hell that followed. I lost track of how many times you took him to physical therapy. He knows you love him. And you have to know he feels the same. You'd be a fool to think otherwise."

"How," he started to say, but the rest got caught in

his throat. "How is he?"

"Oh, Bob. He's a goddamned train wreck. Unconscious since they brought him in. They're taking his arm first thing tomorrow morning—lopping it clean off, above the elbow—thinking that might head off the infection. I'm trying to say positive, but it's not looking good."

"What the hell happened, Jo?"

"It's too crazy to mention. I'm not even sure I believe it, to tell the truth. I keep waiting for someone to wake me up and put an end to this nightmare. That's what this is, Bob—a goddamned nightmare."

"Can I see him?"

Jodi wagged her head no. "He's in bad shape, Bob, comatose and coming apart at the seams. No one wants to tell me outright, but he's probably going to lose this fight."

Bob excused himself, presumably to find a restroom where he could wipe the snot from his nose in private.

Jodi watched as Bob wandered off with his head in his hands, nearly knocking an elderly man out of his wheelchair. With Bob gone, she had to deal with Bonnie, the dumbfounded wife. Jodi thought she could see Bonnie's throat move up and down, as if swallowing something distasteful. She had a good idea what it was.

"Three and a half hours."

"Pardon me?" Bonnie said.

"Three and a half hours—that's how long it took for you two to drive here from home. I know because I've made the drive myself. That's a long time to have to think about what was waiting for you here. I knew Bob would come, but I honestly didn't think you would show. *Hoped* you wouldn't, to tell the truth."

"Why wouldn't I? Martin was like …"

Bonnie struggled to finish the sentence.

"I know exactly what he was to you," Jodi said. "You know, Bonnie, when you get to be our age, you learn not to put up with the bullshit you did when you were younger. At least I have. I'm not stupid, so don't pretend that you and Martin weren't off together doing whatever it was that you were doing to each other, with each other. It doesn't take a detective to tie the ends of those threads together."

Bonnie tried to look shocked.

"You can quit the play-acting," Jodi said. "There's a good chance I'm about to become a widow and you're about to become an ex-mistress, so let's stop pretending."

Bonnie opened her mouth as if to say something, but the words would not come. Jodi imagined stink lines wafting from the open sore of Bonnie's mouth—an awful permutation of cigarettes, coffee, and tuna. She wondered how Martin could have tolerated it—being so close to her, his mouth on hers, the air leaving her lungs as he climbed atop her. With breath that toxic, Jodi figured, Bonnie must have been one hell of a good lay.

"Jodi," Bonnie finally managed to say.

"Don't say another word. Just stand there and feel sorry for me as if you're real flesh and blood. After today I don't want you within a hundred feet of me. Bob? Now he's family, and he's always welcome. You … well, I don't have to say it. You know what you are."

"Jodi." Bonnie's eyes roved the waiting room. "Please."

"I'm not going to blab to Bob, if that's what you're worried about. He's an idiot if he doesn't want to admit what happened between you and my husband, but deep down he knows. Because it kills you a little to discover that two people who are supposed to love you would hurt you so bad. So no, I won't say a goddamned word. With your looks fading as quickly as they have the past few years, I can't risk Bob leaving you out in the cold with nothing to your name. I refuse to have something like that on my conscience."

Bob had suspected something was going on between Martin and Bonnie, just as Jodi had suspected before she knew for certain, before Martin came clean.

One night in June, maybe a decade ago, while Martin and Bonnie were both "out of town," Jodi and Bob met for dinner at a BYO in Glendale. After Bob popped the cork on their second bottle of chardonnay, he remarked how wonderful it was that their significant others were out of town at the same time—Bonnie visiting a college friend in Philadelphia, and Martin in Boston to pitch a prospective client—so he and Jodi could enjoy each other's company. He added, with the slightest suspicion, that Martin and Bonnie had both been away the last time he and Jodi had the chance to dine together. He remembered because he and Jodi last dined at a Midtown restaurant specializing in North Indian cuisine, which he loved but Bonnie detested. He then suggested maybe Martin and Bonnie were "off making the beast with two backs," and then joked that if their significant others ever stooped to such depths, he and Jodi would be obligated to abscond to the nearest seedy hotel and do the same. The idea crossed Jodi's mind for a split second, purely because they could have if they wanted, because who would know? Not that she found Bob the least bit attractive, physically, but appearance played only a small role in desire. Conversations with Bob moved along with ease and good humor, and that was enough to make her love him. Still, she knew herself well enough to realize she would never betray Martin in such a way.

Not then, not ever. At least not since Leonard Strohm. She still regretted her dalliance with the boy from high school, the one who took her virginity while Martin was getting shot at in Vietnam.

"I love my husband," Jodi told Bonnie. "That doesn't mean I always understand him, nor does it mean I've forgiven him or forgotten his missteps. I cannot fathom what he saw in you, especially considering his friendship with Bob. Martin's been through more than most people could stand, but his little tête-à-tête with you made me lose respect for him."

"He had his demons, Jodi."

"You haven't the faintest fucking clue." Jodi imagined taking two steps forward and planting a balled fist in the middle of Bonnie's face, popping her beak-like nose as if it were an overripe berry. "Don't you dare suggest that you know more about my husband than I do."

"I would never."

"Here's what's going to happen, and listen closely because I'm going to say this only once. When Bob comes back, I'm going to thank you both for coming, and then I'm going to tell you to leave, nice as pie, because there's nothing either of you can do to improve the situation. Bob will insist on staying because that's what Bob does, but you're going to grow a backbone for once in your life and take him home to Phoenix. The last thing Martin needs is another spectator to his demise."

"Do you need us to watch the house? Water the plants? Anything at all?"

"There's nothing at the house that can't take care of itself. If there is, my daughter is here. Besides, if I'm forced to stare at your painted-on eyebrows and over-injected fish lips for the next three days, or however much time Martin has left on this planet, I'm likely to decorate the floor with my vomit."

Bonnie pursed her lips and tensed her shoulders. Jodi smiled sweetly in return.

"Jodi, what happened between Martin and me … that was years ago, a decade or more, and it lasted maybe ten months, a year at the most. I regret it. He did, too. We both realized our mistakes. I think we just wanted to find out for ourselves."

"Spare me the details."

"Just know that Martin never stopped loving you."

"No shit, Petunia. Now get the hell out of here before I slap that look off your plasticized face."

CHAPTER 18

Take the Sow

Martin steers the UTV up the gentle incline, across a path strewn with downed pine branches and jagged crowns of greywacke. A puddle gleams in the blare of the headlights. He weaves to the left so the front right tire dips into a rut. Icy water sprays his companion in the passenger seat.

"Dousing me with glacial shit-water as punishment?" Frank yells above the growl of the engine. "That's piss-poor vengeance, pal."

"If you didn't want to get dirty, you shouldn't have chartered an expedition into the heart of the Canadian wilderness."

A cough rattles something loose in Frank's lungs.

Martin pedals the gas to gain on the quad's taillights maybe a quarter mile ahead. By his best guess, thirty minutes have passed since they set out on the midnight-black trail. The lightening sky suggests dawn's imminent arrival.

"I still don't know why you want to do this," Martin tells his friend.

"So I can say I did," Frank says. "When I'm long gone, Marilyn will have the beast's hide stretched across the floor and its head mounted on the wall to remember me by."

"I doubt Marilyn will look at a decapitated bear's head every day and say, 'Hm, Frank sure was a great husband.' A new vibrator would have been a hell of a lot cheaper, and I'm sure she'd get more use out of it."

"Fuck you, Martin."

"When the time comes, you really think she'll give a shit about you killing some defenseless bear?"

"It won't matter, because I'll have already done it."

Frank McGoldrick had a hard head the day Martin met him, when the two were nine-year-old boys in a just-built community in suburban Phoenix. His stubbornness has worsened in the decades since. When Frank got the cancer diagnosis—liver, stage four—no one could tell him anything he did not already know. He gave Martin and Bob Sweems, the third member of their trio, a bullet-pointed list of twenty-two items detailing the accomplishments he wanted to check off in the time he had left. Most of his goals were tame and ordinary: test drive a McLaren and push the speedometer over one-fifty; get a reservation at a new Brazilian steakhouse downtown; take a spin on a mechanical bull at the nearest cowboy bar. The list also had a few surprises: have one last fistfight; steal something worth the trouble; and, worst of all, hunt down a brown bear and take its head and hide as trophies.

"Imagine," Frank said during the conversation in which he tried to sell Martin and Bob on the idea. "We'll be walking through the feral wilderness, stalking our prey, knowing something lethal might be lurking just around the corner. It's either us or them."

"Already did it—Vietnam," Martin replied. "Can't say I recommend it."

Bob refused to go on the trip on principle, but Martin would not deny Frank, thinking his friend would not go through with the deed anyway. Besides, Martin wanted to spend as much time with Frank as he could; the doctors said he had less than a year left.

Each of them played a specific role in their trio: Bob was the level-headed one, Martin was the loyal one, and Frank was the hot-headed dick. Their respective roles had not changed since childhood. Now, driving a UTV on a worn stretch of double-track, miles from their dingy hotel in Dawson City, Martin wishes he had followed Bob's lead and steered Frank toward gentler, more worthwhile pursuits.

The trail curves, and Martin accelerates to see blazing red taillights closer than expected. Their guide, a thirty-something Canadian named Gord, waits on his quad for them to catch up. Martin brakes, and the UTV whines to a stop a few feet from the quad's rear tires.

"Maybe another ten minutes on this trail," Gord says. "Then we hoof it the rest of the way."

He palms a lime-handled skinning knife out of its sheath. The edge of the black blade gleams in the blare of his headlamp.

"Remember what I told you," Gord adds. "When and if we find what we're looking for, we take only the head, the pelt, and the claws. The carcass stays put, to feed whatever has an appetite. Agreed?"

"Fine with me," Frank says. "That's all I want anyway."

Gord speeds off, and Martin follows. His nerves dance. His breathing quickens. He loves the idea of being deep in the Yukon wilderness, but he wishes he were here for any reason other than to watch a friend assassinate an apex predator.

"Where'd you find this guy?" Martin asks.

"Recommendation from a buddy at the country club. Gord's outfit is different than the rest, I'm told. They really put the client first."

"I don't know what that means."

"All I know is I came here for a grizzly, and I'm not leaving here without it."

Martin jerks the wheel to avoid a fallen pine. Surprises abound on the lightless path, too dark to see anything until it meets the reach of the UTV's weak headlights.

"I'm beginning to think Bob had the right idea," Martin says. "He's probably still snoozing, dreaming about a lazy day in the recliner, sipping martinis and watching golf."

"Bob has no guts," Frank says. "He knows it, but tell him I said so."

Martin turns the discussion toward more urgent matters. "You okay to shoot? I know you're hurting, man."

"I get that bear in my sights, and he's meat. That's the only thing I'm sure of."

"Did you tell this guy about your condition?"

"The damn guide, you mean? I don't see how it's any of his business."

Every fiber of Martin's being tells him this enterprise will end badly. At the very least, it will end badly for a bear that wants nothing more than to go about its business in peace. Only the deeply set sense of obligation keeps Martin's foot on the gas pedal.

"It's not too late, man," he says. "Coming out here, gorgeous scenery and all, that alone has been worth the trip for me. Let's lose the Canuck and head back to town. Have a couple steaks, a few drinks. Play some cards for money."

"You think I came all this way to stay inside and play fuckin' Blackjack? You're not that stupid, Martin."

The trail widens and leads them into an expansive valley carpeted in heath, sedge grass, and berry bushes. Snow-capped mountains loom in the distance, their peaks like jagged teeth. Centuries-old pines rim the valley's edge. Gord kills the quad's engine at the trail's end, and Martin pulls behind.

"Where to, chief?" Frank asks.

As Gord unfastens the compound bow and the quiver of razor-tipped arrows from the quad's rear-mounted rack, he points toward the base of a mountain directly in front of him.

"We head straightaway, across the plain, maybe two kilometers in, until we come to the stream where the bears fish," he whispers. "Another guide spotted two or three boars—male bears—fighting over an elk carcass nearby. He put up a makeshift blind yesterday, ready and waiting for us. Rifle up and let's move."

"Who put the elk carcass there?" Martin says with suspicion.

"Accidents happen," Gord says.

Martin slings a Remington over his shoulder and waits for Frank to fall in line behind Gord. Frank does everything more slowly these days, making Martin wonder how much time his friend has left, the disease having taken too much already. Martin follows, a distant third, into the open space. The single-file experience reminds him of Vietnam, only tranquil and beauteous, and the temperature in late September climbs no higher than fifty degrees, compared with the high nineties when he landed in Luong Hoa. Perhaps, he thinks, he can replace the horrors of Vietnam with more serene memories of the Yukon. With any luck, they will find no evidence of a bear other than scat or tufts of fur, and remember this trip as a peaceful walk across a sedge meadow with a reasonably affable Canadian.

The sky, once hard and black, turns soft and periwinkle. To his right and left, Martin sees nothing but waist-high grass, where anything could be hiding. They reach the primitive blind within forty-five minutes, only to find the flimsy structure toppled and torn. Martin wants to blame the elements for the wrecked blind, but he knows it is likely the work of a curious predator that outweighs him by three-hundred pounds. A break in the sedge grass winds through the meadow maybe sixty feet beyond the blind. The stream, Martin assumes, is likely an offshoot of the Yukon River. Gord motions for them to settle in and get comfortable, to prepare for the task at hand.

"I'm not shooting anything," Martin says.

"Then why the fuck did you come?" Frank replies.

"I came for you, asshole."

"I don't need a fuckin' babysitter. If I knew you were

going to be such a pussy about it, I would have told you to stay home with Bob."

Frank grows anxious. He turns to the guide and whispers, "Can we get closer?"

"Why?" Gord says.

"If I'm going to do this, I'm going to do it right—with the bow. I'm not sure I can hit my target this far back. The eyes aren't as sharp as they used to be."

Gord scans the meadow and points to the trunk of a downed tree maybe twenty-five feet closer to the stream.

"That's our best bet," the guide says. "It's a little too close for comfort—no shit, Frank. If you miss your shot, the bear's going to charge and our morning's going to get a lot more exciting than any of us would like. I'm going to cover you. If you miss, I won't. Understood?"

"Good ol' Gordy," Frank says. "I knew I liked you."

Gord leads the way, staying low, and Frank follows. Martin wonders if he should stay with the blind, because getting closer seems stupid, if not dangerous, but he follows for the sake of his friend. He feels exposed, much like he did almost every second of his time in the war.

They creep across the meadow, the ground soft beneath Martin's feet, until they reach the downed tree trunk. Gord settles behind the sun-bleached wood.

"Better?" he asks.

Frank peers over the edge of the trunk and says, "Perfect."

The minutes pass slowly. They have little to do but swat mosquitos. In terms of number and determination, the maddening little pests rival the ones from the jungles of

Vietnam. Sunlight spills over the easternmost peak and paints the meadow orange.

"Getting late," Gord says. "We'll give it another hour."

Martin puts his back to the trunk. Clouds drift overhead. A cool wind sweeps the meadow. The sedge grass undulates, the motion reminding him of waves in the ocean. His eyelids grow heavy.

Three raps on the trunk nudge Martin out of a light sleep.

Gord trains his field binoculars on the tree line, maybe twenty yards past the stream.

"Christmas has arrived, Frank," he whispers. "Nock an arrow."

After nearly fumbling the quiver, Frank guides an arrow onto the bowstring.

A hulking brown mass lumbers through the tall grass and stops at the stream. The grizzly stops to sniff the air. It must weigh a quarter of a ton, Martin thinks. The bear dips its massive head toward the water, presumably scouting for trout or salmon. Martin wonders if Frank could make a shot from this distance even if the cancer had not sapped his strength and screwed up his faculties.

"Don't do it, Frank," Martin whispers, though too quiet for Frank to hear. Besides, the time to bail out has long passed. Either they kill the bear or …

There is no *or*, he realizes. Every other option defies belief.

"Wait," Gord says.

Two cubs scramble out of the heath. One tumbles into

the water.

"What do I do?" Frank asks.

Gord pauses. "How much do you want this, Frank?"

"More than anything," he says.

Gord stays silent for half a minute. Then: "Take the sow."

"You can't be serious," Martin says, louder than he should. "It has cubs."

"I can keep a secret if you two can."

"I'm in," Frank says.

"Absolutely not," Martin says.

"Don't fuck this up for me, Martin."

"Then we're agreed," Gord says. He turns to Frank and whispers, slowly. "Bring down the sow. She'll smell you before she sees you, but stay as low as you can."

"You piece of shit," Martin says.

"Take your shot, Frank. I'll take care of the cubs."

Gord trains the scope of his rifle on the mother grizzly, covering Frank in case his shot misses the mark. As Frank pulls back the release, and the arrow along with it, the sound of the bowstring reminds Martin of a breath being drawn. Frank takes aim, one eye closed. The slightest of coughs escapes his lips. His right arm trembles more than it should.

"You okay, Frank?" Martin whispers.

A tremor seizes Frank's body. His arm fails. The arrow cuts through the grass and stabs the mud maybe ten feet short of the stream.

The mother grizzly raises her head. Her nose scouts the air. Her lower lip curls as she sees them. She squints, and then charges.

"Fuck!" Gord hollers. He lifts his rifle, aims, fires off a round, no telling if the shot lands.

The bear covers the distance in seconds. She crashes over the tree trunk and knocks Gord clear. She homes in on Frank. He falls backward, and she seizes him by the left arm. She thrashes him from side to side, tendons popping, flesh tearing. Blood droplets spray Martin's face. Gord gets to his feet, reloads, fires. A bullet rips into the bear's shoulder hump. She turns and rakes his face with a massive forepaw. The force of her swipe turns his head almost completely around, his cervical spine crackling like kernels of corn in a hot pan. She descends on his fallen body and promptly removes his face.

Martin backs away, in shock.

After the bear severs Gord's head, she returns to Frank.

Martin races forward and swings the rifle as if it were a sledgehammer, cracking the bear across the neck. As she turns toward him, her golden-brown irises burn with rage. She bowls him over, punching the breath from his lungs. Her shadow covers him. Stone-hard claws slash his face and chest, like daggers striking bone. He uses the rifle as a brace, trying to fend her off, but he has never met such strength in another living thing. His finger finds the trigger. As the rifle kicks, his finger breaks. He draws a sharp breath as the bear's weight eases in retreat.

The bear circles him. Blood flows from the hump on her back and, now, her demolished forepaw. He fumbles for the rifle's bolt. As he retracts the bolt, a used casing spits onto the meadow floor. His hand throbs as he thrusts the bolt forward to chamber another shell. She charges again, and in the second before she reaches him, Martin raises the muzzle.

He does not recall pulling the trigger.

The bullet drills a hole through the bear's skull, just above the left eye. Her body falls forward, her shoulder slamming into his pelvis. Her body covers his. The air leaks slowly from her deflating lungs. Blood warms his lap. She makes a noise that sounds like a whimper, as if only now she realizes the precious gift she has lost.

Martin squirms out from beneath the dead bear and crawls to his friend's side.

Frank's eyes stare sightlessly into the unending sky. He could be sleeping if not for his wounds. A hole in his forehead leaks dark blood. Crimson ruts bisect Frank's cheek and chin, courtesy of the bear's canines. His lower lip is absent, as is most of his throat.

Martin kneels by his dead friend to remember the deeds they had done, the times they shared, the messes they made. Gord's lifeless body lies several feet away.

"Why, man?" Martin cries. "Why did you want to come here?"

After a while, Martin lifts his head to check the sky, to gauge how much daylight he has left. He wants to take both bodies, out of respect, but he knows he has enough strength to carry only one. As he lifts Frank's body in a fireman's carry, a ball of blood spills from Frank's mouth and slicks the ground. Blood trickles down Martin's forehead and drips into his eye. Any predators within a mile can likely smell his wounds, taste his sweet scent. He checks his pocket to make sure he still has the key to the UTV. He then begins the long trek across the meadow to his only means of escape. His right knee throbs, some essential part of his anatomy likely broken or torn. He nearly vomits from the pain that accompanies each step. He walks with one eye closed.

A presence looms. Pappaduffus.

"I know you're out there," Martin says. "I can feel you. … Take what you want and don't say a damned word. Just let me get back to my family."

Family.

He thinks about Marilyn, Frank's wife, now widow, and the words he will speak to her if he lives through this nightmare—about Frank's friendship, about the mark he left on the world, about his death. The slaughtered sow's cubs mewl in the distance. With no mother to protect them, they will be dead by nightfall. Martin remembers the guide, Gord, regrettably left behind. At least the cubs will have a good last meal.

Martin's energy drains as Pappaduffus sates his appetite.

Martin stops at a patch of low sedge grass and eases Frank's dead weight off his shoulders. He thinks about how easy it would be to close his eyes and wait for the end to come. Like falling asleep. Cool air seeps into him through his many wounds, claiming whatever energy Pappaduffus has not already sapped. Minutes later he forces himself to get up and keep going. Frank's body seems to have gotten heavier, the combination of his adrenaline wearing off and Pappaduffus having fed.

The distant tree line seems no closer than when he

started. The path disappears beneath his boots. He hopes like hell he is stumbling in the right direction, because he has only so much energy to spare before his body fails.

CHAPTER 19

Battle Hardened

The transport staffer wheeled Martin into his room. The man waited while the ICU nurse reconnected her patient to the computers on casters and other devices that helped keep him alive for the past five days. Or was it six days? Jodi refused to look at Martin's shoulder, where his right arm used to be, or the abhorrent ventilator tube jutting from his mouth. Doctor Stephens waited by the door until the nurse and transport staffer left the room.

"Doctor Till told you the surgery went well," Stephens said.

"Yes, she was very kind and reassuring," Jodi said. She wanted to add, "You could learn a thing or two from her," but held her tongue. "She said he might need revision surgery after he's healed up, but it was nice to have some good news for a change."

He paused, mouth partly open, which Jodi took as him getting ready to spoil the picnic.

"The next forty-eight hours will be critical," he said. "His heart can't keep up with the work the body is asking it to do. It looks like edema will be a persistent problem, but as long as we can keep his lungs clear …"

Jodi exhaled in mild relief. She could deal with a little fluid, or Martin could. Then Stephens kept talking.

"I am concerned about his potassium levels—elevated and continuing to climb—and his urinary production, which is almost nonexistent. Acute tubular necrosis, most likely, which Exelby tells me is an unfortunate side effect of the venom from the scorpion that supposedly stung your husband. You often see it with rattlesnake bites, too. Ischemia of the kidneys, essentially."

"Ischemia." She knew the term, never good.

"Inadequate blood flow. Kidneys can self-heal, and we have some options to help stimulate function, but the organ may not survive if the damage is too severe. We also may want to consider a feeding tube. Fluids are most important right now, but he's going to need sustenance in the coming days so his body can keep fighting and disrupting the disease process."

Fresh tears filled Jodi's eyes, though she was surprised she had any more to give. The thought she had been wrestling with for the past several days returned like a boot to the gut. "Did we just hack off his arm for no good reason?"

Stephens contorted his face and wagged his head from side to side, unable to hide his distaste for the question. He seemed astounded that Jodi might doubt his judgment.

"There's a war being waged inside your husband's body, and we have to fight it one campaign at a time," he said. "The amputation was necessary. Think of it as a lost battle, as territory we had to cede so we have a better shot at winning the big one."

"You know," she said, "I'm really starting to hate this fucking place."

And then she started to sob.

CHAPTER 20

Procession of Losses

Martin climbs out of the AMC Gremlin, its copper paint dulled by road dust. He follows the well-worn trail into Boxelder Park, a ten-minute walk from his first home in Arizona. The contents of a crinkled brown bag adhere to his right hand. He wears his civilian clothes, which make him feel like a pretender. More than a year has passed since his return from Vietnam, but he feels naked without his combat boots. He cannot part with his dog tags.

Quiet reigns in Boxelder, the same park in which he found solace in the lonely days after he and his mother uprooted them from the lush climes of Oregon and dropped them in the arid Southwest. A woman in her sixties or seventies—gray and wrinkled, yet lean and fit—passes him on the trail. He nods out of respect, and gives her a wide berth so she can feel safe, so she can know he is not a predator. An overwhelming feeling weighs him down as he considers the long life she has lived. He identifies the feeling as an amalgam of pity, envy, and grief. Pity, for everything and everyone she left behind; envy, for the years she has spent on the earth; and grief, for the life he knew he would never have. He views old age as a procession of losses and loneliness, a whittling down until the soundtrack goes quiet and the screen goes dark. Whether lucky or unlucky, this old woman has outlived friends, family, pets, and co-workers, yet she finds the will to keep going despite the mounting losses. He wonders if the bad memories will lose their sharpness over time until they become something softer and kinder than pain. If fortune finds him, he will live a good, long life, too—if, and only if, he can get his mind right. At present, he figures he has only a few more years left in him.

The trail leads him to a bench beneath an ironwood tree, where he sweats in the shade. He twists the wedding band on his ring finger, still getting used to the feel. A branch rustles overhead, lifted by a warm, stiff wind. He reaches into the bag and retrieves the revolver—Smith & Wesson Model Nineteen, walnut grip and blued finish. His lips kiss the carbon steel. He turns the weapon inward so he can peer into the muzzle's inky eye.

He cannot handle this life, not here, not anymore. Nothing makes sense, and he does not fit—an outsider, an outcast, a pariah. He wonders if he made a mistake leaving the military. As much as he disliked KP, clerical work, and just about every other duty his superiors had handed him while in uniform, at least he had a sense of purpose as a cog in a wheel. He is not qualified to do anything but follow someone else's orders and bull's-eye targets at the firing range. In Vietnam, though he despised almost every minute, he had a reason to go on living, if only to survive the year and make sure his band of brothers did the same, though that did not work out either. Here, in Western civilization, life seems shallow and empty, a pointless game he prefers not to play.

Jodi.

She is his reason. His sole reason. She makes it worth sticking around, to see how the story ends. He opens the revolver's barrel and checks the cylinder to remind himself he did not load the weapon. Ammunition is a luxury he cannot quite afford, not yet, not with more mouths on the way—progeny. Maybe he should make bullets a priority. He lifts the gun to his forehead, to see how it feels, if it feels right, if this is the way to go. If not now, someday.

"Why, dear boy, would you go and do something silly like that?"

Dead leaves flutter to the ground—a few at first, and then dozens—shaken loose from the nest of branches. The canopy parts for a small man in a gray herringbone suit and matching derby, holding a bone-white walking stick. Inhuman hands guide the figure down the boxelder tree's furrowed trunk. His face has not aged a day.

The memories flood black.

"Pappaduffus," Martin says. "I thought I was rid of you."

"I have been watching your progress, dear boy," Pappaduffus says. "The boy I knew became the man I had always hoped he would be."

"That was you over there," he says, referring to Vietnam, specifically the humid night he lost his friends, Samuels and Horowitz. He remembers the ragged voice whispering to him as he skulked through the jungle, and those bluish-white pinpricks cutting through the darkness. He will never forget those eyes, appearing hot and cold at the same time. "You saved me. Why?"

"Imagine my surprise to see you there, after we had been apart for so long. The last place I wished to see you, considering the time and circumstances. I never wanted any harm to come to you, and surely it would have if I did not intervene. Imagine my disappointment to find you here and now, despondent and pondering an act as selfish as removing yourself from this beautiful, glorious, perfectly backwards and broken world. Believe me when I tell you I have seen far worse. The earth on which you live, you will find no grander place among the stars. Would be such a pity for you to say your goodbyes prematurely, having seen so little of it."

"Nothing makes sense to me here."

"The human world is a senseless place. No need to despair, dear boy. Not yet."

"I don't know how to live here."

"Perhaps you would rather be back in the jungle—hunting human prey, and being hunted in return?"

Martin wants nothing of the sort.

"Let me help you, and help you I shall," Pappaduffus says. "I can spare you from the horrors of your time. Nothing terrible will happen to you with me beside you. Nothing from which you can't recover, at least."

"I don't understand. What are you?"

"Just your old friend, Mister Pappaduffus. Adopt me as your guardian, your protector, and I will take just a little in return, so little you'll barely notice. You just have to promise not to do the kinds of silly things you think you have come here to do."

"I'm crazy. I'm dreaming. I'm dead. Tell me it's one of those."

"Pish posh. You are alive and as awake as they come, dear boy, and I can make sure you stay the same for the remainder of your days. I promise to let nothing stand in your way."

"Why now? Why come back after all this time?"

"My dear, you live on a big blue marble with so much to offer. And there are so many of your kind, but so few like you. You have always been my most favorite of all. Everyone but you can see how special you are, it seems, how much you have to give. You have my undivided attention. Cross my heart."

Pappaduffus swipes two eel-like fingers across a black rose pinned to the lapel of his herringbone jacket. A withered petal slips from the loosening bud and turns to ash as it touches the ground.

"Nothing in life is free," Martin says. "What do you want from me? What exactly?"

"Just the most insignificant of things, really, the things you would wish away," Pappaduffus says. "Bring me your pain, your grief, the tears no one sees. Give them to me and I will ease your burden. Accept me, and in that acceptance, your path will be made easier. If you covet something, you will have it by my hand."

"And if I don't?"

"I understand you will be a family man soon. Bring them along, too. I promise to keep them close, and to protect them just as I would protect you."

He thinks of Jodi back home, and the mass growing in her belly. Twins, the doctors say.

"Leave them the fuck out of this. Understand me?"

"Fine, fine, fine," Pappaduffus says curtly. "No need to get crass or cross. Accept me and they will neither see me nor hear a peep out of me."

Martin leans forward, his head in his hands. He thinks of the mother he has lost, of Samuels and Horowitz, of the agonies of childhood, and the crushing weight of those losses, one piled on top of the other.

"Okay," Martin says. "Take what you want and leave the rest."

Pappaduffus descends from his perch among the branches. Icy pinpricks stare into Martin's eyes. Pappaduffus's chest heaves with excitement. Lines of drool squirt from the spaces between needle-like teeth. The look on the Little Gray Man's face reminds Martin of a tiger ready to pounce. A tentacle-like hand slithers across the back of Martin's neck. The Arizona heat melts away, and Martin feels chilled to the core.

CHAPTER 21

The Minds of the Wind-Makers

Roy's purring usually helped Jodi drift off to sleep, but sleep would not come. The cat settled in the nook of Martin's pillow at a few minutes before three a.m., and later kneaded Jodi's chest as an invitation to stroke the silky fur on its back and tail. Hours passed with Jodi staring at the featureless ceiling. The light began to soften enough for her to see the patterns in the cat's multicolored fur. Dawn would arrive within the hour. A full night's sleep—even a partial one—would have to wait. At least she got to spend a night in her own bed.

Jodi and Alison had left the hospital in Tuba City just before ten p.m. the night before. Unable to stand the confinement, the smell of Martin's room, the sight of Martin unmoving in his bed, Jodi needed a night of rest "away from the torture rack of this hellhole," as she told the doctor, the nurse, and anyone else who would listen. More than anything, Jodi needed time to herself, away from the hospital staff, to process the turn of events. The pressure had been building behind her eyes, in her chest, in the depths of her gut, and she knew something would blow if she did not take a break—even if it meant leaving her husband unattended after a surgery that would alter the rest of his life. The way she saw it, Martin was still unconscious and would not notice her absence. The hospital staff would take care of him if any further madness came to pass.

Assuming he survived the night.

Now, having realized what she had done, she wished she had never left.

Alison did not stir as Jodi tiptoed past the guest bedroom and descended the stairs for the kitchen. As she stood at the sink and filled the coffee pot beneath the spigot, Jodi stared out the window. The sky turned shades of purple, red, and orange. Her eyes drifted toward the shadowed woodpile, wondering where the devilish little bugger that had felled Martin might be hiding. Never before had she felt so lost in a fog. Never before had her life been turned so completely upside down. My, what surprises came with old age. She likened the experience to an accident so tragic it bordered on farce—which, she supposed, it was.

Her phone dinged, a text from Andrew: DAD DOING BETTER?

She began typing a response, suggesting the likelihood of his father's demise, but it hardly seemed appropriate for text. Instead, she wrote: CALL ME. She imagined the difficulties Andrew would face in getting away, in leaving *Turista*—his restaurant, his baby—in the hands of someone who cared less than he did so he could fly home and deal with a disaster. She also knew she and Alison would be the ones to deal with the brunt of the shitstorm even if

Andrew had been by their side. A pang of resentment fluttered through her, wondering what it must be like to leave messes in other people's laps. She shook the thought away, reminding herself that she was happy for her son, for everything he had achieved since leaving his family behind, especially because he fought so hard to attain every award, a top spot on almost every "best of" list, every ounce of praise. She and Martin had visited Andrew once in Valencia, just after his restaurant had "hit." Almost overnight, Andrew's worries became less about finding labor and reliable vendors, and more about satisfying critics, living up to guests' skyscraping expectations, and answering the question, "What next?"

If only Alison could find the same contentment. Jodi's daughter struggled through her teens and early twenties, and eventually found her way thanks to the interventions of psychotherapy and inpatient psychiatric treatment. She had since forged a career in health care, on the operations side, and apparently made good money running offices for same-day surgeries and urologic procedures. While Alison seemed to excel at the work, she confessed to hating every minute of it. Jodi hoped her daughter would find something that made her happy, even if she had to go halfway around the world to find it.

The drip coffeemaker gurgled as it finished its cycle. Jodi usually drank tea rather than coffee, but she needed the boost. She dropped two ice cubes into a mug, followed by a stream of fresh brew. Each ice cube crackled and popped. As the sun inched above the horizon, the world outside her door came to life. Barrel cactuses, chollas, and prickly pears took shape. Daylight painted the striated walls of distant mesas. She understood why Martin had chosen this place to call home—so wild and alive, so different from the dull muteness of suburbia. It called to her, too.

She gulped down the coffee, filled a stainless-steel water bottle to the brim, and tucked a rosewood-handled folding knife into her back pocket. She then fished a notepad from the drawer, penned a terse note for Alison—*Went for a walk*—and stepped outside. The morning air carried a familiar chill, but she knew the coolness would not last long. She passed the woodpile and stepped over the dilapidated fence, onto the dusty earth beyond. Her right knee creaked with an awkward step. She took one last look at the farmhouse, its rooms quiet and not fully awake, and set off into the desert.

After walking for thirty minutes or so, the mesas seemed no closer. She was in Navajo territory now, no doubt, and the feeling of hiking on native land thrilled her. Primordial, in a way, somehow removed from the everyday world. She stepped cautiously, her eyes scanning the scrub for dozing rattlesnakes curled at the base of each brittlebush.

Thoughts of Martin consumed her: the day they met, their first kiss, their courtship, their last night together before he left for Vietnam, the day he found her upon returning from the war, making love for the first time, the fights they had, the birth of the twins, his gift for making her laugh, the disappointments he handed her, and, above all, his tenderness. She hated to think all that would be wiped away by something no one could really explain, as if none of it ever happened, as if Martin never existed.

She squinted as she walked, cursing herself for forgetting her sunglasses. Somehow the discomfort sustained her. The temperature had risen perhaps twenty degrees since she first set out. She took water from the stainless-steel bottle. Sips at first, and then gulps. Her foot sunk into a hole likely made by a prairie dog, and she cursed every member of the pest's species. Despite having nearly turned her ankle, she doubled her pace toward the nearest mesa. The journey would take another hour, by her best guess. It felt good to push her body again, especially after so many days of inactivity by Martin's side—mourning her altered life and the end of her marriage as she knew it, even though her husband's heart continued to beat.

She approached a break in the desert scrub. A double track of primitive road stretched east and west, into the infinite nothingness. She stood there for a moment, knowing each direction would lead her back to some form of civilization, toward humans and comfort and safety. A black bird with ragged wings circled overhead. She pressed forward, toward the flat-topped mesa.

Finally, as she reached its base, she realized she should turn back—should have turned back long ago, in fact. Some internal force compelled her to climb. She scrambled across boulders of hot red rock and found a faint trail, following switchbacks toward the top, until she reached a jut that led to the mesa's vertical walls.

The sun pressed on her like a searing stone, and she tipped back her water bottle only to find it empty. Her heart raced, which she thought strange considering her level of fitness. A terrible word formed in her brain: *dehydration*. She skirted the mesa toward the shadowed side. The surface temperature cooled out of the sun, but her heart would not stop hammering. She found a throne-like rock behind an outcropping. A wave of nausea and dizziness nearly buckled her knees. Her mouth yearned for moisture. She stared out onto the desert, seeing no signs of human life—no stores or houses, no billboards or roadways, nothing or no one who could help her. Yes, she had succeeded in finding a wild place, though her triumph would cost her. How foolish to have come so far so unprepared. She knew better, but knowing better had not stopped her from doing something stupid.

How laughable it would be for her to die out here, she thought, leaving Alison and Andrew motherless, if not parentless.

A stone tumbled down the mesa wall, followed by another and another, the rock and dirt coming down in a sheet. Jodi shielded her head to keep from getting bludgeoned. She opened her eyes to see the source of the small-scale rockslide: a man scrabbling down a worn path, presumably leading to the mesa's plateau.

"Holy Christ!" he said when he saw her. His boot treads skittered on the loose rock. "You nearly scared the ghost out of me!"

The man's body resembled a bowling pin, bottom heavy. He wore a leather fedora, khaki vest and matching shorts, and polarized Ray-Bans. A backpack dangled limply from his slight shoulders. Likely he had plenty of water.

"What in blazes are you doing up here?" he asked.

"I could ask you the same." An ache built in the space

behind her eyes. "I don't suppose you have a few slugs of drinking water to spare."

He knelt and pulled the pack from his shoulders, retrieved a full Nalgene, and unscrewed the plastic top. He passed the thirty-two-ounce bottle to her trembling hands.

"You can keep that," he said.

She gulped insatiably, and her stomach nearly protested. Her heart continued to stammer.

He produced another full bottle and poured half its contents into the Nalgene she held.

"How someone comes out here without water is beyond me," he said. "Do you have a death wish?"

"I didn't expect to come this far."

"You're trespassing on Navajo land, you know," he told her.

"You don't look Navajo to me, so that makes two of us."

"They make exceptions for qualified educators," he said. "How did you get up here?"

"Same as you, I gather. One foot in front of the other."

"You're the first gringo I've ever seen this far out, so far from town. Certainly the first person I've run into on foot. Are you a glutton for punishment? One of those extreme athletes or something?"

"Hardly." A wave of nausea passed through her. She stifled the urge to vomit. "I'm a wife, a mother, and a retired librarian."

"You sure as hell could have fooled me. You've got guts anyway." He stared off, presumably scouting for anyone who might be watching. "Do you live around here?"

"I live …" She turned her head, realizing she could no longer identify the direction from which she had come. "I went for a walk and just kept going. I saw this mesa and thought: *Hey, I should climb it.* Guess I'm just another unprepared fool."

"Nonsense. You were drawn here, like I was drawn here. Funny thing about this place. The Navajo used to come up here to commune with the gods. They believed life began here, atop mesas like the one we're standing on, having descended from the stars. They made pilgrimages here to give voice to their fears and tribulations, so the winds would carry their troubles far away and place them somewhere else, at someone else's feet. The Navajo were thankful for the reprieve, but they also had the wisdom to realize their suffering would return to them when the winds decided they were ready."

"*When they were ready*," Jodi repeated. She thought of Martin's plight, and of her own. Perhaps her life of ease had reached its end and the universe had decided it was time for her to writhe. "How did the winds know when the Navajo were ready?"

"I don't pretend to know the minds of the wind-makers."

"How is it you know so much?"

"Like I said, I'm an educator of sorts," he told her. "Hugo Keczmer—anthropologist, archaeologist, adventurer. Think of me as a modern-day Indiana Jones, minus the bullwhip, the professorship, and any measurable charisma. I do, however, have the fedora."

He tipped the hat's brim to reveal a thinning hairline.

"Archaeologist, you say. So, you're a graverobber, stealing things that don't belong to you."

"That's one way of looking at it." He patted his belly nervously. "Listen, I really should be getting a move on. You sure you'll be all right up here?"

She clutched the Nalgene, which she had mostly drained. Less than twelve ounces of water remained.

"Ma'am, you know where you're going? You know how to make your way back home?"

"Down there and to the right." She didn't want to come across as a helpless old lady, though she realized, in this sense, the description seemed perfectly apt. "I think."

"Look," Hugo said. "I won't be able to sleep tonight if I leave you out here by yourself. Finish your water and we'll make our way down together."

The descent seemed even more difficult than the ascent, strangely. Her legs and lungs both felt weak, her heart still racing. Almost an hour later, they reached flat land, and Hugo led Jodi toward the opposite side of the mesa, back into the blast furnace of full sun. Goosebumps pimpled her forearms.

"You going to be okay from here?" he asked.

A sound perked up both their ears: the distant whine of an engine. A cloud of dust tore across the sun-scorched plain. Hugo groaned as he scaled a boulder of red rock. He waved his arms with fury, and nearly lost his balance at least once.

"What is it?" she asked.

"Someone who can help, most likely." He looked

worried. "Fingers crossed."

The dust cloud ceased for a moment. The engine noise then seemed to grow closer.

The SUV bounced across the landscape and pulled up to the base of the mesa. The words NAVAJO NATION POLICE blared on the driver-side door. The door opened, and out stepped a woman of no more than five feet tall. A long, streaked-gray braid hung across her right shoulder and dangled down to her waist. Her hair and the creases around her mouth and eyes suggested she was in her early fifties.

"Damn it, Hugo," the woman said. "Didn't I tell you last time was the last time? I'm taking you in."

"Sheriff, this woman needs help," Hugo said. "She wandered out here with no water, no food, no nothing. She's probably dehydrated and ready to fall over."

The woman gave Jodi the once-over. "Is she demented?"

"I can speak for myself, thank you," Jodi said. "Foolish, yes, but hardly demented."

Jodi offered the woman a hand to shake, and the woman reluctantly accepted. Jodi's hand folded in the woman's steely grip. A ridge of calluses contrasted the soft, smooth flesh of Jodi's palm. A nameplate pinned to the sheriff's right breast read: CHOOLI ETSIDDY. Jodi explained who she was and where she lived, gave the name of her farm's previous owner, as if dropping the predecessor's name might move the conversation along.

"Get in the front seat," Etsiddy said.

Jodi did as she was told, thankful for the respite from the heat and the sun.

Etsiddy then approached Hugo, who backed away with his hands raised in protest. His eyes darted left to right, making Jodi think he might run for it. The sheriff handcuffed him without incident, and then carefully guided him into the backseat. She palmed his head to prevent him from whacking the door frame. Her captive secure, she climbed into the cab and did Jodi the kindness of turning the AC on full blast, but even that did not cool Jodi down.

"You're on Navajo land, ma'am, which means you're trespassing," Etsiddy said. "People get hurt out here, sometimes worse. We find too many of those folks only after they've been picked over by every critter with an appetite. The mesas are sacred to my people. Too few of our shrines remain intact, with so many others already spoiled by trespassers and thieves. If you want to know more about the Navajo, just ask."

"I didn't know it was sacred," Jodi replied. She disliked the scolding and wanted to say so. Instead, she added, "I didn't know anything at all until Hugo educated me."

"Ha! Whatever Hugo gave you, it's no education. He knows as much about the Navajo as I do about astrophysics, and I can barely spell the word. Just stay on your side of the fence."

Etsiddy turned the SUV onto the double track. The front left tire dipped into a rut, and Jodi's head rang off the window glass.

"I didn't do anything I wasn't supposed to, Sheriff," Hugo insisted from the backseat. "You know how easy it is to get turned around out here."

"And you just came out here for the sunset view, right? Save it for the judge, Hugo. As far as I'm concerned, you're all out of second chances."

Etsiddy lowered her voice to Jodi.

"Where are you folks from? I mean, before you came to Crum."

"Just outside of Phoenix. We came here …" She paused. "For a fresh start."

"You ever need anything in an emergency, just holler. We're all connected out here."

The double track led them to a wider dirt road, which fed into a seam of asphalt Jodi recognized as the road that ran past the farm. A few minutes later, Etsiddy turned into Jodi's driveway. She killed the engine and exited the vehicle.

"Sit tight, Hugo," she said. "Not a lick more trouble from you today."

As Jodi climbed out of her seat, she whispered to Hugo through the gridded metal partition, "Thank you, and good luck." It took some doing to close the passenger door, making her realize how much the day had taken out of her.

She followed Etsiddy to the front porch. Her toes tingled with each step.

"You sure you never met Hugo before today?" Etsiddy asked. "Just a coincidence I found you two together?"

"Never before. Never again. One minute I was alone, the next he was right there. He *did* help me. He saved me, in fact, if that means anything."

"He's harmless. I just don't want him poking around up there, doing something stupid to get himself hurt. That goes for you, too."

"Consider my curiosity satisfied, Sheriff. I appreciate the lift home. Not sure I would have made it otherwise."

"Call me Chooli. You sure you're feeling all right? A day in the sun out here is nothing to take lightly. Bad business. Too many people realize they're in trouble only after it's too late. I can run you over to the hospital if you need it, if only to replenish your fluids."

Fluids. Jodi thought of Martin alone in his hospital bed, the flesh of his legs and remaining arm as soft as a sponge, swollen with excess fluid.

Martin, adrift in a black sea on a moonless night, encircled by hungry mouths.

Martin, drowning, his waterlogged lungs about to burst.

"I'll be heading there soon enough, funny you should ask," Jodi said. "Thank you for the offer, but I can do without an escort."

CHAPTER 22

Fighters

artin leads his young son down the stadium's concrete steps, toward the first-base line.
Andrew keeps his baseball glove close to his chest. Even though the chances of catching a foul ball are probably no better than one in a million, the sliver of hope in a child's mind makes the possibility of going home with a game-used souvenir all but certain. Martin smiles at Andrew's innocence, not yet hardened by cruelty, corruption, or disappointment.

They find their seats, two at the end of the aisle, seven rows up, to the right side of the metal railing separating Section 120 from Section 121. Martin guides his son into the row, but a stranger sits in the third seat. Andrew looks up at his dad and asks, "Do I have to sit next to him?"

"Take the aisle, pal."

Before the game begins, Andrew asks about the rules of the game, how a strike differs from a ball, what the shortstop does, if the players are allowed to hang out with each other as friends when they go home at night. Andrew wrinkles his brow at the vagueness of Martin's answers, but he stands in awe of the spectacle: so many people gathered in one place on a field of grass—actual grass in the middle of the desert, so green and perfect. It must seem like a miracle, impossible for his fledgling mind to grasp.

"Hey, Dad. Why didn't Mom and Alison come, too?"

"I just wanted to hang out with you today, pal. We don't get too much time to each other, you and me, doing manly things."

Martin does not want to admit what Jodi sees in their son—a "tenderness," as she calls it, that will make him different from other boys and, later, other men. *Straight* men. He has no idea how soon a child's preferences become fixed, but he imagines nine years old is too soon. He knows how silly it is to think a baseball game will have any impact on his son's trajectory, because his son will be exactly who he will be no matter how much fun they have at the ballpark. In truth, he just wants to see if a day alone with his son will help him see what Jodi sees. If her assessment turns out to be correct, fine with him. He will love his son regardless, always and forever. His only wish: that each of his children will have a life of ease, free of every avoidable pain.

Dishonorable memories from basic training at the base in Sierra Vista make him cringe. Each memory pertained to Anderson, a fellow private the others called a "dandy," though that was the kindest epithet they hurled at him. Strong and fit, Anderson was among the best of them physically, but everyone saw him as different, a weaker-than. The torment started slowly, subtly. Tying his bootlaces together. Nailing his footlocker shut. Then came the increasingly cruel confrontations in the mess hall and at least one humiliation in the communal shower—one in which Martin participated, however reluctantly—that he would rather forget.

One of the privates, Carr, who came from somewhere outside of Tucson, bragged that he was going to tell the staff sergeant about Anderson's "preferences," and why his "compromised" status made him "a danger to us all." Martin saw Carr for who we was: full of shit, just another talker, because in the end, all of them were in it together. One day Anderson just disappeared, his footlocker emptied. Discharged. Martin hoped the experience had not ruined Anderson's life in any way, because, if it had, Martin bore some responsibility.

Andrew will grow up in a different world, in different times, hopefully in which people realize they all share the same blood, no matter who they are or who they love. Martin would give his last breath to keep his children safe, but at some point they would leave him. He prays that, when the day comes, they will walk in a kinder, gentler, and more accepting world than the one that reared him.

The PA announcer barks out the starting lineups for the Phoenix Dust Devils and the Albuquerque Peccaries. Men in pinstripes take the field and toss hardballs back and forth. The warmup complete, the game starts with a whimper. Two strikeouts, each on four pitches, and a popup to shallow center field bring the top of the inning to a close.

Vendors in white paper hats parade through the stands offering peanuts, beer, hot dogs. Martin indulges each time, drawing the line at cotton candy. Andrew smiles as he gnaws on the end of a hot dog. Fluorescent-yellow mustard streaks his chin and right cheek.

"Having fun, little man?" Martin asks. The phrase hits Martin the wrong way, like a sour taste on his tongue, so he corrects it. "Having fun, pal?"

Andrew nods his head and squints into the sun. His feet dangle off the edge of the seat, swinging in delight.

The bottom of the first inning picks up with another strikeout. The next batter strides to the plate. Tall, maybe six feet five inches, and thicker than most ball players tend to be. The guy should be playing football or rugby, Martin thinks, or maybe ice hockey, if he knows how to throw a punch. The pitcher hurls the first pitch—strike, right at the knees. The next pitch comes, and the batter swings. With a piercing crack, the ball screams down the first-base line, skips off the dirt, caroms off a guard rail, and bounces into the crowd. The ball skims off half a dozen people's hands and rolls to a stop in the landing right next to Andrew's seat.

Andrew hesitates, so Martin reaches across and grabs the ball a split second before the man across the aisle does the same. The man's grip closes around Martin's left wrist. Martin stands, and he towers over his opponent. The smaller man's grip eases for a millisecond, but then squeezes even harder.

"Damned ball cracked me in the mouth," the man says. "Nearly knocked my teeth loose."

"Sorry," Martin says.

"This one's mine." The man tries to pry the ball out of Martin's hand.

Martin's fierceness takes hold. His free hand closes

around the man's throat. He squeezes. The man's eyes widen, and his grip on Martin's wrist loosens. Martin releases the chokehold.

"Asshole," the man says. He coughs, holds a hand to his throat.

The stands go quiet. Martin's eyes scan the crowd, and he can feel his face go red. A wee gray derby blends into the field of sun-scorched faces. An unseen siphon saps his energy. Vertigo turns his legs wobbly. He collapses into his seat and places the ball in his son's mitt. "Now hold onto that," he slurs.

The color drains from Andrew's face.

Andrew does not watch another pitch. His eyes, full of fear and worry, travel from his glove to the man across the aisle that Martin choked. When Andrew declines an invitation for cotton candy, Martin understands the graveness of his error. Shame builds in his gut as he realizes what he has done, right in front of his son. Dozens of other children, too.

At the start of the fourth inning, Martin turns to Andrew and says, quietly, "You want to get out of here?" Andrew hesitates for only a second but then nods furiously. Martin guides his son into the aisle and tells him to wait at the top of the staircase. He taps the shoulder of the man across the aisle and offers an apology, but the guy just waves him away without taking his eyes off the pitcher.

At the top of the staircase, Martin whispers in his son's ear.

A girl sits at the end of the aisle in the last row of Section 121. Andrew walks up to her and hands her the baseball and, to Martin's surprise, the mitt.

"My dad caught this, sort of," Andrew tells her. "You can have it."

Martin takes his son's hand on the way to the parking lot.

"Hey, Dad?"

"Yeah, bud."

"Why did that happen? The fight you had with that man?"

Martin grins and replies, "Because that gentleman and I lost sight of our priorities. Listen to me: Your dad did something silly today. Something stupid. Putting your hands on someone else is no way to solve a problem. I forgot my words."

"I'm glad we gave the ball away." Andrew pauses. "It was dirty."

"Well, you could have kept the mitt at least. And we could have cleaned the dirt off the ball when we got home, if you wanted to keep it."

Andrew wagged his head and said, "Not that kind of dirt. I would think of the fight you had every time I picked it up or even looked at it."

"I wouldn't call that a fight, pal, especially if you're telling your mother about this. Let's call it a misunderstanding."

"Whatever it was, I want to forget it."

Martin feels as though he has ruined baseball forever for his son, ruined his son forever. He has failed yet again.

"Dad?"

"Yeah, pal," Martin says, trying to hold back the tears.

"I had fun today," he says, "but I'm glad we're going home."

"Me, too, bud. Me, too."

Martin creeps out of the bedroom, toward the light emanating from the kitchen. Alison sits at the kitchen table, looking much too tired for a twenty-seven-year-old woman. The clock on the microwave suggests one a.m. will arrive in seventeen minutes. He drags a chair across the tile floor and takes a seat beside his daughter.

"I couldn't sleep either," he tells her.

She hides her face.

"Talk to me, Al."

She twists toward him and says, "I feel like such a disappointment."

"Huh. Me, too. I'm just glad you're here, so us losers outnumber your perfect mother."

"Shut up, Dad." A smile brightens her flushed face.

"Listen," he says. "The only one in this family you'll ever disappoint is yourself. Your mother and I couldn't be prouder. Same with Andrew. We're your biggest cheerleaders. I almost cried when you accepted that diploma today. My daughter, the college graduate. That's certainly more impressive than anything I've ever done."

The chair's wooden feet squeal against the kitchen tile as he pushes away from the table and goes to the cabinet.

He returns with an opened bag of Hershey's Kisses, dumps the foil-wrapped confections into a loose pile at the table's center.

"I felt like such a pretender up on that stage, a fake," Alison says. "Looking around that crowd, seeing a bunch of kids who are already two steps ahead of me because they didn't lose the time I did, I wanted to be anywhere but there, among them. I didn't feel like I *deserved* to be there. It felt like a fucking funeral."

"So, it took you a couple extra years to straighten out and get your degree. Who the fuck cares? Now take what you've learned and go do something cool with it. I have every confidence in you, always have."

"I have no idea where to go from here. Like, zero. Not like Andrew."

"Andrew had it easy."

"How can you say that? He was tortured mercilessly until the day he left here, just 'cause he was different."

"That's part of growing up. Everything your brother went through only convinced him to get the hell out of here and go someplace better. He had a beacon to lead him away. All he had to do was find the courage to follow it, and he did. People like you and me? The universe makes us work harder to get where we're supposed to go."

"I honestly didn't think I'd have to worry about it," she says. "Ten years ago, you couldn't have convinced me I'd still be here, living and breathing."

Martin gets up and wanders into the next room. Bones creak in his knees and feet. He returns with a half-empty bottle of Tanqueray and two glasses. The tumblers clink against the table's maple surface. He pours a few fingers of gin for himself. She stops him as he tries for the other glass.

"I knew you'd fight through whatever troubles had their teeth in you," he says. "Did I want to wring your neck sometimes? Sure. Did I have a few sleepless nights because of you? Absolutely. But I knew I'd catch up on my sleep sooner or later."

"I don't think I can find the words to adequately express how sorry I am for the messes I made."

"You have nothing to apologize for. The fact that we're able to sit here and talk like two civilized adults, that's a miracle. Remember some of the fights we used to have?"

"I wouldn't call those 'fights,' Dad. It was more like me screaming my head off and flailing my arms like a madwoman, while you locked me in a bearhug, trying to get me to calm down. Mom always stood on the sidelines, sobbing her eyes out."

"Well … yeah."

"Again, sorry."

"Al," he said. "Twenty-seven years ago, the day you kids were born, I knew you'd be a scrapper. Could see that spark in you even then. You dealt with everything as it came, scratching and clawing. You struggled, but you never gave up." He dipped his head and lowered his tone. "That's why you're my favorite."

"Dads always love their daughters more. The same way moms love their sons."

"I must have missed that chapter in the parenting manual." He pops another Kiss in his mouth and adds the foil to the pile gathering in front of him. "You're going to find your way just fine. You'll stumble once or twice. You'll fuck up, but that's what you're supposed to do when you're young. Then one day you'll look around and say, 'How the hell did I get *here*?' And you'll be perfectly content, happy. But guess what: You'll never stop making mistakes, even when you're an old fart like me, because you're human."

Gin fills his mouth, slicks his lips.

Alison peels the foil and brings a piece of chocolate to her lips. She bites off the nipple-like tip and places the remainder on the table.

"Christ, just look at me," he adds. "I went from slinging beers at the VFW and dodging bullets on the graveyard shift to somehow becoming director of sales for Kerfe, selling bulldozers and dump trucks to builders across the U.S. and Canada. Don't ask me how it happened, because it shouldn't have. Doors just have a way of opening up if you're paying attention. And they'll open for you, too."

"I know you went through a lot of tough times, Dad. More than anyone I've ever met. How'd you get through it all?"

"There's no magic pill, no silver bullet," he says. "The key is to become shatterproof. Life will surprise you, and sometimes it'll thrash you. You can bend, you can brood, you can take all the time you need to recover, but you cannot let it break you."

"You'll have to teach me that trick, because I've felt broken for too many years."

"But you're better now, and you'll continue to be better because of your experience. Life is a balance between darkness and light. My advice to you is to stay in the light for as long as you can, and let it become part of you. So, when the dark of night comes, because it always comes, you have the light to guide you home."

He stares into a lightless corner of the dining room, far beyond the reach of the kitchen's overhead lamp.

Alison follows his line of sight into the darkness.

"Off to bed, Al. That's all the wisdom I have to share anyway. Tomorrow will be here before you blink."

"Thanks, Dad. You always know what to say."

She rises from her chair, pats him on the head, and exits the kitchen.

Martin waits to hear the click of the lock on her bedroom door. The bulb in the overhead light dims, then flickers. His belly warms as he empties the glass of its last sip of gin. He stands and collects the few remaining Kisses in his hand, and returns them to the drawer next to the pantry. A foul smell, like that of burnt fish, finds his nose. A sound similar to the snapping of twigs comes from the darkened living room. He leans against the kitchen counter and shuts his eyes, because he dislikes the sight of shadows taking form.

CHAPTER 23

One Tragedy at a Time

Icy water massaged the crown of Jodi's head, followed the contours of her body, and spiraled down the drain. Despite the bloat in her belly from having siphoned nearly a gallon of water from the kitchen sink, she opened her mouth and took more from the showerhead.

She felt wrung out and beaten with a baton. An afternoon in the desert sun seemed to have sucked every molecule of water from her body. She should have known better, and in fact did know better. Alison had wasted no time reminding her mother of her idiocy; she laid into Jodi the moment she walked through the front door.

Slowly, Jodi turned the dial from cold to hot, then back to warm. She steadied herself against the wall, because her knees felt like they could give out.

Hugo Keczmer's words returned to her—about the winds carrying the Navajo's suffering away and returning it when they were ready to deal with it. Hugo may have been a fraud, but his words comforted her in a way she did not expect. The winds had placed this catastrophe at her feet, and she would have to deal with the days ahead regardless of whether or not she felt up to the challenge.

Her shower finished, she went to the bedroom and flopped onto the comforter. Her left arm dangled over the edge of the bed. She could have slept for hours, if only she could turn off her brain. Maybe, when they returned to the hospital to see Martin, she would ask Stephens or one of the other doctors to prescribe some sleeping pills. An hour passed before she gave up any chance of rest and went down to the kitchen.

The day's dying light cast long shadows on the kitchen floor. She lifted the teapot from the stove, happy to discover it half full, and turned on the rear burner. Roy sat at the window above the sink, eyes trained on the backyard, tail sweeping furiously at the counter ledge.

"What do you see, girl?"

Three young people—two men and one woman, none older than twenty-five—scoured the earth by the woodpile. Two more people Jodi didn't recognize shined flashlights beneath the shed. As Jodi turned toward the backdoor, a dark silhouette with a brimmed hat filled the doorway.

The hat. Pappaduffus. The Little Gray Man. He had found her.

"Hi again!"

The man lifted his hand and waved. Douglas Exelby, the venomologist.

Jodi clutched her chest and said, "Holy effing Christ!"

"Sorry to startle you." He raised both hands in apology. "Just wanted to let you know my grad students and

I are here, checking out the property for any evidence of an *H. cavestanii* infestation. We discussed this in your husband's ICU room, remember?"

"You nearly shook me out of my boots. That's not hard to do these days."

Jodi held the screen door open. "I'm putting on some tea if you'd like to come in," she said.

"Too hot for tea, isn't it?"

"Have gin for all I care," she said. "The way I was raised, if someone is kind enough to welcome you into their home, you accept. Besides, tea is never tea, just like coffee is never coffee. I want to talk to you. Now get in here."

Exelby removed his hat and tripped across the threshold. Roy leapt from the counter and scrambled for the basement.

"Any luck out there?" she asked.

"We pulled up maybe twenty minutes ago, so it's too soon to tell," he said. "Most scorpions are crepuscular, meaning they become active at twilight and feed into the night. We'll give it a few hours."

"Good luck finding the Angel of Death."

"Death angel scorpion." He paused. "How's your husband?"

"No better. Far worse, actually. They took his arm, not that it seems to have helped much."

"I heard."

"Then why did you ask?"

"Just being polite, I suppose." Another pause. "Listen: I owe you an apology. People tell me I have a knack for saying stupid things, as I'm sure you've noticed. When we first met, I got so excited about the possibility of *H. cavestanii* being right in our backyard, I probably came across as a bit of an unsympathetic jerkoff. Sometimes I lose sight of the fact that the things I study affect the lives of real people, like you and your husband."

Jodi nodded in agreement.

"Last month, when I was in Costa Rica, I nearly got into a fistfight with a guy whose daughter had to have her foot amputated because of a bite from *Lachesis stenophrys*, a Central American bushmaster. Beautiful snake—my favorite, in fact—so I just couldn't fathom why this gentleman didn't want to talk about it. Then he let me know in no uncertain terms that he'd had enough of my nonsense."

Jodi had no trouble envisioning Exelby with his back to the wall and someone else's blade pressed to his throat.

"One of my instructors in medical school once told me I missed out on the empathy gene," he added. "Naturally, I went into research, studying animals rather than humans."

"Don't worry yourself, dear," she said as she prepared the tea. "I know you didn't mean anything by it. Honestly, I feel indebted to you for giving me an explanation of what happened to Martin. Better than anyone else at that butcher shop of a hospital, at least."

"If it means anything at all, I have a good idea of what you're going through. Two years ago, I spent two weeks at a hospital in Tempe, watching my father take his final breaths. Cancer, of course, because everyone dies of cancer these days. Now, every time I step foot into a medical building of any sort, I feel the same pall of dread all over again."

Jodi poured two cups of tea and set them on the

kitchen table. She nudged the fuller cup toward Exelby's hand.

"I'm no stranger to hospitals," she said. "Birthing the twins—that was a big one. My husband had both knees and a shoulder replaced. I'm used to the tedium of waiting rooms and uninspired hospital food." She could have mentioned Martin's recuperations, after the shooting and the bear mauling, but doing so seemed like bragging. "I guess it's different when you're there to watch someone die. Right, Mister Sunshine?"

Jodi enjoyed antagonizing Exelby, and he seemed to think he deserved the ribbing. They had as much chemistry as two strangers could have. In truth, she was thankful to have human company other than her daughter.

"Exelby," she continued, "can you tell me where Martin goes from here? The doctors don't seem to know."

"The Pac-Man analogy comes to mind. You're a bit older than I am—"

"Kind of you to remind me."

"I didn't mean to suggest—"

"You're too easy, Exelby." She smiled at her ability to make him uncomfortable. "Tell me what you were going to say. I'll shut up."

"So, Pac-Man, the video game. Pac-Man moves around his pixelated maze, gobbling up pellets and trying to evade the ghosts who want to do him in. *H. cavestanii* venom is like Pac-Man, and it's going to keep eating and trying to outfox the ghosts—in this case, the body's immune system— until it has cleared every pellet from the gameboard."

"And what are the 'pellets' in Martin's case?"

"Nerves, muscles, cells—the architecture of his body."

Alison stomped down the stairs and into the kitchen, likely eager to give her mother another earful of vitriol as punishment for her misadventure in the desert.

"Oh," Alison said, surprised to find her mother sitting at the table with a stranger. Exelby stood to greet her.

"Alison, this is Douglas Exelby, a doctor from your dad's hospital. Well, he's sort of a doctor. Exelby, this is Alison, my daughter."

"Hi there," Alison added and left abruptly.

"Don't mind her," Jodi told Exelby. "She's been having a tough time."

"Been there." He looked around the rustic kitchen—scuffed cabinets, cracks in the ceiling, cobwebs in the highest corners. "I guess I'm obligated to say you have a nice home."

"It's a work in progress, but at least it's quiet. I used to be a bit of a social butterfly, but living out here has taught me how awful and annoying and useless most people are. I've gone back to Phoenix once or twice to meet with the few friends I still care to see, but that list keeps getting shorter and shorter. You can make a small life very satisfying if you put in the effort."

"I couldn't live out this way. Too dull and remote for me."

"I like you, Exelby. You're a complete idiot, and you don't even know it."

They laughed together.

"Well," he said, "thanks for the tea."

"You haven't touched yours."

He lifted the cup and drained it. "Happy?"

"About Martin, my husband. I appreciate you leveling with me. I know how difficult it can be to tell the truth, especially when it involves bad news."

He pursed his lips and nodded in understanding.

"We're heading back to the hospital in an hour or so," she added. "I'll keep the back door unlocked in case you or your students need to use the restroom. You're welcome to anything in the pantry or the fridge—anything that hasn't gone sour, stale, or rotten, anyway. If you do come in, just mind the cat. She's always pawing at the door, wanting freedom she wouldn't know what to do with if she got it. I don't have to tell you, of all people, why we don't want her prowling around outside. If anything happened to my Roy Boy, I'd pitch myself into the nearest rattlesnake den and end it all."

"We'll stick to the home's exterior, ma'am, but I appreciate the hospitality. I'll let you know if we find any trace of *H. cavestanii.* The last thing I would want is for you or your daughter, or your cat, to suffer the same fate as your husband."

"Whatever you do, safety first. One tragedy at a time is all I can stand."

After she escorted Exelby out the back door, Jodi sighed as she looked around the bedraggled kitchen—so much dusting and cleaning and tidying up to do. All of it would have to wait for another day. She hoped to leave for Tuba City before sunset so she could find the route back to the hospital without her eyeglasses. She padded into the hallway and lifted her smartphone from the basket atop the console table. The screen suggested she had a missed call from Andrew and three others from an unfamiliar caller in Tuba City. Her voicemail inbox showed three messages waiting. Her fingers shook as she pressed the button to play the first message.

"Alison!" she screamed. "We have to leave now!"

CHAPTER 24

Penitence and Punishment
in the City of Big Shoulders

The ornate spire looms among scores of two-flats and other squat buildings as Martin cuts through the tangle of Chicago cross-streets. Cool spring air pours through the half-open driver-side window and fills the car's interior. He trains his eyes on the road, mostly, but his gaze keeps wandering to the spire's million-dollar gold cross, seeming to glow against the backdrop of baby-blue sky.

His meeting at Kerfe's headquarters office in hardscrabble Cicero ended early, so he has a few hours to kill before heading back to Chicago Midway. If he's going to do this, he might as well do it here, far from home, far from anyone who knows him—and, hopefully, far from the reach of Pappaduffus. He makes a right without using his blinker and circles the church twice before finding a spot on a side street. His rented Charger idles as an old woman with bluish-gray hair, her salvation having been granted, eases her Cadillac battleship out of its spot and veers into oncoming traffic, nearly decapitating a bearded dude on an all-black-and-chrome Harley.

She's made it this far, he supposes, so what does she have to gain by being careful now?

Martin kills the ignition and considers what he might possibly say to anyone inside Saint Faustina's who might have the patience to offer a way out of his dilemma. As far as he knows, anything he might say to a priest or any other "man of God" is private and confidential, barring criminality, almost as if any conversation between the two never even happened.

Confident in his words, Martin exits the car and lopes up a flight of weathered concrete stairs. He tests two locked doors before discovering the twin oak doors that bid him inside. The familiar smell hits him immediately. Peppery, throat-closing incense fills his core with feelings of powerlessness and wrongdoing. He has not stepped foot inside a Catholic church in nearly a decade, for good reason. He tiptoes around the outer aisles and takes a seat in a pew toward the rear left, familiarizing himself with the church's interior and guessing where certain things ought to be. Older men and women, mostly women—all in their seventies, eighties, or nineties, all awaiting the liberation of death—crowd the first five or six pews. Some pray to lit candles. Some sit silently, staring at Christ on his cross. Others chat quietly, to themselves or their neighbors. Martin figures each of them has come here seeking absolution for a sinner's life.

Or, like him, they seek answers to mysteries surrounding the nature of good and evil.

Above the thin wooden door built into the wall on his

right, a small red light in the shape of a stubby cross blinks out. An old woman in a long gray overcoat waddles out of the confessional, and the door creaks to a close behind her. She looks Czech or Russian, vaguely eastern European. Another woman dressed in almost the same manner takes her place, as if on a conveyor belt. He considers for a second that he might be caught in some weird loop.

A procession of elderly women, and a few men, come and go in their quest to reconcile with God. He catches himself being judgmental, realizing every human sought the same thing: comfort amid fear, reassurance amid uncertainty. While some find what they look for at the bottom of a bottle, others make their way here.

He will leave no stone unturned.

He crosses the center aisle and squats into the opposite pew, sweeping his rear end along the smooth wood until he reaches its outer edge. Without trying to eavesdrop, he catches whispers of conversation from inside the confessional. The priest, he figures, is busy granting another batty old bird the quickest route into the light of God's infinite grace. A full five minutes pass—he counts them off—before the red light above the door goes dark again, and another twenty seconds tick by before the penitent woman inside can bless her forehead, turn around, and fiddle the door open. He stands and grabs the door's edge just as she creaks it open, pretending to hold it for her. She gives a surprised "Oh!" as she sees him, and shuffle-steps backward. Her jowls flop with her rocking movements, and the crater-like pocks in her ancient cheeks seem to deepen.

"So sorry, ma'am," he mouths. He ducks into the

confessional before she can smite him with some sort of primeval Slavic hex. As he eases the door to a close, a soft lightbulb fizzles to life overhead.

Surreal, he thinks, as he considers the closet-sized room. The peppery incense intensifies in this place he is tempted to call a punishment room. He smiles uneasily, though not sure why. He eyes the kneeler, which is covered in a nubby material not unlike worn felt. It doesn't seem right to kneel, considering his loose beliefs, so he squats and struggles to get comfortable. Muscles and ligaments burn with a familiar strain. Things have begun to wear and tear inside him, right down to the bone.

The occupant of the other half of the confessional slides a panel across to expose a brown honeycombed slit. Through the honeycomb Martin sees the suggestion of an aging man—not old, but no longer young—with a thick lawn of finely coiffed hair, tamed by a fine-toothed comb slick with pomade. His frosted gray sideburns and freshly shaven face suggest the paternity and kindness of a man skilled at putting Band-Aids on skinned knees. A foot-long crucifix hangs on the wall beside him, its tacked-to-the-wood Jesus looking gruesome. The sight of it reminds Martin of his childhood, and makes him wonder, if it's all true and Jesus endured the agony and indignity to save humankind, has the Son of God ever had second thoughts? Regrets, even?

Martin has not been this close to a priest since the one came to his childhood home in Oregon after Pappaduffus revealed himself to his family in the kitchen. It takes him a moment to realize the priest is speaking to him.

"Son," the priest says, "can I help you with

something?"

The priest's curtness belies his fatherly appearance. Then again, Martin remembers, his own father wasn't exactly a paragon of warmth and civility either.

"I think I'm supposed to say it's been a while since my last confession," Martin says finally.

Martin's father was Catholic, though his father did not care enough to send him to Catholic school or take him to church on Sundays. His mother had no faith, so neither did Martin. On the few weekends he slept over the house of his childhood friend Frank McGoldrick, Martin accompanied the family to Sunday morning Mass. The experience made Martin think he might one day become Catholic, but something always came up.

"That's fine," the priest barks. "Your sins?"

Again, curt and annoyed, just like dear old Dad. Martin feels eight years old again. His backside burns as if lashed by a belt—muscle memory, he supposes.

"That's not really why I'm here, Father."

The priest sighs.

"I was hoping for an informed opinion," Martin says.

The priest squints through the honeycomb.

"I've lived a kind and decent enough life, but—"

"Everybody thinks they've lived a kind and decent enough life," the priest interrupts. "The world would be a better place if they were right."

"Well, see—"

"Say two Our Fathers and two Hail Marys. Your sins are forgiven. Try to do better."

"Thank you, Father, I think. No, see—"

Another sigh.

"Father?"

"Yeah."

"Something's wrong with me. I've been cursed."

"Come again?"

"I'm not doing this right."

"No, you're not."

"Sorry. I'm not exactly the religious sort."

The priest brays three coughs of laughter that suggest, "Why me?" Martin imagines the priest has already had a long day, and now *this* is sitting in front of him.

"Let me cut to the chase," Martin says.

"By all means."

"So … do you … do you believe in demons?"

The priest leans forward, directly beneath the light, and presses his nose into the lattice separator. Springs squeal and soft wood groans beneath him.

"Demons," he repeats. "You want to know if I believe in demons. *That's* what this is about?"

"Yes. You know. Demons."

"Jesus Christ."

This can't be good, Martin thinks.

The priest backs away from the lattice, his face bathed in shadow. He makes a noise that makes Martin thinks he's laughing or choking.

"Father? You all right over there?"

"I don't know what you expected to gain by coming here." The priest's voice sounds gravelly, pained. "Best to open the door and head home, back to where you belong."

A new smell tamps down the smell of incense. It

smells like fish … and *burning.*

"I don't want to be here, in this wreck of a place, any more than you do, Martin. Now run along like a good boy and get back to doing what you were put on this earth to do."

"Did I tell you my name?" Martin asks. Of course he hadn't.

"You've tried this once before. At least your old man did, the rotten sadist. Or was it the wife he used as a punching bag who made the call? Whole lot of good it did you— nothing but a skinned backside and the death of your parents' marriage. I thought you had more sense than this, dear boy."

The tip of a tentacle-like arm caresses the delicate honeycomb. The brim of Pappaduffus's derby catches the dim yellow light. His eyes, little more than white-hot pinpricks, burn through the darkness.

"You try something like this again, and I'll come for *her*, Martin. Understand me? I will take her, break her, and tear her to pieces—two, threes, fours, too many bits to count. You think you know pain now, boy? Imagine coming home to find her scattered across the house like the pieces of a jigsaw puzzle, never to be put back together again."

Martin grasps the doorknob and turns, but the door does not budge. The temperature seems to rise twenty degrees. Sweat soaks through his shirt. His throat threatens to close.

"I should do just that, you know," Pappaduffus seethes. "It would only serve my cause, and it would help you too, dear boy. Imagine how powerful you would become to be free of her."

Martin puts his back to the wall, bracing, and thrusts

his heel into the door's center. The door splits down the middle. One half clatters to the floor, nearly bulldozing an old man and his walker. Martin stumbles through the opening and faceplants on the polished marble. As he struggles to get his feet beneath him, he ducks his head and hurries for the exit.

The sound of Pappaduffus's cackling echoes throughout the church.

Martin beams as he nears the highway exit, because he knows he will soon be at peace, beyond the manmade constraints of walls, windows, and doors.

The simple joy of a traffic-free road on a cold and clear morning makes him grateful for the invention of sunlight, the presence of which means he has made it to another day. Unremarkable miles pass without protest. He likes the openness of the Midwest—boring and almost post-apocalyptic, a sanctuary worthy of his time and spent gallons of gasoline.

He steers his rented SUV off the highway and passes through a small town, seemingly abandoned. The vehicle's passenger-side tires shudder across the rumble strip. The last time he saw this place, Starved Rock State Park, leather-vested bikers and families shared space outside a roadside dairy stand, everyone looking happy and care-free, eating ice cream and sucking down bottles of frosty root beer. It was summer then. Now, in winter, the dormant landscape looks withered and dead. The road curves to the left and then sharply to the right, one serpentine after another. He turns a final corner and angles the car into the parking lot. Only six cars dot the frozen grid, including a red Audi that seems to have spent all winter in a garage, and a forest-green Jeep with a dented driver-side door and bumper stickers papering every inch of the tailgate not obscured by the spare tire: Soundgarden, NIN, Black Sabbath, an American flag that has cracked and begun to flake away, "Hike," "Coexist," "Be Kind."

During his last visit here, on a Friday afternoon from the prior June, more than a hundred cars, SUVs, and motorcycles crowded the lot, each outfitted with a rooftop kayak, a bike carrier, a strongbox filled with summertime playthings, or some other outdoorsy adornment. Memories made during warmer days, from happier times, scrolled through Martin's mind. Parents pushing toddlers in Fisher-Price fire engines. Teenagers riding motorized ATVs, wind combing their hair. Finches and wrens chirp-chirp-chirping on low-hanging branches. Fathers and sons tossing footballs and baseballs. Barefooted college-age dirtballs winging Frisbees or juggling Hacky Sacks to the soundtrack of Baez, Cohen, Dylan, and Guthrie strummed on an acoustic. Dirty little boys turning over rocks in streambeds, terrorizing crayfish and salamanders. Lovers reading books of poetry on quilted blankets in the high grass. Dogs on leashes everywhere, tongues lolling. Extended families cooking over rock-lined barbecue pits, the smell of sizzling pork wafting for miles. Perfect nuclear families, smiling kids and their parents, a few grandparents, all looking as if they understood the point of being alive.

No trace of any of that now, in the dead of winter.

Starved Rock State Park has become a regular stop on his twice-yearly tour of Chicago to visit his company's HQ just outside the city limits. It's his first visit in the middle of winter, early February, and the temperature hovers around the twenty-degree mark. In summer, people came to enjoy the view and bask in the sunshine. In winter, they came for different reasons: to forget, or to swim in the pain of remembering people or things they lost.

Martin realizes there is another reason to venture to a natural wonder far from civilization: to murder things with shotguns, crossbows, and razor-edged knives. Martin is no hunter, but he has come to slay something, too: the parasite within. He just hopes it can be slain, or that he has the courage to snuff it out.

He puts the SUV in park and removes the ignition key. He expels a deep breath and closes his eyes to prepare for the shock of cold. No matter how many layers he has on, it will not matter. Midwestern winters always find a way in, right down to the bone. He counts down from three and pulls the door handle. Icy knives rush in, slicing through his jeans, his flannel shirt, his wool socks, even his North Face jacket. He does not mind. At least he feels something.

He scales a hill of frozen earth, over tread marks in the mud long since fossilized. His feet bounce around in his pale-brown boots, his bones absorbing the impact of each step. He should have worn a second pair of socks. Punishment, he thinks, and he deserves every knuckle of it.

He follows the incline, not reading the few remaining signs, until he finds himself at the top of the first peak.

Memories of better times come flooding back—either with Jodi, or with Jodi and the kids, though Jodi is the constant. Visions of lazy afternoons with Jodi, his arms cradling her body, her sandy hair whipping his face, not saying anything, just letting the world blow over them as clouds passed overhead. Blood warms his body as he savors the quiet times, when he was unbothered by obstacles, most of them involving Pappaduffus.

Seasons came and went. People died. Empires collapsed and were replaced by well-meaning revolutionaries. He finds himself staring at a promontory overlooking the river, icy and barren, and imagines lying beside Jodi on a bed of pine needles. Far below, the mostly frozen Illinois River creaks and cracks. Crooked sheets of ice plod downriver, crackling as if on fire. As he stares, the broken ice sheets seem to align, forming a colossal face with demonic eyes and a jagged seam of a mouth—the gateway to an icy grave. A faint but distinct shriek of ragged laughter cuts through the whistling wind.

No escape, it tells him.

He sighs as he proceeds up the staircase, itself sheathed in ice and sprinkled with rocks of gray salt. He steps carefully, his calves burning, until he reaches the landing for the top platform—named for something about eagles, he remembers. Eagle's Peak or Eagle's Nest or Eagle's Point or maybe something not related to eagles at all, something along the lines of Alpine Terrace or Lookout Bluffs. The name does not matter. Someone removed the sign: a park ranger, perhaps, or a determined vandal.

He then reaches the top of the world, considering flat-as-a-glass-sheet Illinois. He longs to let it all go, all the weight, all the pain, every bad thing that has ever happened. If only he could push a button or swallow a pill or click his heels to make it all fade away. He does not mind remembering the bad things—the shit. The good memories—those are the ones that hurt, because he knows he will never return to them. At fifty-eight years old, memories and pictures are all he has left, and both fade just a little every day.

Martin plants himself on the nearest bench. The cold bites through three layers and sinks its teeth into his rear end. He sits there, frozen to the bench, the wind boring holes through the pores of his knit hat and into his skull. His ears ache. He sits and does nothing but think.

His brain takes him nowhere productive, dragging him back into the morass, attempting to solve the problem that has gone unsolved for decades. All talk aside, he would gladly drive a screwdriver into his temporal lobe if it might push him in the right direction.

"Phillips head or straight?" he asks himself, smiling.

He abhors this self-pity, though he supposes he is entitled, considering the malevolent parasite that has tormented him for most of his life. He will leave it here, this misery, so it does not follow him back to the real world. Back to Jodi.

An hour passes, maybe longer, and he will stay put until his misery's appetite gets its fill. It eats so much sometimes, sinking him deeper into despair. Real men are not supposed to have these kinds of problems. Real men are not supposed to feel anything. No room for mourning.

His peripheral vision catches the hint of movement in the open space to his left. A hawk or falcon or some other magnificent raptor soars on an updraft. He feels sick for it, out there, floating a half-mile above the river on a cushion of air, with nothing below but empty space and, far below that, a frozen landlocked sea. He considers the immense risk of flight, given the assurance of death if the natural laws suddenly come undone. Countless numbers of fledglings have fallen to their ruin by testing boundaries before their time. Might he join them?

The raptor fades to a speck in the endless gray sky. Wisps of snow fall from the clouds and dapple his shoulders. At least he has company now, he thinks. He pulls his hat down to cover his frost-pricked earlobes. His nose and cheeks have gone numb.

Life out here, he begins to understand, does not exist. No problems, no urgencies, no blame to be cast, no cause for hurt. This place is reserved solely for pause and reflection, spending time alone to work out all the kinks. Up here, on the roof of Illinois, he sees himself dreaming again, an end to the nightmare. The scene reminds him of a not-long-ago trip to Acadia National Park in Maine, stark and simple, just shy of perfect.

The wind whistles between cracks in the floorboards. It sounds alive, as if trying to tell him something important. He wonders, what would the wind say? "Go piss up a rope," perhaps. "Stop being such a wuss, all this Pappaduffus business, and get on with your goddamn life," maybe. A common refrain, one that has been stuck on repeat for too many years. Even the wind does not understand the depth of his predicament. He knows how stupid and self-important his thoughts would sound to a stronger person, a sane person.

A test, Martin determines. He climbs the guardrail and leans into the wind, his weight and strength versus the unstoppable force of nature. The edge of the two-inch-by-four-inch railing digs into his shins as he hovers above the frozen plain a quarter-mile below. Beyond the plywood barrier, an outcropping of boulders bleached white with bird feces—black vultures, most likely—stands between him and the void.

He sees something else down there, clawing its way out of the river's churn. At first, he dismisses it as his eyes playing tricks. Slowly, the object's edges sharpen. Its silhouette takes shape. Pappaduffus clambers up the cliff's steep face. At the base of the outcropping, he doffs his derby in recognition. He should be soaking wet, with icicles dangling from his nose and chin, but his clothes are bone dry.

"What now?" Martin asks. "What else do you want from me?"

Martin's life has come to a standstill. He is sick of being stuck, trapped by Pappaduffus, but cannot figure out how to get unstuck, or how to free himself from the jaws of his tormentor's trap. If he cannot solve the problem, then someone, or something, would need to make up his mind for him so he can get on with it already.

He will let the wind decide.

He leans out farther, the wood digging deeper into his shinbones, and the wind pushes back. Maybe it does care after all, he thinks. The wind weakens for a second, and he tumbles forward. His gloved hand grabs the rail's edge to keep from hurtling to sure death. As his grip slips, his body goes end over end. His foot catches the rocky outcropping just past the guardrail, stabilizing. He laughs—actually *laughs*—but the sound turns into something between a sob and a cry of pain.

"What are you doing, boy?" Pappaduffus asks. He hovers in the open space, maybe ten feet distant from the rocky ledge. "Sometimes I think all you want to do is give your old friend Mister Pappaduffus reason to worry."

"You couldn't care less what happens to me."

"Pish posh. Oh, how I wish you would stop telling yourself such terrible stories. If not for me, then consider the woman you decided to marry. Consider the progeny you fathered."

Pappaduffus's words remind Martin of everything he has to lose. His heart pounds through layers of cotton and synthetic fiber.

"Don't do it," says another voice, this one farther off.

The wind, Martins wonders.

He grips a rocky handhold and climbs back over the rail until his boots touch the wooden platform. He rests his backside on a patch of rock-salted ice.

"You all right, fella," says the voice again.

A man in rust-colored coveralls stands at the top of the staircase. A green emblem shows on the left breast: park ranger.

Shit.

"Yeah," says Martin, out of breath. "Just a little slippery is all."

Shit. Shit.

"Right," says the ranger. "Slippery."

The wind speaks between them. To Martin, each gust sounds like a hurled insult.

"Why don't you come down with me, pal?" the ranger says. He takes two steps forward.

"I'm fine, promise. Be along in a few minutes."

"I'm going to have to insist, sir."

Shit. Shit. Shit.

Martin feels the weight of his own shame. He ducks his head and approaches the ranger, fully expecting to be tackled, shackled, and hauled off to the nearest nuthouse. On the way down the icy stairs, he wants one more look at the chasm before being dragged away in a straitjacket.

Just one more look.

No sign of Pappaduffus.

The ranger waits at the bottom of the first landing, looking up.

"Hell of a day, huh?" he says.

"Sounds about right," Martin replies.

Martin hurries past with his head lowered. Snot drips from the tip of his nose. He checks over his shoulder to see the ranger standing with a hand on the railing leading up to Eagle's Peak or Eagle's Point or Eagle's Nest or Eagle's Suicide Leap or whatever its proper name is. Martin smiles, feeling as if he has gotten away with something.

Ten minutes later he stands at the driver side of the rented Ford Explorer, its exterior wearing a film of road salt. He pats down his pockets, wondering where he put the key. Finally, he locates it in the zippered pocket on his chest. As he seals himself inside his rental car, the leather seat crinkles as if frozen. Ice crystals coat the wrong side of the windshield. His brain asks the question: Why has he come this far, out to the frozen desert of Starved fucking Rock? To kill himself. Not really, but maybe to try on the idea and see if Pappaduffus would let him get away with it. The correct answer: He has come to convince himself he still has something to live for. He realizes he has more than most, almost too much.

Anger wells within him. He does not want this turmoil, any of it. He wants only to be free of it because it has done him no good so far. But the brain is too insistent. Or maybe it is his heart—not the muscled-up organ, but the one of love songs and poems about grief, pain, and lips never to be kissed. Or perhaps it is Pappaduffus, trying to keep Martin's feet rooted to the earth. Whatever it is, it still wants to work him over for a little while longer.

"Cry, dammit," he pleads. "Fucking cry."

He takes the steering wheel in both hands. Leather groans in his grip, and his bare knuckles turn white. He wants to rip the leather right from the wheel and gnaw on it, maybe strangle someone with it, but his wants mean little to the world. The wheel does not break or budge or tear, his outburst useless. His anger passes a moment later, leaving him spent and worthless.

The phone buzzes in his pocket: an incoming call from Jodi, quickly accepted.

"Where the hell have you been?" she asks. "I've been trying to reach you for an hour or more."

"What's wrong?"

"Nothing's *wrong*, really. Just wanted to say hey. I

miss your face."

He laughs. "My face misses you back."

"You're coming home tomorrow, right?"

"Funny you say that. I'm on my way to the airport right now, as it turns out. Hoping to catch an earlier flight."

He has no reason to shed a tear for the trials he has been given.

The engine growls and grumbles as Martin backs the Explorer out of its spot. The wheels dodge disks of frozen ice as the SUV makes its way out of the lot. Tires trudge through slush and wet gravel, and then peel out as they find dry asphalt, leading him back to Chicago, back to Midway.

Back to Phoenix.

Back to Jodi and the life they have built.

CHAPTER 25

Turning to Dust

Paarush Mehta, M.D., yammered away, wasting precious time on what Jodi considered small talk: if she was feeling anxious or depressed, if she was getting enough sleep, if she was taking a daily multivitamin. As the doctor droned on, Jodi's eyes studied Martin's inert mass. He looked fine—or, if not fine, at least unchanged since she had seen him last—despite the urgency of the messages the hospital staff left for her.

Then Doctor Mehta dropped the bomb.

"His heart stopped."

"He had a heart attack?"

"Not exactly. An interruption of the heart's electrical system. Truth is, we don't know why, but likely it's a consequence of the venom. Your husband is showing signs of advanced heart failure. That means his heart cannot pump enough blood to do what the body requires of it, and that's causing secondary problems, like the edema. You've noticed the swelling in his legs, of course. The good news, at least for now, is that he responded to resuscitation."

Jodi collapsed at Martin's side and took his hand—his *remaining* hand—in hers.

Doctor Mehta seemed like a kind man, but Jodi wished Stephens had been there to deliver the news. Stephens had an imperfect bedside manner and failed to save Martin's arm, but he also got right to the point, often without tact. Besides, Stephens had been with her since the start of this ordeal, and she believed in continuity.

"I'm afraid there's more," Mehta added. "Your husband seems to be in the latter stages of renal failure. His heart may respond to medication and further treatment—another round of ultrafiltration, possibly—but to me the kidneys present a greater challenge."

"Dialysis," Jodi said. "Will dialysis help?"

Her father had spent the final eight months of his life on thrice-weekly dialysis treatments, though he despised each one. Or so her mother told her, because he never talked to Jodi about it, never grumbled about his fear, pains, or concerns. In the end, the therapy could not keep him alive long enough for a donor transplant—no second chances for him.

"Dialysis may help to some degree," Mehta said. "The damage to the kidneys is severe and, in your husband's case, likely irreversible. Even in the unlikely event that your husband does regain consciousness, he will not have an easy road."

"Take one of mine," she said. "He can have one of my kidneys."

Mehta shook his head as if he had heard something ridiculous.

"Ma'am, even if your tissues are compatible, I do not see your husband as a candidate for a transplant at this point."

"I'm confused. Doctor Stephens said the amputation would help. He wasn't the only one who thought so."

"The infection is still working its way out of the body. Your husband's arm needed to be excised no matter what. Yes, the body is healthier for having shed the diseased limb, because it gives his body a chance to keep fighting, but …"

Jodi noted his hesitation, his inability to let his eyes meet hers.

"But what?"

"He is not likely to wake up."

"Like … ever?"

"No, ma'am. I do not believe so."

A scream built in her chest but got caught in her throat. She wanted to put her fist through a pane of glass. Wanted to tell Stephens and Mehta and the rest of the ICU staff their medical degrees were worth as much as dog shit smeared on a slab of cardboard. Wanted to destroy the whole damned building. Instead, she said, meekly, "Our options?"

"Only one that I see," Mehta said. "Dialysis, as you noted, to see where that takes us, along with cardiac care to sustain the heart. Another round of ultrafiltration will address the edema, but that's a short-term fix. Maybe another year of life for your husband, maybe less. Or we forgo dialysis and let things play out."

"*Play out*," she repeated.

"Yes, ma'am."

"Let him die, you mean."

"He will expire, yes."

"Your best advice is to let my husband die."

"I did not say that, ma'am, but it is an option."

"Would he have a peaceful death?"

"Some say."

"Will you please give me one straight answer, goddammit! Look at my husband! Look at everything he's gone through! Look at where listening to you people has gotten us!"

Her foot connected with a spin stool. The stool glided across the room, crashed against the wall, and toppled. A rogue wheel skittered along the tile.

"I understand this is difficult, ma'am."

"Difficult, yes. Thank you so fucking much for understanding how fucking difficult this whole fucking shitshow has been."

Hugo's words returned to her. Was it her duty to suffer now, just as Martin had suffered so long without complaint?

"You want me to do nothing and let him die?" she said. "Fine, let him die. And put me out of my misery, too, while you're at it."

<hr>

The notes of a Muzak version of "You Don't Bring Me Flowers" drifted from the overhead speakers in the ICU waiting area. Jodi sat on the edge of the chair and cried. Alison held her tightly.

"Nothing's for certain, Mom. Dad has surprised us

before, right?"

Jodi wiped the tears from her eyes. She was sick of crying.

"What am I doing here? I'm useless, pointless. Your dad deserves better."

"Can we get him out of here? Transfer him to a better hospital, in Phoenix? You can stay with me."

"The geniuses here say he wouldn't survive the trip. For once, I think they're right."

Jodi supposed she should start thinking about what life might look like "after." Given the likely ridiculous price tag associated with Martin's care, and the siphoning effect on their savings, becoming her daughter's roommate was a logical option. As was selling the house in Crum. Even so, she would find an alternative if and when the time came. She loved Alison dearly, but the two of them quarreled like banshees even on their best days.

"The kindest thing a parent can do for their children is stay out of their way," she said. "That's as true today as it was when you were seven."

Alison insisted, but Jodi held up her hand as if the argument were not worth having. "All the Avec-Georges women I've met are strong and resolute, as are the women in my family," she said. "I'll be fine in Crum, no matter what."

"Mom, think of how lonely you'll be in that big ol' farmhouse. I mean, if Dad …"

"I love the people you and your brother became— independent, fierce, unique," Jodi added. "At the risk of sounding boastful, you got those qualities from me. I've spent most of my life by myself anyway. Truth is your dad was often someplace else even when he was home."

Jodi took Alison's silence as understanding.

"No offense to your father, dear, but sometimes I prefer being alone. The problem with the world these days is too many people haven't taken the time to find out who they are. I know who I am."

"Do you think he's in pain?"

"Seeing your father in that bed, it's the most peaceful I've seen him since we were teenagers."

Jodi paused for a moment, as if to take in her surroundings. Some internal mechanism told her to commit each moment to memory, down to the finest detail—her untied shoelace, the scuffmarks on the wainscoting, the uninspired wall paintings of woven blankets and potsherds, the desiccated insects turning to dust in the overhead light panels—to remember Martin's final days on the earth so she could return to them later.

"Your father," she began. "I don't know what else to do."

"Have ... have you prayed?"

Jodi wrinkled her brow at the suggestion.

"Have *you*?" she asked. "We didn't raise you kids to pray."

"I have a mind of my own, you know. Years ago, with everything I went through, I tried anything that would help me find answers, give me comfort. Prayer helped. It still helps, sometimes."

"Honey, I wouldn't know where to begin."

Olivia Leary, the head ICU nurse, hurried toward the waiting area, barking into her cellphone. The urgency in her voice struck Jodi, because the whole floor had been deathly quiet since the day Martin ended up in the ICU.

"Do *not* let them up here. … I don't care what he's *suspected* of doing. … The patient's barely conscious. … They can apprehend him the second he leaves the ICU, for all I care, but not a moment sooner."

Nurse Leary offered a reassuring smile as she passed them and slipped through the double doors leading to the ICU. Her insistent words became duller with each step.

"Sounds like we're not the only ones having a shitty day," Alison said.

Jodi sniffed back the wetness trickling from her nose and added, "Shitty is an understatement. It's not like this day could get any fucking worse."

***

Jodi supposed Alison was right. Neither prayer nor positivity could hurt Martin's chances of pulling through. An hour later she took the stairs to the first floor and entered the chapel— the so-called nuclear option. Empty, quiet, and tranquil, though poorly lit, the chapel had six pews on the left and six on the right, bisected by a center aisle. She walked down the aisle and sat in the second pew, because she figured she did not deserve a seat right up front. She closed her eyes and thought: *Here goes nothing.*

"I don't think we've spoken before, but if we have, it wasn't a particularly memorable conversation," she began. "We might as well be strangers, you and me. I wasn't even sure where to go to say what I have to say, thinking I might get a better signal in an honest-to-goodness church, synagogue, or some other house of worship, not some dingy chapel in a second-rate hospital. But if you are all knowing and all seeing, like they say, then I suppose my longitude and latitude don't really matter.

"And if you are what they say you are, the master and maker of all things, you know why I'm here. My husband, Martin Avec-Georges, born in Eugene, Oregon, now a resident of Crum, Arizona, a man who right now is unconscious and fighting for his life in a hospital bed one floor above. At least I hope he's still fighting.

"I've had to say goodbye to parents, pets, friends, but I could handle those losses. This one will be different. Martin has suffered his whole life—sixty-something years of blood and tears. Too much for one person. Now he's had to give up his arm, not that it seems to have done him any good. If you're as powerful and forgiving as they say, you can stop what he's going through. You can wake him up. Hell, you can probably turn back the clock as if none of this ever happened, as if all this has been the worst kind of bad dream.

"I don't mean to sound flippant, and if you love me and know me as well as my daughter insists you do, you already know who I am and accept me, warts and all. So, please. Please. Stop this war raging inside him. Do what's best for Martin. He's already lost a limb. Give it back, if you can, or at least give him—give both of us—the strength to carry on. If not, ease his pain. Stop his suffering. Don't let *us* suffer anymore. His daughter, Alison. His son, Andrew. Spare them the pain of seeing their father die slowly, one piece at a time, one day at a time, like I did with my dad.

"I don't want to lose Martin, but take him if you must, in the gentlest way possible. If you have something else in mind because it's your way of being mysterious or whatever, I'm sorry, but you can go fuck yourself."

She opened her eyes, and looked around the chapel to make sure no one had entered and, more to the point, no one had heard.

"I hope you've been listening. I hope I haven't been blubbering to an empty cloud this whole time. Please give Martin more time, and the right kind of it. Heal him. If he lives through this but ends up as an invalid who has to spend the rest of his days drooling into his lap and wishing for a merciful death, I swear I'll do him the kindness of ending it for him."

She waited a beat.

"And then I'll find a way to come for you, you hardhearted son of a bitch."

CHAPTER 26

A More Permanent Option

Martin flicks on his turn signal and eases off the gas. His car squeals to a stop in front of a shop called The Wild and Gentle Earth. Rusted iron vines wreathe the aging sign above the door. He closes his eyes and concentrates, to ascertain whether he can feel Pappaduffus's presence. He feels nothing but a faint burning in his right side, likely an aftereffect of last night's frybread.

He drove toward The Wild and Gentle Earth twice before, but each time he kept driving as he got closer because he felt Pappaduffus lingering. He will not let this opportunity go to waste.

He hurries inside the store to find two women talking at the counter. The clerk at the register has short brown hair, khakis an inch or two too short, and a button-down blue shirt with an alligator stitched into the left breast. She looks normal—kind and motherly. The customer, on the other hand, has long graying hair and a sari-like dress, long and flowing, a silver ring on every finger. She fits the part. The two women laugh as Martin paces the aisles. He coughs to make sure the clerk knows he is waiting. Finally, the woman in the sari departs.

"Let me know if you need help with anything," the clerk says from behind the register.

He hurries to the counter and begins, "This may sound crazy."

She smiles and adds, "I'm listening."

He expels a breath, and the words come easily. He tells her about Pappaduffus, a creature that has spent decades feeding on his misery, since he first saw the Little Gray Man hovering outside the window of his childhood bedroom in Oregon. Her straight-faced expression does not falter. He explains that he has come to her for solutions, to see if she can somehow help him sever the link between him and this otherworldly creature.

"Dispatching a malignant entity is easy enough with the right tools. Do you know its name and sigil?"

"What's a sigil?"

She shakes her head at his response.

"My parents tried evicting this thing years ago, when I was a child," Martin adds. "A priest dropped by the house, blessed every room, and that seemed to piss it off enough to drive it away. Years later, it came back to me. How can I send it away for good? I can't risk enraging this thing again and having it return to torment my wife, my children—my grandchildren, if I ever get any. I need a more permanent option."

She pauses to consider. "Come with me," she says, and hands him a red basket similar to the ones he uses to pick up dinner fixings at the Safeway in Glendale.

She leads him to a bookshelf, squats into a lunge, and retrieves a shrink-wrapped tome: *Brockum's Last Stand: Defensive Enchantments Against Devils, Demons, and Malevolent Spirits*. She drags the sharpened nail of her index finger down the spine and peels away the shrink wrap. The pages flicker past, and she stops at a chapter titled "Binding and Displacement." She dogears the chapter's third page and hands the book to Martin. He turns the book over in his hands. The back cover bears a black-and-white photograph of the author, Dennis Brockum: bald, unsmiling, wearing a thick silver chain with a many-pointed charm that reminds Martin of a bizarro version of the Star of David. He opens the book to the dogeared page. Strange symbols and phrases in a language Martin does not recognize stretch from margin to margin, along with numbered directions penned in Latin and English. Even the English words seem like gibberish.

"Consider this your how-to manual," she tells him. "It shows you precisely how to perform a ritual distilled from the ancient grimoires, updated for modern times. You have only one opportunity to get it right, so study up. Follow the instructions down to the last letter. Every letter, understand?"

She then moves to a shelf with an array of tinctures, plucks out several small bottles, and drops them in the basket. She shows him one of five bottles filled with some sort of red dust, explains its use, and describes the protection it will afford him while he prepares for "the rite." They turn a corner and face a floor-to-ceiling rack of candles. She stops to consult the book, and then chooses ten candles—three white, seven black—adding an eleventh for good measure—red, "just to have around," she says.

"Please don't take this the wrong way," Martin says, "but you don't look like much of a witch."

"Yeah, well, they stopped handing out uniforms a long time ago."

He had expected the proprietor to be a woman in a black robe, with Elsa Lanchester's *Bride of Frankenstein* hair and dark eye makeup, wearing lots of tinkling jewelry, not a soccer mom with a bob. He hopes she knows what she's talking about.

"What will this spell do, exactly?"

"Call it a rite. A ceremony. A ritual. If successful, it will erase the malignant presence from your physical life. You will essentially bind the entity to your nonmaterial self—the part of you that lives on, *ad infinitum*. These creatures do not tolerate the transition between planes, so when you die, you would essentially be killing or at least severely weakening the one that seems to have latched itself onto you. Some theologists believe these creatures can be reborn over time, though eons would pass before they would gain enough strength to break through the veil separating our realm from theirs.

"Based on experience, most entities such as the one you describe will flee the scene quickly, never to be heard from again."

"By binding it to me, I'll drive it away? I'm confused."

"It's a paradox, but it's a bit like human behavior. You do something wrong, you're going to do everything you can to not get caught, right? Same with the kinds of entities we're talking about. They can't stand the thought of what awaits once their host's heart stops, and they think they can somehow be forgotten by making themselves scarce. You'd be amazed by how sensitive they are—petty, bashful, almost delicate."

"So what happens to him"—*him*, not *it*—"when my time comes?"

"The entity?" she says. "Truth is, no one knows. If you believe the Christian theology, Heaven and Hell and all that, when your soul goes north or south, the entity will follow. If you go to the good place, the entity likely won't be able to survive. If you go to the bad place … well, what's one more problem to add to the pile?"

Her expression turns serious.

"I find honesty to be the best policy," she adds, "so a word of caution: What you're about to do *could* make things worse. Some of these entities—the most powerful ones, the ancients—will choose vengeance rather than escape. They will see your act as a betrayal deserving of swift and severe reprisal."

"Lovely."

"Either way, follow the instructions to the letter. A mistake could result in the opening of a door you would much rather keep closed. Besides that, your fate after the death of your physical body may hang in the balance."

"I don't really believe in that kind of stuff," he says. "Heaven, Hell, the afterlife."

"Maybe you should," she says. "If you're telling me the truth about the things you've seen, you must be a fool to think this plane of existence is the one and only."

"Well," he says, "your help means the world. Thank

you."

She takes the basket from him and hurries to the register.

"Nothing gives me more satisfaction than helping someone in need, especially when it involves something as gravely important as the wellbeing of the eternal self," she says. "You would be surprised at how often people come in here looking for help vanquishing some sort of malignant entity. I hope you let me know how it goes. As often as I ask, few people return to let me know the outcome. You would be the first, in fact."

She arranges everything in a crisp brown bag, finishes with a broad smile. He thanks her profusely, promises to follow up after the deed is done, and goes to take the bag from the counter. She pinches the bag's lip between two fingers.

"Let's call it three-hundred even," she says. "Cash or credit?"

⁓

Martin spends the next three days poring through *Brockum's Last Stand*, not only reading the ritual outlined on the dogeared page, but also studying the horrifying illustrations of supposed demons and the incantations needed to summon them or otherwise control them. Each disturbing page makes him wonder about the dangers of disrupting ancient organisms of cosmic provenance that should be left to their slumber, about gateways to a shadowy world he would rather not see. Nausea roils his stomach.

Early on a Saturday, Jodi catches him at the kitchen table muttering phrases from the book and sketching strange symbols on a napkin. She merely shakes her head, presumably because she has grown used to his peculiarities.

"I'm meeting the girls in Glendale on Tuesday," she tells him. "We're having lunch at some new Thai restaurant Tracey keeps raving about. You should come, too. Maybe afterward we can wander the Taft for a few hours, see the latest exhibit. I think they're doing American folk artists now. Edward Hicks, Grandma Moses. We can pop in on Alison, too, see how she's faring. You said you've been worried about her."

And there it is—the opening he has been waiting for.

"Have fun without me," he says. "Give your friends my love."

He means every word. He knows how deeply Jodi misses her old life: the co-workers she left behind at retirement, memories of her work as assistant director of programming for the Greater Phoenix Public Library, the friends who have begun to forget her.

"But you love the Taft," she says. "Of all the art museums in Phoenix, you always say it's your favorite."

A big part of him very much wants to accompany her, to revisit old haunts, maybe have a beer with his oldest surviving friend, Bob Sweems, but he has important business to conduct in private. With Jodi out of the house for half the day, he can complete the ritual to evict Pappaduffus from his life, and from hers, because no one suffers alone.

"You go. Please. I need to get a little work done around here anyway."

Martin joins Steve Miller in belting out a verse of "Abracadabra." The zip of a chop saw and the metronome of a hammer sinking nails drowns out the chorus.

He has spent two days carting sheets of plywood, a stack of two-by-fours, and almost every power tool he owns from the garage to the basement. The fruit of his labors: a fort of sorts, a four-walled shell designed to inform anyone who might see—Pappaduffus, mainly—that he is tackling a boring old home-improvement project, nothing more. He must be careful, as the simple act of whacking his thumb with a hammer could draw the imp right to him. Even negative or self-defeating thoughts would do it, so he keeps his mind focused on the task at hand.

With the structure mostly complete, he prepares the battlefield. His thumb depresses the button on the utility knife to expose the razor's edge. He slices into the carpet and lets the razor do its work. Jodi will want to kill him for ruining the carpet, but the book insists on a hard, natural surface— "bare stone or unvarnished wood," the instructions make clear. Hopefully concrete qualifies. He pulls up the carpet and padding beneath, tosses the refuse into a pile, away from his workspace. His lips hum in time with Steve Miller.

He opens *Brockum's Last Stand* to the dogeared page. The contents of the witch's brown bag sit before him. He twists the corks off two of the five small bottles and sprinkles redbrick dust onto the concrete, enclosing himself in a perfect circle. The fragrant substance reminds him, at turns, of topsoil and cinnamon. He double-checks his work, cheek to the floor, to make sure each section of the dust circle stands at least half an inch high. "Shore up any points of weakness in the circle through which the malevolent spirit may enter," the book insists. Carefully, he uses the tip of a wax pencil to draw a rectangle inside the circle, and then inscribes one of four sigils at each corner, north, south, east, and west. He then positions the seven black candles and three white, with each talisman—an ampule of cloudy water, a lump of amethyst, a charred piece of wood, an animal's shriveled claw, reptilian by his best guess, or possibly taken from a long-dead rodent—arranged beneath the corresponding sigil, in accordance with the book's precise instructions.

Although he has the ritual almost memorized, he runs through each step to ensure he has missed nothing. One final adjustment to one arc of redbrick dust, and the circle is perfect and complete. He makes minor adjustments to the talismans and then darkens a few lines of the sigil at the northern point. He stands to admire his creation.

At last, he is ready.

The Steve Miller Band has moved on to "Give It Up." Martin lifts a leg over the wall, to turn off the CD player. His right foot catches the lip of a two-by-four, and he tumbles forward. His left knee lands on the clawed end of a framing hammer. The metal teeth pierce his flesh, down to the bone. Blood darkens the knee of his blue jeans. He winces, doing his best to think about anything else, anything but the pain. He punches the top of the CD player, and the plastic cracks. Steve Miller goes silent. He struggles back over the wall and kneels inside the circle. His ruined knee throbs. Anger and agony replace the tranquility he fought so hard to cultivate. Blood smears the exposed concrete. A drop touches the edge of one of the sigils.

He closes his eyes and breathes slowly, to reclaim his sense of calm. He shifts his weight onto his right leg, to ease the pain in his knee. His eyes open to the makings of the ritual, and so it begins.

The words flow freely from his lips—in Latin. He does not stumble. He does not hesitate. He lights each candle as he finishes the first incantation.

The CD player comes to life, the disc starting over from the beginning, with the opening riff of "Abracadabra."

"Gotcha," Pappaduffus says in a sing-song-y lilt.

The Little Gray Man perches on the corner of Martin's wooden enclosure. "What do we have here, dear boy? Dabbling in the dark arts?"

Martin ignores him and proceeds to the second incantation.

"Quit this nonsense. Before you hurt yourself more than you already have."

Martin finishes the second incantation, and snuffs out the white candles, as instructed, leaving only the black ones lit, "for protection." Pappaduffus rises from the edge of the enclosure. He moves to enter the circle, but he cannot. The boundary holds. Martin locks eyes with him. Pappaduffus's pupils, usually white pinpricks, burn with a fierce blue glow.

"I'm going to tear you apart, boy."

Martin moves to the third and final incantation, the binding. He fumbles one word, recites the whole line again, finishing with the name of his tormentor. The incantation ends more quickly than he expects, the ritual complete. He feels no different. He anticipated fireworks of some sort—a ferocious breath of wind, the walls splitting down their middle, the ground quaking beneath his feet. Instead, it ends with silence.

Pappaduffus, however, seems to notice a shift in the balance of power.

"What have you done?" he implores. His voice has a ragged edge, tinged with strain and alarm. "Tell me now, boy."

Martin kneels with his eyes closed. He recalls the witch's warning, that some entities seek vengeance rather than escape. As long as Martin stays inside the circle, surrounded by the talismans, the burning candles, the sigils, Pappaduffus cannot touch him. Martin knows the protections will not hold for long. Eventually, Pappaduffus will find a way in, and Martin will have to answer for his actions.

"Talk to me, boy. Don't make me beg."

The flame of one of the black candles winks out.

"You're bound to me," Martin says. "In my death, you die with me."

"Idiot! You don't even know what you've done. You've sunk me, haven't you? When your heart stops and you leave this earth, you're going to drag me down with you. Guess what, boy: Unless you undo this betrayal, I will spend all of eternity putting a cudgel to your back."

"I can issue threats, too." Martin picks up the utility knife and holds the blade to the side of his neck. The tip pierces the skin, kissing the carotid pulsing beneath. A trickle of blood turns the collar of his white shirt red. "You know I'll do it. I've already made peace with anyone who matters."

Two more candles die in a tremulous breeze.

"*Wait! Wait! Wait!* … Dear boy, we have too much to discuss."

Another candle burns out, leaving only three. Pappaduffus senses a weakness in the bulwark and weaves a snakelike arm through a point in the circle where the dust has grown thin. The barrier dissolves. Pappaduffus wraps an arm around Martin's throat. Barbs pierce the skin, burning as if scalded. The utility knife tumbles from his hand, and tip of the blade breaks off as it hits the exposed concrete.

"This is how you repay me?" Pappaduffus growls. "I should make you watch as I tear apart everyone and everything you love, piece by filthy piece."

Martin's foot clips two of the remaining lit candles. Wax seeps into the circle and spills over the rim of redbrick dust. Martin's strength melts away, like an appliance disconnected from its power source.

"Every shred of pain, every squirt of suffering I have taken from you since you were a mealy-mouthed fidget unwanted by his parents, I give back to you now."

The final candle dies, and Pappaduffus rushes into the circle with the impetus of an enraged bull. His tentacles clamp onto Martin's chest, burn through his shirt, and sink teeth into his flesh. They seem to bore into him, latching onto something inside him, infusing him with venom. The edges of Martin's vision go white. He has never felt such pain, each pulse so intense he cannot find the sense to scream.

"Let it out, boy," Pappaduffus says through locked shark's teeth. His voice seems to echo. "Cry and scream like a toddler who has skinned a knee. I will extract the same agony from your lovely wife. Imagine the squeals bound to come from her aching mouth."

As if on cue, the front door cracks open. The unmistakable din of Jodi's heels clacking on travertine filters through the floorboards above Martin's head. Three terrible words bounce off the walls and find his ears: "Martin, I'm home!"

"Well, well," Pappaduffus whispers in Martin's ear. "Your perfect wife has perfect timing."

As the tentacles retreat from Martin's throat and chest, each one takes a chunk of flesh with an audible *pop*. Pappaduffus fades into mist. A trail of vapor, like smog, swirls through the basement and up the stairs for the first floor, toward Jodi. Martin attempts to rise, but the consequences of Pappaduffus's torture slow his response.

Shadow creatures crawl through gaps in the ceiling and turn the eggshell-colored walls dark. Roused from their slumber, Pappaduffus's legions slither across the floor and descend on Martin. The swarm has come to feast.

CHAPTER 27

Blessings and Bullets

Jodi stopped at the nurses' station, where Nurse Leary hunted and pecked at her keyboard. The women locked eyes, each recognizing the toll of exhaustion in the other. The nurse said nothing, seeming to know the grave decisions Jodi would soon have to make.

"No emergencies, Liv?" Jodi asked.

"A rare moment of calm," Leary said.

"Another day in paradise, huh? Any news about Martin?"

A small part of her expected her plea in the chapel to have worked its magic in short order.

"Doctor Stephens should be in within the hour," Leary said. "I know he wants to speak with you."

"About nothing good, I'm sure. It's never anything good with him."

"Don't even get me started. In the four years I've been working here, he hasn't cracked a smile or told so much as a bad joke. He should lighten up for all our sakes."

"I suppose it goes with the territory, trying to keep

dying people from crossing over, day in and day out."

"Jodi, I've been an ICU nurse for almost twenty years. You don't see me being a miserable SOB to everyone in my path."

Jodi recalled the last time she had seen Leary, barking into her smartphone.

"You seemed a little harried earlier. Out by the waiting room. Everything all right?"

"Oh, that. Some excitement involving one of the patients on our floor." Leary pointed to a room almost directly across from Martin's, at the opposite end of the hall. She leaned toward Jodi and said under her breath, "Seems the cops have taken a special interest in the guy. Suspected of murder, I'm told. Supposed to be a nasty SOB, but he's so banged up he can barely speak, let alone walk on his own. Thank God for small blessings, right?"

Jodi must have made a face, considering the swiftness of the nurse's follow-up.

"Don't worry, Jodi. The patient is as weak as a baby bird, and the cops are going to take him in as soon as he's strong enough to stand."

Jodi tapped nervously on the Formica counter, killing time before she had to return to the chill of reality waiting for her in Martin's room. She stood in the doorway for a while, looking at what had become of her husband. The poets had it right, she thought, especially Frost. "Nothing Gold Can Stay." She stepped into the room and draped her body across Martin's legs. She wanted to slap him awake, to yell and scream and demand that he stop his nonsense, to yank the tube from his throat and force him to return to his old self.

But she knew.

"I'm done with this, Martin. I really am. I imagine you are, too."

Her smartphone rang in her pocket. Andrew's name and image appeared on the phone's face.

"Sorry I kept missing you, Mom," he said. His voice sounded far away, fittingly. "How's Dad doing?"

"It's time for you to come home. Listen to me: When you hang up with me, buy a ticket and book your flight. Not an hour from now, not even a minute—the first chance you get. Your father's dying. You might not make it here in time, but you at least have to try."

As much as it hurt to say the words, voicing her worst fears felt freeing, because they were true. She spent the next few minutes listening to Andrew rage and cry and rage again, until he calmed and asked what she needed, how he could help. Finally, she told him she had to go, reminding him one more time, "Come home, and be safe."

A figure blurred past the door to Martin's room.

"Sir?" said Leary from the nurses' station, her voice sharp with alarm. "Sir, you're not supposed to be up here."

Jodi watched as Leary followed the intruder into the room of a patient at the far end of the hall.

Jodi rose from Martin's bed and peeked out the doorway. She squinted for detail her aging eyes would not give. Her ears tried to fill in the blanks. Leary shouted, and a male voice shouted viciously in return. Something heavy and metallic clanged to the floor.

Seconds later, Leary hurried back toward the nurses' station, blood trickling from her nose. She screamed a code into the handset.

Jodi's heartrate doubled. Her eyes focused on the doorway of the room down the hall. Two silhouettes emerged: a stocky bald man in a patient's gown, his throat bandaged, his arm draped across the shoulders of an even larger man with a familiar face—Mister *Blut und Boden*, the skinhead who days earlier had shown her the kindness of sharing a cigarette. The man with the bandaged throat dropped to his knees, and *Blut und Boden* helped him back up, dragged him into the hall.

Time seemed to freeze. Jodi felt removed, helpless, as benign as an observer in the audience of a stage play.

"Get up!" *Blut und Boden* yelled to his companion. "You wanna fuckin' die in here?"

Two men in blue spilled through the door beneath the EXIT sign, maybe ten feet from where *Blut und Boden* stood. The skinhead reached for the pistol tucked into his waistband. Two shots rang out. One of the cops fell to the ground, a bullet to the gut. *Blut und Boden* abandoned his sprawling friend and raced down the hall, toward Martin's room, toward Jodi. Another gunshot cracked the air. The bullet whizzed past Jodi and spider-webbed the glass of Martin's window. *Blut und Boden* turned the corner of the nurses' station and sprinted toward the elevator just beyond the glass double doors. As the elevator door opened, two more officers stepped out with their sidearms drawn.

Jodi withdrew into Martin's room.

To her horror, *Blut und Boden* followed her through the doorway and took shelter behind the frame. Jodi could smell him—a combination of sweat and tobacco smoke and fear.

Jodi moved in front of Martin. *Blut und Boden* stepped toward her. Something animalistic glinted in his pupils. For a brief moment, Jodi thought she saw the flicker of recognition in the dark wells of his eyes.

"Please leave," Jodi said calmly. "My husband has had enough of this. So have I."

He looked past her, at Martin in his bed, tube down his throat, machines doing their work.

"You gotta help me get the fuck outta here," he said.

As the skinhead reached for her wrist, she slapped him across the face. The blow stunned him for only a second. She slapped him again, and once more, and then her open hand became a fist, pummeling the side of his head until her knuckles cracked against his bristled skull.

He turned away from her assault, lifting the beef of his left forearm to stave off her punches. As he raised his head toward her again, she saw his expression had changed, as if something had been shaken loose. He stood there, struck, while angry voices yelled from the hall. A soft sigh escaped his lips. He placed the pistol at his feet and turned for the open door.

"Remember what I told you about fighting for what you believe in," he said. "Good luck, funny lady."

Arms at his sides, he made a right into the hall, toward the elevator. Jodi jumped at the jolt of a fired bullet, and two more close behind. The first bullet sent *Blut und Boden* reeling, and the other two took him down. Officers screamed cusswords and demands from the hall, even as a red puddle gathered on the floor beneath their target's unmoving body.

Jodi turned away from the carnage and eased her weight onto Martin's bed. She would not permit her gaze to linger on the dying man just outside the door. Why, she wondered, did people have to make a beautiful life so damned ugly? Why must everyone suffer? She squeezed Martin's rigid calf, thankful her husband had not been awake to witness more needless bloodshed.

Small blessings, she thought, remembering Nurse Leary's words. The smallest.

CHAPTER 28

Nothing Left to Do,
Nothing Left to Take

Two men in pin-striped ties, dark slacks, and rumpled button-down shirts crossed the threshold to Martin's room. Jodi retreated to the farthest corner.

The man in front—balding, fifties, the potbelly of a man who liked his beer—folded a stick of Wrigley's into his mouth. He tossed a stick of foil-wrapped chewing gum to his peer—thin, late thirties, a head of thick, dark curls—and it fell flatly to the floor. The younger man snagged the gum stick with the toe of his shoe and swept it beneath Martin's bed. The older of the two took a seat by the window and nodded toward Jodi.

"Detective Holtz," he said, hand on his chest. "This is Detective Lopez. Sit down if you like."

Jodi sat in the chair closest to Martin. Wind whistled through the bullet hole in the window someone had ringed with yellow tape.

"Sorry you got tangled up in this mess," Holtz said.

"I've seen worse," Jodi replied.

"When the suspect entered your room, did he say anything?"

"He asked me to help him, and I asked him to leave. Then he came toward me and my husband. So I hit him. I just kept hitting him until he understood I was going to be of no help to him. I can't tell you exactly what happened after that, but I must have awakened something inside him, hidden deep in his brain. Decency, maybe. He wished me luck, said to remember what he told me, and then he left. That's when you guys shot him."

"Wait," Lopez interrupted. "Remember what *who* told you?"

"The dead guy," Jodi said. "The sad-sack son of a bitch your guys used for target practice."

"Let's back up," Holtz said. "Did you know the deceased?"

"Barely. I met him about a week ago, outside. He gave me a cigarette. We talked for a bit. He was here visiting a friend who got stabbed in the throat—the guy down the hall, I guess. Despite the garbage he had tattooed on his arms, he was kind enough. Kind to me, anyway, 'cause I had the right skin color."

"How so?"

"Speaking of the guy down the hall," Jodi said. "Do you know what happened to him that landed him in the ICU?"

"It's an open investigation, ma'am," Holtz said. "I can't share specifics."

"My memory suddenly got fuzzy," Jodi said.

Holtz sighed and said, "The patient down the hall, his name is Robert Lee Braun. Goes by Nero. He came into the hospital with numerous stab wounds, including one to the throat. He's a suspect in the murder of a family down in Gray Mountain. Guatemalan folks. A young mother and her three kids. Savage stuff."

Jodi rubbed her temples. Her bones craved sleep.

"We want to talk to him about another incident in Willow Springs from about a week ago," Holtz added. "Two more people dead, another clinging to life—senseless, stupid gang shit. We're guessing that's how he ended up in the room down the hall. From what the nurse tells me, Braun was all but unresponsive until yesterday. Still can't say a word because of his wounds, but that didn't stop him from using his phone. He's been texting his buddy here ever since"—he pointed his chin toward the spot on the floor where *Blut und Boden* had fallen, the tile stained dark with fresh blood—"letting him know the local PD was sniffing around. Looks like his buddy finally tried to bust him out."

"The man outside my husband's door. What was his name?"

Holtz and Lopez shared a look.

"Duncan Reisinger," Holtz said. "Another troublemaker. I need to know if he told you anything about where he'd been the past few days, who he was with, where he was going. Anything at all."

Jodi took a deep breath and spilled her guts—every detail she could remember about her conversation with the man who died on the cold floor just a few steps away.

Lopez waited until she finished and added, "Anything else?"

"I know how he feels," she said.

"Who feels?"

"Duncan Reisinger. Someone he cared for was in a bad way, and he was going to do everything he could to help, even if it killed him. I guess he and I weren't so different after all." She waited a beat. "I wish I never met him."

Holtz handed Jodi a business card.

"You think of anything else, you let us know," he said. He glanced at Martin's inert form. "I hope your husband gets better soon."

"Yeah," Jodi said. "Wouldn't that be nice."

Jodi struggled to catch her breath as she hurried down the hall. As she entered the ICU's waiting area, she felt a tug on her arm. Alison embraced her, asking if she was all right, if her father was all right, if anyone had been hurt. Jodi pulled away. No doubt Alison had heard the gun shots, had seen the police, and maybe even saw them wheeling Duncan Reisinger's bagged body off to the morgue.

"Your father's fine," Jodi insisted. "I'm fine. Just need some air."

Tears obscured her vision, but Jodi knew the route all too well. She passed the elevator bank and followed the red EXIT light above the stairwell. The light dimmed as she opened the door. She sobbed as she went, nearly slipping on the last stair before the landing. The overheads buzzed and flickered. An uneasy feeling hurried her steps. As she reached the bottom floor, she pushed the bar handle, but the door would not open. Twice more she depressed the handle, but the door did not budge. She wondered if the shooting had somehow triggered the door locks and sealed her in. The lights flickered again, a briefer interval this time, leaving her in darkness for longer than she would have liked. With an audible click, the overheads died for good. A red-tinted haze took their place—emergency lights.

Then the smell hit her.

"Lovely to see you again, my dear."

She turned to see him—*it*—floating on a thin, black cloud. He stood no more than two and a half feet tall, outfitted in a loose herringbone suit and matching derby. His hands resembled snakes, eels—slinky, slimy things. The red haze seemed to deepen the creases in his ghastly face.

"You have no reason to fear me," Pappaduffus said. "Surely no harm can come from an innocent conversation. My, how long I have wanted to speak with you. After all, I feel like I *know* you after so many years. Martin gushed over you every chance he got, and color me embarrassed to admit I have had eyes on you for longer than you might suspect."

His voice sounded vaguely wet. A ball of phlegm rattled around in the back of his throat.

"You're behind all this, I gather," she said. "The mess upstairs, the scorpion that took my husband off his feet, every bad thing that's ever knocked Martin on his ass."

"None of this is my doing, dear. I have merely come to clean up the *mess*, to use your word. Whatever catastrophes Martin has had to stare down, whatever sticky holes he thrust his fingers in, those troubles are of his own making. Same old story. I know his prognosis is grim, but I can assure you I would much rather see him stay put."

He ran the tip of his alabaster cane along the rungs of the metal railing. The sequence sounded eerily musical.

"Which," he added, "is why I have come to see you again."

Again. She recalled the brief moment in which she had seen him in his more diminutive form, in her yoga studio back home in Rio Vista, the day before they fled their home for good, before Jodi learned of the dark forces that had their hooks in the Avec-Georges DNA. The putrid odor. His ragged lips nipping hers. The absurd scene her eyes showed her. Then she thought of the next night, their last in Rio Vista, when she came home to find Martin apoplectic in the basement, while toothed and clawed creatures slithered in and out of the shadows, and Pappaduffus in his true demonic form lumbered up the hall astride a crocodile-like monster.

How such an aberration could be breathed into existence …

"You can wash away Martin's duplicity," Pappaduffus said. "This *binding*—most inconvenient for yours truly. Most troubling. He did what he did for your sake and that of your progeny, bless the man. You can return the favor by helping him now. Naturally, if a man cannot speak for himself, his wife speaks for him. You can release me with a word."

"Let me go," she demanded, though she knew he had something else in mind.

"In a minute, dear." He stabbed the air with the point of his ivory cane. "First, the matter of Martin's chicanery. By binding me to him in death, wherever he goes next, I follow. Wherever his *soul* goes, you might say. Frankly, I have no desire, and no intention, of returning to that dreadful place, yet that is precisely where your fool of a husband intends to drag me."

"Do us both a favor and spare Martin's life. Please. You've put him through enough. Let us go about our lives as if nothing ever happened."

"I could lie to you and say, yes, I would be happy to perform such a service in exchange for a small recompense, but that is hardly within my power. I can, however, help you in the event of Martin's passing."

"How?"

"Why, whatever you want, dear," he said. "Riches, fame, infinite pleasure for the remainder of your days. Vengeance upon your enemies, perhaps. Name your desire and you shall have it. Simply undo Martin's folly."

"And if I do? Where would you go?"

"Off to sail with the wind, like a gull, like a dandelion spore, like a plague." The tips of his eel-like arms massaged his face. His smile broadened to reveal a mouthful of silvery shark's teeth. "You would hear not another peep out of me. A promise made is a promise kept."

"So you'll go off and terrorize someone else. Martin did what he did for a reason. If you think I'm going to lift a fingernail to help you, you're even dumber than you look."

"No, no, no," he corrected. "You have it all wrong, backwards, and upside down. I can assure you I played no part in the pains of Martin's life, which would have come to him even if I never entered his path. I merely profited from his suffering, and just in the slightest. Some people are meant to suffer more than others—marked from birth, from *before* birth, a code written in the cracks between time and space—and the stink of them makes them stand out among all others. The stink is what drew me to your better half. I merely had to point my nose in the right direction to claim him as my own."

"Suffering," she whispered. "Martin certainly had his share."

"Precisely, and I was his savior. Rescued him more times than I care to count, from whatever abyss he was about to tumble into. He spent most of his life wanting to hurt himself, irreparably, if not fatally. Did you know that? If not, I find your ignorance quite sad. Such a dangerous mind he had. I saw him in his weakest moments, his worst moments, trying to find his way out of the many troubles he did not see fit to share with anyone, not even you. Who stayed his hand time and time again? Me. I meant more to that dear boy than you ever did."

Pappaduffus's pouting lips made *tsk-tsk* noises, as if he pretended to pity her.

"You're a nasty little shit, you know that?" she said. "An inconsequential shrew of a thing."

Shadows discolored Pappaduffus's features. Dark veins rose to the surface, and fractures cracked the mask of his face. Flakes of pale skin around his mouth, beneath his eyes, across his forehead, tumbled to the floor like bits of ash.

"You dumb cow," he hissed. "Your insufficient mind cannot possibly imagine the sting of my blade. Heap agony upon your shoulders until your bones break, reduce you to a bundle of nerves and set the pile alight until you beg me to end your trifle of a life. You have no idea the depths I could reach. Push me one step too far and I'll liquefy your old bones, lap you up, and dribble you out in a puddle of piss."

The rage drained slowly from Pappaduffus's porcelain face. He exhaled a billowing cloud, reeking of hardboiled eggs, car exhaust, and week-old halibut.

"Forgive me, dear. Let us not discuss such unpleasantness. Best if we could reach an accord."

Jodi leaned against the wall and crossed her arms. She did her best to hide her terror.

"Are you going to open the damned door?" she asked. "I have better things to do than listen to the nonsense of a little shrew whose days on this earth are numbered."

Pappaduffus snaked his tentacled fingers along the cinderblock wall and said, calmly, "Or perhaps I just bring down the walls on the crown of your head, X marks the spot."

"But you won't," she said, hoping she was right.

"You humans are oblivious to the forces that exist beyond this insignificant little world. But Martin, *he* understood. He gazed into the eyes of the insatiable machine that keeps this cursed orb spinning, that keeps the fabric of this universe stitched together. He fed it, in fact. All of creation will mourn the loss of the sustenance he provided. A pity his remainder will linger in nothingness for eternity, his gifts gone to waste, all for the fuel of a lousy furnace at the bottom of an ash heap. He is so much more useful here."

Jodi had never fully grasped the idea of life after death. Rather, she chose not to believe it. When Martin died, he would be gone. Same with her and everyone else on the planet. If that were true, though, why did Pappaduffus care so much about Martin's supposed soul?

"You sound completely apeshit, you know that?"

"No need for nasty language, dear. If we lose our decency, what do we have left?"

"Martin sent you away and sealed your fate. I'll do nothing to undo his will."

"You don't realize what he's done, your brain too primitive to even touch the edges. You don't realize anything. Allow me to show you."

Pappaduffus twined a tentacled arm around Jodi's throat. As his flesh met hers, her eyes went dark, and her whole body went rigid. Slowly, a vision unfurled in her mind: the surface of a rocky planet from a distant cosmos or an alternate reality, thousands of stars pricking the black and purple heavens above. Mammoth blob-like creatures beyond human comprehension—all eyes and mouths bearing formidable teeth, translucent flesh reflecting the star-choked cosmos, as if sprinkled with glitter—encircled the base of a towering edifice made of black rock. Veins of blue metal striated the stone column. Despite its inert makeup, the tower seemed somehow organic, somehow alive.

Pappaduffus's voice echoed in her head, a soundtrack to the horrifying scene.

"Upon Martin's death, he will return to the Warm, Dark, Bleeding Place. Abysmal, as I know all too well. The Warm, Dark, Bleeding Place manufactured me, raised me, reared me, kept me until the Hungry Ones came calling. Have you heard of them before? A dud like you, unlikely. Think of the Hungry Ones as builders, the ones who stitch worlds together, turn the big wheel that powers the universe. They freed me from the Warm, Dark, Bleeding Place, made me a

Collector, to seek out humans like Martin to feed the machine, to prevent time and space from collapsing in on themselves.”

“You’re … making … no … sense,” Jodi said, reeling from the nightmarish vision Pappaduffus showed her.

Atop the jeweled pylon sat a five-pointed windmill, of sorts, with each spoke resembling an Aztec war club. Iron blades shaped like shark fins lined the outer edges of each spoke, a gnarled knob like the head of a femur at its tip. Comets streaked the night sky and fell to the rocky surface, all converging on the same point: the base of the pylon. Upon their arrival, a horde of thick, thorny tendrils clambered out of the earth. The tail of each comet burned away to reveal a vaguely humanoid shape: a bipedal figure dressed in formal haberdashery, including a bowler or a fedora. Each figure approached the pylon and disgorged a ball of black ooze from its gaping mouth—food for the machine. As tendrils soaked up the ooze, the windmill spun more quickly, the veins of blue metal glowing like the bellies of fireflies.

“The Hungry Ones have become complacent, I can admit,” Pappaduffus said. “They no longer have an interest in the art of creation. All they want is to fill their bellies and watch themselves grow fatter and fatter.”

On the screen in Jodi’s mind, the Hungry Ones lumbered in from all sides, coming to graze. The titanic blobs took turns at the pylon’s stony teats, hugging the stone and drawing sustenance through lamprey-like mouths. The glow of the blue metal dimmed, and the wheel’s pace slowed. One by one, the blobs wandered off, bloated and unsteady, as if inebriated.

"Martin does his greatest good when he cries and squeals and bleeds and wails," Pappaduffus added. "I merely collect the byproduct, nourishing myself and taking the rest to the Hungry Ones so they can steam their engine, you might say. Humans like Martin are extraordinary in terms of how much punishment they can take. You cannot imagine how much power one human's pain can generate.

"Your husband is an anomaly. Females tend to suffer more by nature, so they tend to be infinitely more useful to someone such as myself—and so much more valuable in matters of the grand design. So much more put upon, the fair sex, so many more obstacles placed in their path. But Martin, oh that dear boy has few peers in terms of the pains and problems he's had to swallow. It would be funny if it were funny, as you humans like to say."

"Stick to the cancer wards, burn units, and the centers for spinal injuries," Jodi said. "Maybe you can do some good there."

"Oh, I could and certainly have," Pappaduffus replied. "Don't look at me as some kind of opportunistic bloodsucker—a feeder or taker. I make investments in your kind; relationships strengthened over time. Like Martin, I find them when they're young and lead them through life. The terminally sick and injured, surely they produce more than their share of misery, but they do not tend to last terribly long, as you can imagine."

Tendril to his chest, the imp twisted his face into a look of concern, as if he did not want Jodi to think badly of him.

"Do you think I *enjoy* seeing Martin writhe and brood

and break his back?" he asked. "Hardly, but it is his purpose to struggle, you see. His sole purpose, just as with every other human. It is all you are good for, to put it plainly, though some have much more of a talent for the work—hurting each other and themselves and enduring the agony that follows. By comparison, look at my existence. I do not suffer, other than tolerating the tedium of humans. Some lives are worth more than others."

A cough erupted from Pappaduffus's lips.

"When Martin dies," he continued, "I will deal with the inconvenience of nurturing another in his place. At least I would have, had he not bound me to him. Now, because of his insolence, and because of your refusal to intervene on his behalf, I will follow him to the Warm, Dark, Bleeding Place. Your inaction will rob the universe of what it needs most, what it craves. If it all comes tumbling down, the burden will be yours to bear."

He unfurled his tentacled hand, and Jodi dropped to her knees.

"I know your name," she said, panting on the floor.

"And?"

"I can use it to control you." A bluff.

His tiny body shook with each ear-shredding cackle.

"Just try, you fuddy-dud. Now stop this preening and undo your husband's cowardly act. For your own benefit, if not for his."

"If you're as powerful as you claim to be, why not put it to good use by batting down the world's problems? Solve the hunger crisis. Cure cancer. End homelessness. And start by putting Martin back together."

"I simply cannot fathom why someone as remarkable as Martin chose someone as dense as you for his partner." His face became a mask of frustration. "After everything I've told you, and everything I've *shown* you, you still don't get it. My dear, the problems are the entire point. Without them, there'd be no reason for your world. Now stop your posturing and undo Martin's nasty little deed. I've asked so nicely up until now."

"I will do nothing to help you. Follow Martin wherever he goes. When he sees you next, he's liable to put a fist up your ass and wear you like a sock puppet."

"Have you ever reflected upon why this world is such a miserable place? It is by design. A contraption built solely to power the machine. All of that unpleasantness upstairs, the fellow with the bald head who shot up the place? Just another pawn in a meaningless chess game."

She imagined Duncan Reisinger on a checkered board, his body being nudged into position by a gargantuan four-fingered hand with a gleaming black talon at the tip of each finger.

"You must know this," Pappaduffus said. "It is why all humans share the urge to end it all, to stop the pain, because deep down they understand the pointlessness of an earthly existence. The enlightened ones, they know. They can feel it in their bones. Martin has always known. Smarter than most, that one. Which is why he has tried to end it all, by my count, a dozen times. Who do you think stopped him? I admit, he has some strange attachment to you I have not quite been able to pinpoint. Some misplaced sense of obligation, I suppose. I was the one who eased his burden, the only one who knew him well enough to soothe his dark mind. What did you do but add to his suffering, or to be so self-involved that you knew nothing of his troubles? I pity him to have chosen his mate so poorly."

Pappaduffus had gone too far. Her lips trembled with rage.

"You worthless piece of shit!"

"If we're resorting to childish name calling, what a foolish hag you are, destined to end up in the same ditch as her husband. I intend to make sure of it."

"Then fucking do it already! If you're going to do it, do it now!"

Pappaduffus's body ballooned until he burst through his herringbone suit. The fabric turned to tatters, and the tatters turned to ash as they touched the floor. His derby disintegrated in the air, replaced by a flame-tipped crown. His massive reptilian frame filled the stairwell. A mammoth snake-like tail pressed her into the cinderblock wall, and his face came to hers. A slug-like creature slithered out from beneath his eyelid, slid down his cheek, and made a new home of his slit for a nostril. The wall seemed to vibrate behind her. Tiny burrs on his slippery flesh pricked hers, bleeding into hers, biting. A tendril snaked around her throat, drawing her closer.

"Stupid, filthy, rancid whore!" His body felt somehow less than solid, almost gelatinous. The tip of a tendril wove through her hair, tugging at the roots. As he inhaled, his chest swelled to twice its size, crushing Jodi between two walls—one made of cinderblock and another made of barbed, otherworldly flesh.

A drop of his spit fell on her upper lip. The tender skin burned as if doused in acid.

"Un! Leash! Me!"

Jodi did not hear his plea so much as she endured it, the force of it so intense she felt the bones of her skull rattle and smelled her hair being singed. Her lungs screamed. Panic welled inside her, as she imagined her life coming to an end at the hands of a demon. So severe was the pain, she would do anything to make it stop, even if it meant undoing the "spell" Martin had cast to restrain Pappaduffus's power.

"Unleash me now or I swear this to you: Your dear husband will suffer agonies too harsh for your simple mind to grasp. I'll oversee a routine of flensing and flaying and cauterize his wounds with fire. He'll beg for the clock to be turned back, and he'll curse you for lacking the sense to intervene when you had the chance."

An image of Martin's contorted face flashed into her mind.

"Nothing!" she screamed as she found her strength. "There's nothing you can do to me that hasn't already been done, nothing you can take from me that hasn't already been taken. So go *fuck* yourself!"

Pappaduffus reared back, his fiendish profile distorted by surprise. She thrusted a thumb into one of his eyes, the pupil slitted like a cat's.

As the demon wailed, Jodi curled herself into a ball at the base of the steps. She had taken her shot, and she knew Pappaduffus would recover to take his pound of flesh in return. At any moment, her body would sizzle and burn as if zapped with ninety-thousand volts. She imagined her body reduced to little more than a mound of char and ash, Pappaduffus using the tips of his tentacles to trace his name in her powdery remains.

Then, as if someone had flicked a switch, the stairwell went still and silent.

She opened her eyes in time to see the overheads blink back to life. Only Pappaduffus's horrid scent remained. Her knee cracked as she rose from the fetal position. Vertigo unsteadied her, but she fought off the spell and grasped the exit door's bar handle. The heavy door groaned open. She stepped into the hall and stared into the empty stairwell until the door closed behind her with a mechanical click. As she took a step into the lobby, her left knee buckled, and she tumbled to the floor.

CHAPTER 29

Once More to the Splitter

Martin clips the side of the uncut round with the blade of the splitting maul, toppling the wood from the chopping block. The blade sinks into the dirt a few inches from the boot of his right foot.

He bends and hefts the round back onto the block. As he goes to take another swing, a familiar heaviness fills his chest. He lowers the maul and makes a full turn.

"Hello, dear boy."

Pappaduffus sits atop a pile of split wood—the fruits of Martin's labor.

"It's been a while," Martin says, huffing.

"Too long." Pappaduffus eyes the farmhouse and the desert beyond Crum's distant border. "Such a lovely place to call home."

"Don't try to change my mind. What's done is done."

"Cannot one friend drop in on another unannounced without arousing suspicion? I have merely come to offer tidings of housewarming."

Martin leans on the maul. A drop of sweat falls to the

dusty earth. He looks toward the kitchen window, to see if Jodi is watching.

"Our last interaction was, shall we say, regrettable," Pappaduffus says. "I hope you can forgive an old friend for his tantrum."

"Your tantrum almost killed me. Jodi, too. I warned you to keep her out of it."

"As I said, regrettable. Perhaps we can find a way back into each other's good graces."

"I'm happier without you, better without you."

Martin swings the maul with such force, it blasts through the wood and sinks deep into the chopping block. Pappaduffus smiles at the display of brute force.

"Pleasantries offered, fences mended," Pappaduffus says. "On to a more pressing matter. Be a good boy and release me from this bond."

"Why would I do something stupid like that?"

"One friend to another, my dear."

"Some friend you've been."

"The best one you've ever had, you must admit," Pappaduffus says. "Truth be told, I can think of few others among your race I can imagine wanting to spend all eternity with, though I would rather wander in my own way. Think of what I gave you—the tools needed to lead a long and fruitful life. I eased your despair whenever possible. I spared your family."

"Yeah, until you didn't."

"Pish posh." Pappaduffus's voice takes a vicious turn. "Whatever we had, boy, consider it ended. With your last breath, you come with me. To the world of darkness and flame we go. You have not felt true pain yet. But you will, old boy, you will."

"Promises, promises."

Martin can admit he has missed seeing Pappaduffus, missed their talks, missed the way the derby-topped imp would lift him up and remind him of his uniqueness. Despite everything Pappaduffus stole from him, the bugger always made Martin feel … *special*. Of the billions of humans on the planet, Pappaduffus had chosen only a handful, including Martin. They sustained one other, he and Pappaduffus, each drawing nourishment from the other.

"Dude, even if I *wanted* to release you, I have no clue how I'd even go about it," he says. "I'm not even sure the ritual worked."

"Oh, it worked," Pappaduffus replies. "My skin prickled as soon as you did it, and the prickling has since spread to every part of my being. I feel … *tethered*. Most unpleasant, I can assure you. Now make it go away."

Martin returns to the wood pile behind the shed and collects another round in his arms. As he hobbles back to the splitter, he feels a pinch on his forearm—slight at first, like a needle stick, and then a cauterizing fire that weakens every muscle in his arm. The round tumbles to the earth, and Martin dances out of the way. A reddish-brown scorpion dangles from his forearm. Its black pincers cling to the skin, stinger sunk in, doing its devilish work. The thinness of the scorpion's pincers gives Martin a sinking feeling. He learned long ago that the ones with big, lobster-like claws look tough but are almost harmless, while the ones with less imposing pincers pack a deadly wallop.

He yanks the scorpion from his arm and flings it across the yard.

"*Shit.*"

Dizziness comes a second later. His vision blurs. Sweat erupts from his brow and slicks his back. He drops to a knee and leans onto his fists. Nausea builds in his gut, radiating. He plunges forward, face smacking the ground. He struggles to turn himself over, lungs fighting for each breath, but somehow gets onto his back.

Cotton-white clouds pass overhead. The silhouette of Pappaduffus's head, derby and all, blots out the sky.

"Stay with me, boy," Pappaduffus says. "Stay with me."

Martin struggles to respond, a disconnect between his tongue and his brain. He turns his head toward the house. Jodi's silhouette passes the kitchen window.

"Watch over her," he manages to say. "My kids, too. Protect them all."

Pappaduffus snakes the tip of one of his tendrils into the palm of Martin's hand.

"Anything for you, boy," he says. "You have always been my favorite. Despite what you have done, despite your sedition, consider me your forever friend. But you will pull through this little hiccup as you have with every other that has preceded it. Now stop this silliness and get on your feet."

A seizure claims Martin's body. His hands and feet quiver. His bladder empties. He feels the blood drain from his face.

Pappaduffus's ghastly expression turns to one of genuine concern. He seems to realize the seriousness of

Martin's situation. The kindly imp curls a tendril beneath Martin's neck and lifts his head so he does not choke on the foam filling his mouth.

"Listen, boy," he says. "Of all the humans I've met, throughout the millennia, you have enriched my existence more than any other. Watching you build a life, watching you struggle and stew and overcome every obstacle—all of it has brought me more joy than you could know. I will always look out for you, no matter where we go next."

The gray sky turns black. Pappaduffus's face fades from view as Martin's eyelids become too heavy to keep open. The world goes dark and silent.

CHAPTER 30

Too Much

Jodi reposed on the chair next to Martin's bed, her legs propped up on a footstool. Her eyes moved from the needle in her arm to the clear plastic bag dangling from the IV pole beside her. When she came to a few hours earlier, an unfamiliar male nurse told her she was being admitted to her own room so she could be treated for dehydration and exhaustion. Jodi refused. She had enough clarity, despite the crushing headache that seemed intent on splitting her skull, to insist on taking treatment from a chair in Martin's room.

Her headache had since eased, and she was beginning to feel more like herself. She closed her eyes to chase away the grogginess and promptly slipped into the shadows of unconsciousness.

The sound of a man clearing his throat broke Jodi's dreamless sleep.

"Missus Avec-Georges?"

Douglas Exelby, the venomologist, lingered in the doorway to Martin's room.

"Enough with the formality." She wiped the sleep

from her eyes. "Call me Jodi, for chrissakes. I've told you more than once."

He entered the room and took a seat in a chair by the window. His eyes moved to the asterisk of masking tape covering the spider-webbed glass, courtesy of the stray bullet.

"I heard about what happened," Exelby said. "You all right?"

"Oh, you know, like a million bucks. I'm alive, so that's something."

He nodded toward Martin and added, "And how is he?"

"You would know better than anyone. Come to say your goodbyes?"

"Doc Stephens called me over," he said. "Some idiot came into the ER with a bite from a coral snake. The moron caught it during a hike in Tucson and brought it home because he wanted photos to post on Instagram. The bite happened four hours ago. The idiot no longer has the ability to speak. Bad news, coral snakes. Some people just don't have enough common sense to stay out of the crosshairs."

She shook her head and pursed her lips, because she had a good idea how that story would end, too.

"Too much death," she said. "Too much pain. Too much everything, it seems. Tell me: Why does life have to be so difficult? If you can help me understand, I'll shake your hand."

Exelby seemed to consider the question, fishing for the right answer.

"Rainbows and rain," he said. "As silly as it sounds,

you can't have one without the other. Life is a wonderland, but not every day's going to be a birthday party."

"I was hoping you wouldn't say something stupid like that."

He laughed. She mirrored his smile.

She remembered Pappaduffus's explanation—humans as vessels for suffering, or makers of fuel to power some infernal machine, and nothing more. Damn that imp for infecting her brain with his nonsense.

She reached over and placed an arm on Martin's bare leg. The flesh felt cool and rubbery, too soft, the limb twice the size as it should be. The edema had returned as if seeking revenge—another ominous sign.

"Won't be long now," she added. "Your pal Stephens says Martin's heart has had just about enough. We're on the doorstep of the 'final showdown,' as Stephens likes to call it. What a prick."

"We're not pals—Stephens and me. Don't much care for the guy, to be honest."

"Not the point, but whatever." Her eyes wandered to the world outside, beyond the window's marred glass. "Why do bad things happen to good people, Exelby?"

"What does *good* have to do with anything? No one deserves the bad things life brings. Everyone takes his turn beneath the wheel—young and old, rich and poor, black and white. Like Morrison said: 'No one gets out alive.' Or was that Dostoevsky?"

"Fair point. Did you find anything at the house? Any more of those goddamn Angel of Death scorpions creepy-crawling around?"

"Death angel scorpions," he corrected. "Not a trace, but thank you again for letting us poke around. I never turn down an opportunity for grad students to do fieldwork, especially when the work has the potential to save a life."

"You found *nothing*? What the hell, Exelby."

"Nothing out of the ordinary, I should clarify. It's one of those mysteries we may never get the answer to."

"I don't really care for mysteries anymore."

"Science cares."

"Science can go take a long walk off a short pier."

"Of course," he said slowly, "there's the possibility the venom profile of a native species has taken an unexpected turn. Evolution never stops. We gathered up a handful of bark scorpions from beneath your shed so we can compare samples of their venom to what we took from your husband. It's an unlikely outcome, damn near impossible, but we can't rule out anything."

"So, you're saying this could happen again, to someone else?"

"Afraid so."

"Well, that really sucks."

"Welcome to the world we live in."

"Exelby, is he in pain? Martin, I mean. Is Martin hurting?"

"Probably not. That's one good thing about what he's going through. In response to the venom, the body protects the brain. Martin's probably having some of the craziest, most vibrant dreams of his life."

Jodi smiled, grateful for another small favor.

"That is," he added, "if his brainstem has not died

yet."

She looked at him cockeyed. Damn the man, he could make the most insensitive and insulting pronouncements. Knowing he meant no disrespect was the only thing that kept her from slugging him.

"I have one more question for you," she said, "likely to my peril."

"Anything."

"What do you think happens when we die?"

"That's hardly my area of expertise."

"I don't give a shit about your expertise," she said. "I'm asking you to talk to me like a human being. I haven't given much thought to what happens when the lights go out—until recently, of course—but the idea of an afterlife seems pretty damned appealing right now. Tell me something good, even if it's a lie."

Exelby paused. His face contorted as his brain prepared a response.

"Well, I like to think we go on," he said. "I want to believe we go to a place with the potential for complete understanding and immersion in a universe of knowledge—not joy, exactly, but a place where we can have every question answered and indulge in only the experiences we choose. Someplace where conflict has no seat at the table."

"I'll take that answer."

"Energy cannot be destroyed, right? It has to go somewhere. Why not some other plane of existence? If you don't care for the word *soul*, use whatever term you want to refer to the energy that leaves the body of any living thing. I hope I'm right, selfishly. I wouldn't mind seeing my parents again. A few of my aunts and uncles, too. Maybe one particular colleague who got too sloppy while milking venom from a fer-de-lance."

The far-off look in his eye suggested a once-happy memory since turned bittersweet.

"Oh, and Sparky—my pet iguana," he added. "I'd love to see him again."

"Of course you had an iguana." She laughed at the thought of him with a big, green lizard perched on his shoulder. "Why wouldn't you?"

"When I was twelve, Sparky escaped his enclosure and went on the lam for three days before my father cornered him in the laundry room. Sparky was never particularly friendly, at least not to anyone but me, and going without food and water for a few days probably hadn't helped matters. Most people don't realize it because they look so harmless, but male iguanas can deliver a nasty bite— disfiguring, if you're not careful. He wound up taking off the tip of my father's index finger, right to the first knuckle. Quite the bloody mess. Well, that was the last of Sparky. Buried him in a patch of dirt beneath a Japanese maple outback. Loved that iguana as much as anyone could."

"A moment of silence for Sparky," Jodi said.

They sat in silence, looking anywhere but at each other.

"My daughter thinks you're cute, you know," she said. "I can't say I see it, but whatever. She's her own person."

"I'm married."

"Happily?"

"Most days."

"Good answer." She halved the distance between them, patted Exelby on the back of his right hand, and then playfully swatted his cheek. "It's been a pleasure knowing you, Exelby. Your role in Martin's story has reached its end, I would think. Don't take this the wrong way, but I hope our paths don't cross again."

CHAPTER 31

Parting of Worlds

Martin hovers above his corporeal form, supine on the hospital bed. A tube snakes down his body's throat. His right arm has gone missing. Machines sustain his life, but he knows they will serve their purpose for only a short while longer. The exodus has already begun.

His escort floats at the edge of the bed on a cloud the color of dishwater.

"You still have time to release me, boy," Pappaduffus says. "All it takes is a word, a nod, the simplest of gestures."

"I wish you would shut up and give this moment the respect it deserves," Martin replies. "I'll have plenty of time to listen to your prattle later on. Forever, in fact."

"Please, boy." Pappaduffus's voice changes in pitch, tinted by an emotion resembling fear. "Pretty please, boy, release me. Release me from this *bond*. I cannot go back there. We have but a moment."

A hospice nurse nods to Doctor Stephens.

"It's time, Jodi," Stephens says. The doctor stands at

Martin's bedside, the bell of his stethoscope on Martin's chest. "There's nothing left to be done."

Jodi's lower lip trembles as the words sink in.

Martin can guess the contents of her mind as she surveys the husk on the bed before her. Martin looks nothing like the man she fell in love with, the man she married, the man she made a life with, and the man who battled dark forces for longer than anyone could have known. Missing an arm, legs swollen with fluid, skin the pale yellow of chicken fat.

Of all the multiple iterations of Hell he has faced throughout his life, finally he has run into one he cannot best.

"I'm very sorry, Jodi," Stephens says. "Let me know if you need anything at all."

"You've done enough," she says, though Martin guesses she does not mean her words to sound as harsh as they do, because she tends to reserve her vitriol for the people closest to her. "Can someone please fetch my daughter? She needs to say goodbye."

Martin's eyes remain fixed on Jodi. Sprawled across his body, she raises her head to show the anguish on her face. Her strawberry-red cheeks glisten with fresh tears. A nurse ushers Alison into the room, because this will be the last time she will see her dear old dad alive. He hates to see them in pain, though he feels buoyed by the knowledge that they both loved him, despite his failings and weaknesses and moments he would like to wipe from the slate.

His son, Andrew, will not witness his father's demise. Part of Martin wants to believe his son is wringing his hands on a plane thirty-five thousand feet above the

Atlantic, trying to get home to his family before Martin's heart stops, but another part of him thinks Andrew is still in Spain, unwilling or unable to break away from his many commitments. Deeply disappointing, mainly because Martin knows Andrew will not forgive himself for missing out on another Avec-Georges family milestone.

Flashbacks from Martin's years with Jodi burst in his mind, one after the other, like a fireworks finale. In almost every image, his wife wears a broad smile. He will miss her laugh. He will miss her badgering when he deserves it. He will miss her ability to surprise him, unfailingly, with her bravery, her good humor, and her ability to shift from crass to tender and back again in the time it takes to fry an egg.

Imperfections aside, he has done all right, he thinks. He has seen his wife at her best and her worst, and he showed her the same in him. So few get to experience such privilege. He gave himself to her as wholly as he could, and he hopes he made her comfortable enough to show her vulnerabilities, few as they were. Regret tingles him, from the times he disappointed her, reminding him of how much he adored her, of his desire to do better. Memories of his weakest moments fill him with shame, despair, and disdain, but he also knows he tried—genuinely *tried*—to fulfill her, honor her, and love her.

He will continue to adore her, for eternity. A sense of lightness overwhelms him.

"Make up your mind, boy," Pappaduffus says. "Are we staying or going? If you have chosen the latter, please let's get on with it already."

Martin smiles, knowing Jodi will be fine without

him. She possesses too much strength to let the loss of him break her, especially with Pappaduffus out of the frame.

The monitor next to Martin's bed shows a trio of flat lines. The nurse flicks a switch or pushes a button, and the monitor goes dark. Jodi and Alison collapse into each other.

"I guess that's my cue," Martin says. He turns to Pappaduffus. "Whatever happens next, I suppose we're destined to face it together."

"Like I told you before, dear boy, I always liked you the best. When we reach our destination, be kind to me. I promise to do the same."

Martin feels pulled from his core, slowly at first, and then impossibly fast. The world rushes past, a whirlwind of sound and color, of light and vibration, until everything goes dark. Then he perceives a flicker on a distant horizon. A pained howl echoes in an enclosed space, another following closely behind.

"Never thought I would see this place again," Pappaduffus says, a slight tremor in his voice. "Curse your earth magic, boy."

Their footsteps echo in a cave-like chute, all rock and moisture and the faint smell of burnt rubber. The once-distant spark becomes a wall of flame alive with tongues of orange, blue, and green. The howls build in both number and intensity. Whatever creatures are capable of making such awful noises grow nearer. The walls close in.

"I hope this pleases you," Pappaduffus utters, the words almost too quiet for Martin to hear.

Infected by Pappaduffus's fear, Martin takes a step backward. A cloud of stifling heat and rank odor grows thick in the tunnel. Martin imagines the maw of an ancient giant expelling gusts of hot breath through yellow-brown fangs and wart-pocked lips. He wants to run, but run to where? He wants to hide, but he sees nothing that might shield him from his would-be tormentors. Although his surroundings baffle him, he has enough smarts to know he has nowhere to run or hide.

"Cat got your tongue, boy?"

Martin seems to have lost the gift of speech. Chains rattle. Talons scrape smooth rock. Sonorous booms that remind Martin of amplified beats on a bass drum bounce off the walls.

"Prepare yourself," Pappaduffus adds. "You will likely find the experience ahead of you to be rather unpleasant."

"No doubt."

"Stay close to me, boy. No matter what happens, no matter how much they try to break you, hurt you, pull you apart, do not let go. But listen to me: If they manage to separate us, I will find you. A promise made by your old friend Mister Pappaduffus is a promise kept. There may be hope for us yet."

CHAPTER 32

A Seabird With Its Back to the Shore

The nightmare jolted Jodi awake. The same damned one, harsh and ugly: Martin's death and descent into Hell. Heart pounding, she sat up in a lather, as if she were roasting in the furnace along with him, or perhaps instead of him.

"Son of a bitch," she said as she expelled the poison. She flopped onto her back, the pillow cradling her sweat-sopped head.

Jodi had slept soundly since returning from the hospital twelve days earlier, when she said goodbye to Martin for the last time, though one of two all-too-vivid dreams shocked her awake each morning. If presented with a choice, she would have chosen the other dream, the one imbued with softness and hope and the feeling that she and Martin had done something right with their lives.

A few days had passed since she had had the soft dream, but she remembered it clearly. It always began with Jodi's toes dangling over the cliff's crumbling edge. She would study the jagged rocks below, then back away from the edge until her bare feet trampled a patch of sea pinks. The skin of her face looked softer and smoother than it had in years. The salty breeze tugged at her hair, long and soft, not a trace of gray.

"The wind's good today," Martin would say from behind her, and then step toward the precipice, beside her.

Her response: "You'll need it." Jodi's eyes would wander to the pine forest behind her, down the coast, and into the horizon. A place she had seen only in pictures and in her mind, just as Martin had described it more times than she cared to remember. "It's beautiful here. I see why you wanted to come. I'm glad I finally got to see it."

"You were with me when I saw it, even if you didn't know it," he would tell her. "You were with me for everything—every step forward, every step back, all of it. Can't say I enjoyed every minute, but I'd give none of it back."

He would bend to lift an object at his feet: a scuffed gray bowler, its crown dented and brim ragged, band shredded and coated in dust. Turning the derby over in his hands, he would feel the velvety fabric and then hurl the bowler over the edge of the cliff. It would sail like a thrown discus, straight over the water, until dipping and tumbling end over end into the sea, no more.

Then came the part that hurt: the forest behind them fading into a curtain of darkness, Jodi turning to face the sun rising out of the sea, shadows gathering strength behind her. Waves thrashing the black rocks below. The roar growing louder in her ears. Martin taking her hand and pulling her toward the edge of the world. The soles of her bare feet grinding against bare stone. Pebbles creeping between her toes.

Rather than fear, she always felt an encroaching sense of finality, and the niggling possibility of rebirth close behind it. She would stop a few inches from the precipice and release Martin's hand. He would look back one last time, with a smile and a wink.

"See you soon, Jo."

Then he would lean forward. Gone.

Each time she imagined rock and water rising up to meet him, the wind caressing his face and hugging the contours of his naked body. Her eyes and ears became his. As his descent slowed and leveled out into a graceful arc, the crash of water against rock grew softer, farther away. He became one with the horizon, a seabird putting its back to the shore. The sun burned so bright that his closed eyes—and hers—might as well have been open.

"Find a way," she would whisper to the ghost of him. "Find your way back to me."

She would not have described it as a nightmare, but rather a mix of good and bad, pleasure and pain, joy and misery. Much like life, she supposed.

She felt a presence between her knees. She lifted her head from the pillow to see Roy yawning, the calico showing its fangs.

"Another day on the right side of the dirt," she told the cat. "We should probably get up and do something with it."

Jodi drifted down to the kitchen to put on a pot of drip coffee, just enough for a cup. She had made Martin's coffee every morning for the life of their marriage. Instinct compelled her to make a fresh pot her first morning as a widow, forgetting the coffee would go undrunk. Old habits died hard, she knew. She would have tea at the farm table and run her fingers along the chipped rim of Martin's empty cup. By noon, she would drain the coffeepot into the sink. The routine had become ritual, in honor of her late husband. Someday she would stop, but not anytime soon.

Roy rubbed its head against Jodi's calves.

"I forgot your breakfast again. Sorry, cat."

Martin had always been the one who took care of feeding the cat. Although he often complained about having to breathe in the stink of processed salmon, shrimp, and tuna so early in the morning, Jodi knew he enjoyed owning the chore. He became Roy's preferred human as a result, and now she would have to put in the effort needed to claim the title.

She winced as she emptied half a tin of Friskies—salmon and rice—into Roy's shallow metal bowl. She clanged the spoon against the rim and set the bowl on the stone counter. A moment later, the cat leapt onto the counter and gulped down the pinkish paste.

The front door rattled with a less than gentle knock. Jodi peered around the corner and took a few hesitant steps into the foyer before realizing she was being foolish. She opened the door to find the Navajo sheriff, Chooli Etsiddy—the woman who brought Jodi home after wandering too far in the desert. Etsiddy held a crockpot topped with a bundle wrapped in aluminum foil.

Jodi undid the latch on the screen door with a smile.

"Bad news travels far and fast, I suppose," she said.

"My husband and I wanted to tell you how sorry we are," said Etsiddy. She held out the crockpot. "Some red chili stew and my mother-in-law's frybread."

"You're far too kind." Jodi took the crockpot. "Please come in."

"I can't stay long."

"Good," Jodi said, realizing her gaffe too late. "What I mean is I'm still not feeling quite like my old self, so I doubt I'm fit to entertain for very long. I'm not sure when the old Jodi will show up again, or if she died with Martin and has become someone else."

Etsiddy stepped into the foyer, her eyes roving the barren walls. "You don't have to explain yourself. I know how loss changes a person."

Jodi opted not to press for specifics, because who wants to be reminded of the fingerprints a death leaves on those left behind? She had spent too many days watching Martin die, thinking about his impending death and, one day, hers. The world would be better off, she figured, if she pushed the pain far from her mind.

"I've always liked this house," Etsiddy said. "All my life I've lived within five miles of where I stand, so I must have walked or driven past this place probably ten-thousand times if I did it once. Always wondered what it looked like on the inside. Now I know."

"We moved in only a few weeks, a month at most, before all the bullshit happened," Jodi felt the urge to say. "I haven't had much time to decorate. So, you're close by?"

"Maybe ten minutes from here, on the rez," she said.

"I grew up walking this road—nothing but dirt and dust back then. It was a different time in the world."

"Martin and I thought we'd have ten or fifteen good years here. Then, when our minds and bodies tired out, we'd find someplace boring and more civilized to die. Funny, how this country has institutionalized the nuts and bolts of dying, shaped whole industries around it. But what else are you going to do, just walk into the desert until your heart fails and wait for the coyotes to finish you off?"

"That's one way to do it," Etsiddy said. "How are you holding up?"

Jodi shuttled the crockpot into the kitchen, losing her breath as she considered how to answer the sheriff's question. Etsiddy followed close behind. She removed her hat and held it before her as if it were a shield.

"Oh," Jodi said. "You can imagine. It's been strange trying to find my feet without Martin. You spend so much of your life with someone, then all of a sudden that person is gone and you're left trying to figure out who you are. ... Forgive me. I'm trying not to be so morbid. Clearly, I'm losing that battle."

"I'm happy to listen."

"I'm curious who told you."

"You remember Hugo?"

"Of course." How could Jodi forget Hugo? The man had saved her from certain death atop the mesa, miles into Navajo territory.

"I'm afraid Hugo has passed on, too. Dead. Gone. *Aniné.* Found him at the base of Hunters-By-the-Moon, another mesa, a few miles from where I picked up the two of you. He must have fallen. Broke his leg and tried to crawl his way out, but didn't get far. He'd been out there at least a couple days, based on the severity of the sun poisoning. He lingered in the hospital for a day, unresponsive, but there was no saving him."

"I guess the wind-makers decided he was ready," Jodi said, using Hugo's words.

"Hugo made me think of you, so I looked you up. It didn't take long to find out about your husband, the shooting at the hospital, all that mess. Sometimes it seems like the whole world has lost its mind."

Strange, Jodi thought, that Hugo had saved her life, and now he was gone. Just like Martin. The barrier between life and death was thinner than anyone realized.

"Awful about poor Hugo, just awful," she said, and she meant it. "Did he have a family?"

"He lived with his mother in Burrill, the next town over. With him gone, Social Services felt she could no longer care for herself. She's in a nursing home over in Copperas, at least temporarily. Last I heard she wasn't doing well, not really able to understand what's happening and why her son hasn't come by to visit. But, you know, at least she's still here, among the living."

"Just awful," Jodi repeated.

"Hugo was a kind soul," Etsiddy added. "A pain in the rear end if there ever was one, but he had a good heart. I think he just wanted to feel like he was part of something bigger than him. I was hard on him sometimes, maybe harder than I should have been, but that hardhead just wouldn't listen to reason. No matter how many times I told him to stay away from those damned mesas, to stay off our land, every word I spoke to him went in one ear and just kept sailing through to the other side. And look what good it did him."

Jodi could have understood if Etsiddy felt some responsibility for Hugo's death. "It's certainly not any fault of yours, Sheriff. There's no stopping fate."

A silver ring on Etsiddy's left hand caught Jodi's eye.

"You're married. Tell me about him."

"It's not a terribly interesting story. I met Clyde when I was thirteen. He was twenty. Stayed friends for a few years until I was old enough, and then we became more than friends. We got married the day after my seventeenth birthday."

"What's he like?"

"Cranky now, a few months shy of seventy, but thoughtful, generous, kind. Still knows how to make me laugh, though I don't let it go to his head. Still works nine or ten hours a day—carpentry—despite his eyes. Looks after his mother, who's in her nineties and raises more hell now than she did the day I met her. Doctor says Clyde will be blind in a year, two at the most."

Jodi gasped.

"Oh, it won't be so bad," Etsiddy added. "We're happy. Happy enough, anyway, which I guess is more than most folks can say."

Etsiddy seemed to regret the intimacy of the conversation. She placed her hat back on her head and took a step toward the front door.

"Well," she said. "I'll check in on you in a week. You'll be done with the chili by then."

"Really, you don't need to concern yourself with me. I'll be fine."

"I taped my information to the side of the crockpot, so you have my cell number and my email. If you need anything, if you want to talk or cry or hear a voice to remind you you're not the last person alive on the earth, just call me. It's bound to get lonesome out here sometimes."

"I'm counting on it."

"Like I said, see you next week."

Etsiddy hurried for the door and retreated to her SUV. Jodi waved as the vehicle backed out of the driveway. Minutes passed before the cloud of road dust settled. She appreciated the sheriff's kindness, but she was glad to be alone again.

Alone.

The parade of losses continued. First, the kids starting lives of their own. Then, retirement. Then, the move from Rio Vista to Crum, in which she shed the trappings of the life she had built, including most of her friends. Then, Martin's death. She sighed as she looked at the empty driveway, the empty street, and the empty landscape beyond. A reluctant smile spread across her face. She would be okay. With Alison having returned to her life in Phoenix and all of Martin's arrangements handled, Jodi had little to do but sort out their finances and put her mind to the task of figuring out how to spend the remainder of her time on the earth. She was thankful for the return of quiet, though she knew peace never lasted for long.

The coming days would be so full that Jodi would barely have time to think of who and what she had lost.

Andrew was due to come home in a week—on the anniversary of Martin's birthday, which would have been his sixty-sixth. Jodi would have to pick up Alison at dawn so they could meet Andrew and Mateo at the airport in Phoenix. With her car containing the earthly remnants of her family, she would take the highway south of Gila Bend and seek out the place where Martin had declared his love for her more than forty years earlier, as kids who knew nothing about the years of anguish, bliss, and tedium to come. From the parking lot, they would follow the trail to the edge of the Gila River, and she would twist off the lid of Martin's urn, drifting half of his ashes into the river's torrent. Later that day, Andrew and Mateo would pronounce—or repronounce, given their elopement—their intentions to one another in a small ceremony beneath a vine-strangled portico at Pinyon Pine Country Club in Rio Vista. Once Andrew and Mateo returned home to Valencia, she would board a flight east, to Bangor, Maine, and head for the coast, to sprinkle the rest of Martin's remains into the open mouth of the Atlantic.

"When I'm gone, sprinkle what's left of me here and there," Martin once told her. "With any luck, my remains will come together somewhere in the middle."

Alison would soon leave her, too. Jodi's daughter had quit her loathsome healthcare job and joined an organization devoted to teaching ESL to non-English-speaking people around the world, mostly in the remotest parts of Asia. The group would likely send Alison to either Thailand or Vietnam, the hiring manager told her, due to ship out by year's end. Jodi considered the combination of thrill and terror Alison must be feeling. She just hoped her daughter would stay safe in her travels and, with any luck, relight the fire in her belly that life's dreariness had snuffed out years ago.

Jodi stirred honey into her tea and peered out the kitchen window. Patches of grayish-white stratocumulus clouds streaked the sky. The day seemed somehow unsure of which way it wanted to turn, the sun in hiding one moment, then painting the desert with its full brilliance the next.

She turned her back to the sink and blew heat off the tea's surface. Her eyes settled on the stack of mail that had accumulated on the kitchen table. She pored through the pile, dividing the stack into bills and trash, pulling out a few oversized cards from friends and family, some from as far away as Michigan. She pulled out the first one, from her cousin Marla in Tucson; Jodi had not seen her in ten years, maybe longer. She tore the envelope open to find a dramatic sunrise decorating the card's front, along with some religious saying about eternal life. Inside, Marla had scrawled the following: DON'T MOURN BECAUSE IT'S OVER, SMILE BECAUSE IT HAPPENED.

"Oh, go fuck yourself with a toilet brush," Jodi said. She ripped the card in two and dropped it into the trashcan, along with four other cards, unopened, that would surely offer similarly useless sentiments.

A freeze frame from her dream flashed into her mind. *The derby.* She recalled her encounter with Pappaduffus in the hospital stairwell, and his chilling words to her. Humankind's only role in the universe, its only value, was to manufacture pain and suffering to feed some infernal machine. Somehow, his words made sense, as if she had turned over a rock and discovered an untold truth. If he was right, she would make herself worthless, because she intended to live happily for as long as she could, even without Martin.

"Best day of my life," Jodi said, using Martin's words from the night they ceded their Phoenix home to Pappaduffus and his underlings. Maybe, she figured, if she continued to repeat Martin's words, and celebrate the things that made him special, he would live forever.

Roy lifted its head from the food bowl and made a noise Jodi had never heard before—a meow that morphed into a deep, throaty growl. An oily pink residue slicked the fur beneath the cat's chin. Roy went rigid and pressed its ears flat to its head and then leapt off the counter. Paws clamored on the tile floor in the cat's swift retreat to the basement.

Jodi detected movement in her periphery. She snapped her head to the right and thought she saw a shadow slink out of the kitchen and into the foyer. A rasping sound, like a fingernail scratching bare wood, echoed in the stairwell. She closed her eyes and exhaled. As her feet led her out of the kitchen, her nostrils caught a faint yet familiar aroma: the citrusy zip of gin.

"Martin?"

She felt silly speaking his name, but the events of the past year had taught her to make room for the unbelievable. Her hand gripped the banister to steady her footsteps. As she scaled the narrow staircase, each stair squealed beneath her, until she reached the top. She turned to face the master bedroom.

Sunlight spilled through the blind-less windows. She

took three steps and stopped in the doorway. The lemony aroma intensified, with hints of juniper, pine, and clove, followed by the sulfurous whiff of a just-struck match.

The room darkened as another patch of clouds blotted out the sun. Shadows crept in from the corners, rose from the floor, descended from the ceiling. Her gaze landed on the perfectly made bed, a slight indentation in its center. A gray haze hovered above the duvet.

"I was beginning to think you'd never show up," she said. "Deep down I knew you'd do it. I knew you'd come back to me."

A smile spread across her face as her feet left the threshold. The braided area rug muffled the groan of each aging floorboard. As she came to within a few feet of the hazy form, the silhouette grew darkly opaque, taking on texture, edges, features. The depth and breadth of odor overwhelmed her, hitting her layer after layer. A kaleidoscope of scents triggered every emotion: joy, fear, serenity, sadness, disgust, confusion, grief, lust, rage, contentedness, misery, dread, awe. She opened her arms in a welcoming embrace.

The bedroom door creaked to a close behind her.

ACKNOWLEDGMENTS

I extend my gratitude to the following humans for their time, kindness, and thoughtful criticism, all of which improved the final draft: Donna Schoener Donahue, my partner, best friend, and first reader, for critiques of early drafts and so much more; Don Swaim, founder and leader of the Bucks County Writers Workshop, as well as past and present BCWW members Candace Barrett, Isabel Barton, Chris Bauer, Beverly Black, Jim Brennan, Bobby Cohen, Lee Bigelow Davis, Ef Deal, Natalie Zellat Dyen, Jim Kempner, William Kirk, George MacMillan, Kathleen Madigan, Jackie Nash, William O'Toole, Kristian Rowley, John Schoffstall, Ashara Shapiro, Alan Shils, David Updike, and Jeffrey I. Zimmerman, as well as the late Daniel Dorian and John Wirebach; William F. Donahue Jr., my late father, for his perspective on the Vietnam chapter; LCW Allingham (also a BCWW alum) and River Eno, fellow authors and co-founders of Speculation Publications, for their friendship, support, and skillful content edits; Melissa D. Sullivan (yet another BCWW alum), writer, organizer, and kitten adopter; Jeani Rector, founder and editor of *The Horror Zine*, for the connection; Fred Courtright and Copper Canyon Press, for their permission to use a darkly romantic W. S. Merwin poem as the epigraph for this book; and anyone who read and/or reviewed my first three novels. Also, many thanks to the

Manta Press team, particularly Tim McWhorter, for giving life to this story.

I also want to thank the nonhumans in my life—namely, Marbles, Crash, Baxter, and Sprout, as well as the scores of kittens and mama cats that Donna and I have had the privilege to foster through the nonprofit Forgotten Cats (forgottencats.org). These animals offer the best kind of distraction from writing, editing, and having conversations with characters I need to get to know better.

Finally, thanks to John Errichetti of Tinhouse Design for the amazing cover, and to authors S.L. Coney, Greg F. Gifune, Carol Gyzander, Ken Jaworowski, Daemon Manx, and Diana Rodriguez Wallach for taking the time to correspond and share their kind words.

ABOUT THE AUTHOR

William J. Donahue's previous novels include *Burn Beautiful Soul, Crawl on Your Belly All the Days of Your Life*, and *Only Monsters Remain*. His short fiction has appeared in *The Horror Zine*, as well as in the horror anthologies *Cry Baby Bridge, Heavy Metal Nightmares*, and *House of Haunts*. A writer, editor, and kitten foster, he lives somewhere on the map between Philadelphia and Bethlehem, Pennsylvania. Although his home lacks a proper moat, it does have plenty of snakes.

www.ingramcontent.com/pod-product-compliance
Lightning Source LLC
Chambersburg PA
CBHW061655190726
48289CB00006B/1889